About the Author

Jane Peart, award-winning novelist and short story writer, grew up in North Carolina and was educated in New England. Although she now lives in northern California, her heart has remained in her native South—its people, its history, and its traditions. With more than 20 novels and 250 short stories to her credit, Jane likes to emphasize in her writing the timeless and recurring themes of family, traditional values, and a sense of place.

Ten years in the writing, the *Brides of Montclair* series is a historical, family saga of enduring beauty. In each new book, another generation comes into its own at the beautiful Montclair estate, near Williamsburg, Virginia. These compelling, dramatic stories reaffirm the importance of committed love, loyalty, courage, strength of character, and abiding faith in times of triumph and tragedy, sorrow and joy.

Fortune's Bride

Book Three
of the Brides of Montclair Series

JANE PEART

Zondervan Books
Zondervan Publishing House
Grand Rapids, Michigan

FORTUNE'S BRIDE
Copyright © 1986, 1990 by Jane Peart

Zondervan Books is an imprint of
The Zondervan Publishing House
1415 Lake Drive, S.E.
Grand Rapids, Michigan 49506

Library of Congress Cataloging-in-Publication Data:

Peart, Jane.
    Fortune's bride / Jane Peart.
       p. cm. — (Brides of Montclair series : bk. 3)
    ISBN 0-310-66971-5
    I. Title. II. Series: Peart, Jane. Brides of Montclair series :
bk. 3.
PS3566.E238F67 1990
613'.54—dc20   89–70768
                                     CIP

Edited by Anne Severance
Designed by Kim Koning

Printed in the United States of America

90 91 92 93 94 95 / LP / 10 9 8 7 6 5 4 3 2 1

For "Mayme"
In appreciation of years
of love and devotion

None without hope e'er loved....
But love can hope
Where reason should despair.
                    —Lord Lyttelton

Prologue
Mayfield, Virginia
Summer 1806

What is come upon us: . . . Our inheritance is turned to strangers, our houses to aliens. We are orphans.

Lamentations 5:1–3

THE WHEELS of the handsome black and gold carriage rolled up the winding drive to the large house of mellowed brick, half-hidden by the tall elms surrounding it. Within, a grave young man of twenty-seven and a child of ten rode in silence, each enclosed in private thoughts.

For Graham Montrose, it was a strange homecoming. For Avril Dumont, it was no homecoming at all. Until a few weeks ago her whole life had been spent in a pink stucco house, frosted with white iron lace balconies and shadowed by gnarled oak trees hung with Spanish moss, overlooking the Mississippi River. There she had known nothing but happiness. Now she was experiencing the overwhelming sensations of sadness, loneliness, and anxiety.

Within hours of each other, her parents had died of the dread Yellow Fever that swept through Natchez, leaving virtually no home untouched in its wake. The past weeks had been filled with turmoil and confusion, the servants wandering about without direction, strangers coming and going—a bewildering, frightening time until this kind, quiet man had appeared.

Calmly he had taken charge, explaining that he had been a friend of her papa's and that she would be coming to live with him at his plantation home in Virginia, where he would take care of her as her parents had wished.

Shyly Avril glanced in the tall man's direction, but his head was averted. He was staring out the window, apparently lost in a world of his own. Avril wished mightily that Dilly, her black nurse who had accompanied her all the way from Natchez by barge, boat, and stage, were with her right now. Dilly had been sent ahead to Montclair while she and Mr. Montrose stayed overnight in Williamsburg with his Aunt Laura Barnwell. In her entire life Avril had hardly ever been out of her old nurse's sight and without her the child felt even more lonely and uncertain.

She turned and looked out her window. Since leaving Mayfield, it seemed they had been riding for hours along this narrow road bordered on either side by dense woods. Rounding a bend, she saw a great house with lovely green lawns rolling down to a ribbon of sunlit river.

"We're almost there," Graham said, but she gave no response.

He wished there were something he might do or say to bring a smile to the small, freckled face, to soften the impact of her tragedy. He had lost two dear friends, but Avril had been robbed of her parents. Still stunned with shock from the news of Paul and Eva's sudden deaths, the responsibility as guardian of their only child weighed heavily on Graham.

Their friendship had begun in their school days when, after his own mother's untimely passing, Graham had been sent to Virginia Preparatory for Boys. Paul, then an upperclassman, had taken the lonely Graham under his wing and had become like an older brother to him. Over the years they had remained close friends—so close, in fact, that when Paul married Eva Duchampes, Graham had stood up with him.

The night before the wedding the two friends had signed a noble pact, agreeing that whoever survived the other's death would take as his sacred duty the care and protection of his friend's family. At the time, since both were in the full vigor of young manhood, it had seemed only a gallant gesture unlikely ever to need fulfilling. Now Graham wondered what he, a childless widower himself, was to do with this pathetic orphan, this desolate little girl, alone in the world except for a few distant cousins.

His soul-searching was cut short as the carriage halted in front of the pillared veranda of the house and the carriage door was opened by a smiling black man in a bright blue coat trimmed with braid.

"Welcome home, Mastuh Graham! You's a sight for dese ol' eyes!"

"Thank you, Hector, it's good to be back." Bending his tall frame, Graham sprang lightly to the ground. "And this is Miss Avril Dumont, who will also be living at Montclair." Turning, he extended a hand to the frail child, who made no move to get out.

Hector's grin widened to a white crescent in his dark face as he nodded. "And welcome to you, little Miss. We has been waitin' for yo' comin'!"

Avril smiled tentatively. "Is this Montclair?"

From her vantage point in the carriage, the three stories of the great house rose forebodingly. Then a sliver of late afternoon sun pierced the gloom, striking the polished windows. The reflected rays of light made the glass sparkle like winks of welcome. Suddenly her heart felt lighter.

"Come, dear," Graham urged.

Dutifully she placed her small, thin hand in his and descended cautiously.

Avril was tall for her age and the hastily purchased mourning clothes, a high-waisted frock of dove gray bombazine, hung limply on her skinny, small-boned body. The black straw "shovel" bonnet with its crepe ribbons almost obscured her face but could not hide the carroty curls escaping in tangled clusters from beneath the wide brim.

Standing there, Avril took a deep breath. The flower-scented air was refreshingly cool after the long, dusty ride along the country roads. She glanced around at the velvety green grass and the gardens where flowers grew in profusion. Beyond the hedges flocks of white sheep grazed in meadows that seemed to stretch forever.

As if realizing some comment was expected of her, Avril murmured, "It's very pretty here."

Graham looked down at her and smiled. At length he said gently, "Shall we go in? This is your home now."

She looked up at him and for a long moment their eyes met and held. In that span of time, a message was sent, trust given and received, an irrevocable bond forged. Avril's fingers tightened on Graham's.

Together they mounted the steps and went into the house.

Part I

Montclair
1806

The stranger that dwelleth with you shall be unto you as one born among you, and thou shalt love him as thyself.

Leviticus 19:34

chapter

1

YEARS AFTERWARD, whenever Avril thought of her first weeks at
Montclair she would remember them as a series of impressions—
vastness without emptiness, security without confinement, compassion without pity. For now, she knew only that she loved the
spacious rooms of the great house, the wide shaded veranda, the
smooth lawn where she played under the cool canopy of the elms.
Although warm, the Virginia summer had none of the oppressive
heat that in Mississippi had forced her to rest in the long afternoons.
Avril adjusted with remarkable ease to her new surroundings.

It was Dilly who found it hard to fit in, to become accustomed to
the change of climate, the "pecking order" among the Montrose
servants, and her puzzling role as nurse-mammy to a child who no
longer seemed to need her watchful care.

But for Avril, every day at Montclair offered a delightful
discovery. In his inexperience Graham instinctively did the right
thing, giving Avril the freedom of the house and grounds, allowing
her to wander and explore at will. Thus, she had investigated every
inch of the rambling mansion, with its many wings and unexpected
twists and turns. She enjoyed moving from step to step on the
curved stairway, examining the portraits of the pretty ladies lining
the wall. Some of them were dressed in old-fashioned clothing, and
Avril often wondered who they were.

"They are the brides who came to live at Montclair," Graham told her one day when he found her studying the paintings. Dropping down beside her on the stairs, he pointed to a brunette beauty in crimson velvet trimmed with gilt lace. "That was the first bride, Noramary Marsh, my grandmother. And that"— his voice grew soft with emotion— "was my mother, Lorabeth Whitaker. She died when I was just a little boy." Moving on quickly he pointed to the next painting. "And this was my stepmother, Arden Sherwood."

Avril looked thoughtful. "Noramary? Is she the one who worked the sampler in the music room?"

"Yes," Graham smiled. "That's the one."

"But your mother is dead?" she added softly.

"Yes . . . When I was fifteen, my father married a very wonderful woman. They both died shortly afterward—"

Avril's eyes grew bright. She put her small hand on his, her expression sympathetic. "Then you're an orphan—like me."

Deeply touched, Graham patted her hand. "Well, but now we have each other, haven't we?"

Avril's smile was unexpected, and for the first time, Graham noticed a little dimple at the corner of her mouth. She had not smiled much until now. From that day Graham's determined goal was Avril's happiness, to see that dimple dance again.

It was only a week later that Graham called to Avril from the foot of the stairs just as Dilly, hairbrush in hand, was putting the finishing touches to her toilette.

"Avril, come down! I've something to show you!"

Pulling away from Dilly's restraining arm, she rushed from the bedroom, down the hall, and leaned over the banister. Graham was standing in the front hall, with a mysterious smile on his face.

"Hurry!" he urged, motioning her down the steps.

Avril took them at a skip. Covering her eyes with her hands as instructed, she allowed him to lead her onto the porch. There on the drive stood one of the stable boys at the head of a graceful, cinnamon-colored horse with a silky mane and tail.

"Oh-h-h!" Avril let out a long breath.

"Do you like her?" Graham asked.

"She's beautiful."

"She's yours."

Avril's eyes widened. "Mine? Really?"

"Really. Her name is Fancy. I'm going to teach you to ride, so you and Fancy will become great friends."

With the riding lessons came the beginning of a companionship between the man and the child that grew into one of the special pleasures of the life they were making together.

Each morning, with patient thoroughness, Graham instructed Avril in the intricacies of expert horsemanship, treating her with the same consideration and courtesy he might have accorded a grown lady. And Avril responded with an earnest desire to please him and to become an excellent rider.

These she accomplished in record time. Soon they were taking daily rides along the woodland paths and up into the nearby pine-studded hills.

By fall Avril was riding well and had entered into life at Montclair with alacrity. She loved everything about her new home. Above all, she had come to love Graham with the affection of a young girl for a father-brother-and-best-friend, all in one.

Only two incidents marred the lovely flow of her days during the first year. Both were unexpected and never fully explained.

One afternoon, when Avril was out in the side yard, pushing herself back and forth on the swing Graham had hung for her from one of the branches of an enormous oak tree, she saw a strange carriage coming up the drive. She watched as it stopped in front of the house. A slightly built man dressed all in black emerged. He stood for a moment, surveying his surroundings. Then he spoke to the driver, who was slumped in his seat atop the carriage, and turned to mount the steps leading to the porch.

Curious because Graham had said nothing about expecting a visitor and because the man was a stranger to her, Avril let the swing die down, then went inside. As she stepped into the hall, she heard angry voices coming from behind the closed doors of the library.

The thought of Graham's wrath both startled and frightened her. She had never heard him raise his voice, not even when correcting a stable boy.

Alarmed, she turned and fled outside to the sanctuary of the lilac bushes, where she remained until the sound of booted feet stomping down the veranda steps assured her that the stranger was leaving. Only then did she allow herself a peek at his hasty departure.

"Back to Mayfield!" he ordered and entered the carriage, slamming the door with a violence that sent Avril ducking back into her hiding place.

At dinner that evening Graham announced, "I must make a business trip, Avril. It will require an absence of several weeks, so I want you to stay with Great-Aunt Laura while I'm away. You remember her, don't you? She's a delightful old lady and you'll be good company for her."

There was no mention of the mysterious caller, however, and for some reason Avril felt afraid to ask about him or the reason for the angry interchange she had overheard. Somehow, though, she suspected that the conversation was connected with her guardian's sudden travel plans.

Avril's stay in Williamsburg was pleasant enough. As promised, Great-Aunt Laura was brimming over with vitality and ideas for entertaining a lonely child. She taught Avril to tat, and to tend the several varieties of flowers and herbs that grew profusely in her gardens. In addition, there were children of friends and neighbors to play with. In spite of all these diversions, Avril was very happy to see Graham again when he returned for her.

"You must come back at Christmas," insisted Aunt Laura as they were about to leave for Montclair. "Graham, you must bring Avril for the holidays. Williamsburg at Christmas is an experience never to be forgotten, my dear," she said, kissing Avril on both cheeks.

"Sister Sally will be here with her grandchildren, so there will be plenty of young folks and fun."

But the week before Christmas produced a heavy snowfall followed by plummeting temperatures that glazed the snow-covered roads with a treacherous sheeting of ice.

Thus, Avril's first Christmas without her parents was spent in the company of Graham and the house servants. And while their solitary celebration was a quiet one, there was an abundance of good food and holiday treats and even several intriguing packages under a beautifully decorated tree.

On Christmas morning, Graham watched anxiously as Avril unwrapped one of his gifts to her—a large porcelain doll dressed in satin and lace.

Upon seeing the guarded expression on her face, however, he instantly regretted his choice.

"Ah, my mistake, Avril. You are too old for dolls, aren't you?"

She glanced at him tentatively, but her eyes betrayed her momentary disappointment.

"I should have known. Forgive me."

"Oh, she's very pretty, Graham. I will love her always even though I don't play with dolls anymore." And to prove it, she clasped the lovely gift to her breast.

"Well, never mind," he said, handing her two more boxes. "Perhaps these will be more pleasing to a growing young lady."

In one of the gaily wrapped packages was a white fur muff, lined with satin, with a tasseled cord to go around the neck; in the other, a picture book about horses.

Avril squealed with delight. "Thank you, Graham! This is the happiest Christmas ever!"

"And there shall be many more, Avril," Graham promised, feeling an unexpected tightness in his throat at the sight of her shining face.

Month followed happy month in the company of Graham and the servants who seemed intent on bringing some joy into the life of the orphaned child. It was precisely because life at Montclair was so peaceful that Avril did not have the slightest premonition that something was about to happen to alter the course of her destiny.

With the summer of 1807 nearly past, fall's subtle stirring could be felt in the lavender dusks and misty mornings. On one such morning Avril awoke with her usual eagerness to start the day. She hopped out of the high four-poster bed, ran to the window, and looked out.

The day was splendid—the sky, a cloudless sweep of blue as far as she could see; the meadows, gold and white with goldenrod and tufts of Queen Anne's lace. Autumn in Virginia was by far the nicest time of year, so Graham had said, and Avril had long since ceased to question his wisdom, particularly because he always seemed to be right!

She sincerely hoped he would be able to go riding this morning. The brisk air had sharpened her desire to be outdoors, seated on a sidesaddle atop her beloved Fancy, beside Graham who usually chose a handsome mount named Gallant.

In the last week, she had followed Graham on his plantation rounds and he had pointed out the tobacco fields ripening a golden-brown in the September sun. The orchards, too, blazed with the colors of harvest, and the kitchen help was kept busy canning and preserving the rich yield of apples and pears.

Turning back to the room, Avril left her daydreaming and pulled her nightie over her head, anxious to dress and be off in search of Graham. She raced about the room, gathering up the clothes she had flung carelessly aside the night before. Well, thank goodness, Dilly had not come up to tuck her in, so she had not been around to scold. Her nurse was still smarting from the abrupt changes wrought by the deaths of her master and mistress, and missed her kin in Mississippi. Last night she had been complaining about that very thing when Graham allowed Avril to stay up past her bedtime to finish a chapter in the book they were reading aloud together. Dilly, already vexed, had gone off in a huff to the servants' quarters and hadn't been seen since.

How could one be unhappy on such a glorious day? Avril mused, feeling the slightest bit sorry for her old nurse. But the next minute, as she drew the hairbrush through her long mass of red curls, she was again relieved that Dilly had not appeared. She always made such a fuss over Avril's hair, tugging at each tangle till it broke free and lay smooth and shiny over her shoulders. Now Avril made short work of it, looking around for a ribbon. Spotting one she had discarded on the floor beside her bed, she quickly gathered up her hair and twisted it until she could wind the blue silk around it and tie a bow.

For a moment her attention was diverted by the twin silver-framed miniatures of her parents on the top of her dressing table. Precious Papa and Angel Mother! She felt a momentary pang of loss, then realized that she no longer missed them as much as she had at first. Feeling almost guilty about her newfound happiness, she picked up the pictures, kissed the painted images, then replaced the frames on their stands. *Silly Avril*, she thought. Who would be happier than her parents that things had worked out so well? After all, it was their wish that she come to Virginia to live with Graham. Then, still buttoning her bodice, she ran out of her room and down the stairs in search of her guardian.

Halfway down the stairs, she halted. From the first floor the sound of voices floated up to greet her. *Visitors!* she thought, making a wry face. She hoped they wouldn't stay long. It was so pleasant having Graham all to herself, making plans for the day. Sometimes, when company came, the grownups went on talking forever.

Hesitating on the landing, Avril considered slipping through the hall and out to the kitchen to beg some cornbread from Cookie, who doted on her since there had been no children at Montclair for years. From there she could go out to the stables and wheedle Ben, the head groom, to saddle Fancy for her. Though riding by herself was not half so much fun as riding with Graham, it would be better than sitting out the tedious conversation of adults. But the tantalizing aromas of fried ham and fresh-baked biscuits and the pungent smell of coffee wafted up enticingly, triggering her healthy young appetite. Avril gave a little shrug and skipped down the next few steps.

At the door of the dining room she paused uncertainly. The visitors were strangers, not the Barnwells from Williamsburg as she had supposed. Graham did not entertain, and most callers were relatives.

Seeing Avril standing there, Graham called to her. "Come in, dear. Here are some friends I'd like you to meet."

The dining room was mellow with sunlight streaming in the long windows from the porticoed porch. At the polished mahogany table with Graham sat a lady and a gray-haired gentleman, whose murmured comments ceased as Avril entered shyly.

"These are our neighbors from Cameron Hall, Judge and Mrs. Hugh Cameron, who have been abroad for a year. And this," he gestured almost proudly, "is Avril."

"Avril? What a charming name." The lady's voice was sweet and soft and she rested her dark eyes kindly on Avril as Avril slid into the chair in her usual place beside Graham.

"It's French for April—the month," she explained.

"But, of course!" Mrs. Cameron exclaimed, looking knowingly at her husband. "Her mother was a Duchampes from New Orleans and you know the Dumonts—"

The gray-haired man nodded and continued to regard Avril thoughtfully.

"We knew your mama, my dear," the lady went on. "Actually, we attended your parents' wedding. She was a beautiful bride and Paul, such a handsome young man. What a pity!"

Graham cleared his throat with a note of warning.

"You must bring Avril over to Cameron Hall very soon, Graham," she said, changing the subject adroitly. "Or she could take the trail through the woods. Our boys ride those paths nearly every day. It would do those rascals good to polish up their manners and learn to entertain a young lady." She gave Avril a conspiratorial wink. "Our sons, Logan and Marshall, run quite wild through the countryside, I fear, with no gentling influences. Thank goodness, they'll be going off next year to an English boarding school."

"And you'll be bereft without them," Graham correctly surmised.

"Oh my yes, I suppose I shall! But then, to make up for their absence, perhaps I can take Avril under my wing. I should love having a girl around after putting up with those two madcap boys all these years!" Mrs. Cameron's gay little laugh softened the sharp commentary on her sons' conduct.

After that the conversation passed to other things—local events, people, and other items of interest to the three adults. Avril, who had finished eating, did her best to suppress her restlessness, all the while wishing the Camerons would leave. But here came Hector with the silver coffeepot, refilling the fragile china cups with freshly brewed coffee!

At last, unable to contain herself a moment longer, Avril caught Graham's eye. "May I be excused now?"

He nodded his assent and she slipped out of her chair.

"Say your farewells to our guests first, Avril," he reminded her gently.

Avril went to each and curtsied, as she had been taught to do, extending her hand politely. But Mrs. Cameron took her face in both her cool hands and gazed at her tenderly.

"We're so happy you're here at Montclair with Graham, my darling. I do hope you and I can become great friends." Then she brushed back the straying red locks and smiled at Graham over Avril's head. "Graham, I'd like to see that this child has some new clothes now that her period of mourning is almost passed. A year for one so young is really quite enough, don't you think? I'm sure we could find some lovely materials in Williamsburg and have some pretty dresses made up for her. May I borrow her some day soon and take her into town with me?"

"Of course, May. That is, if Avril would like to go." Graham looked askance at his ward.

But before she could answer, Mrs. Cameron spoke up again. "But of course she would, wouldn't you, darling? There's not a girl in the world who doesn't adore shopping for new clothes. It's settled then. We'll just have to decide on the time. I'll send over a note in a day or two after I've made the arrangements." Then she turned to Avril again. "You see, my dear, since we've just returned from our long journey, there is much to attend to at home. But now that we're back, we shall be seeing a lot of you both. Oh, it will be such fun!" she laughed gaily, almost like a girl herself.

"Thank you, Mrs. Cameron," Avril murmured, now anxious to leave and go out into the sunny morning.

"Oh, child, don't call me Mrs. Cameron. That's much too formal. Do call me Auntie May, just as my sister's children do. It would please me very much." And she gave Avril a quick hug.

Out in the hall Avril stood for a moment, wondering whether she should go find Dilly or go straight to the stables. Unless the Camerons left right away, Graham would not be able to go riding with her until later. As she hesitated Avril heard her name spoken and could not resist lingering to hear what was being said about her.

It was Mr. Cameron's deep, resonant voice that carried first. "It is expedient, Graham, that it be done without further delay. From the communications I have received, I have no doubt they will proceed, and all will be lost. My information is that they are without scruples, with not a shred of compassion. You must act quickly or—"

"Have you not said anything to the child?" This was Mrs. Cameron's anxious voice.

Now Graham's, speaking in a low, concerned tone. "But she is so young—just turned twelve last week. How can I explain so that she will understand the necessity for such a plan?"

"Leave that to me, Graham. As a lawyer I think I can make it simple and clear. After all, it is only a protective measure until she reaches her majority."

Avril stiffened, standing rigidly as the strange words fell on her ears. What were they talking about? What did it mean? Why did Graham sound so troubled?

She felt a chill, and a little shudder coursed through her small bony frame. Outside, the sun went behind a cloud, darkening the little circle of light in which she had stood.

Somehow Avril wished the Camerons had never come. They had brought some kind of news, something that was going to change her life here at Montclair. Avril didn't really know how she knew that. She just knew.

chapter

2

RETURNING from her morning ride one day, Avril cantered onto the cobblestone stableyard, observing that the heat seemed more like midsummer. As she passed the side of the house, she caught a glimpse of a familiar carriage. The Camerons' driver was leaning against one of the elm trees, whittling under its leafy shade.

Avril felt a pang of dismay. In the two years she had been at Montclair Avril had come to love Auntie May, but sometimes her visits proved inconvenient. Like today. Graham had promised to ride with her later in the afternoon. He wanted to exercise his new horse, a powerful gelding, hoping to temper the animal's headstrong nature alongside the gentler Fancy.

She rubbed the nose of the mare affectionately before handing the reins to one of the grooms. Instead of entering the house through the front door and thus risking an encounter with the visitors, Avril took a shortcut through the kitchen garden. She proceeded up the steps of the side porch and slipped into the house through the French windows of the library. Tiptoeing over to the double doors leading to the hall, she opened them cautiously, and peered out.

Noting that the doors of the drawing room were shut, Avril debated the advisability of running lightly past, on the chance that she could escape being seen. Certainly it wouldn't do for Auntie May to find her in this state of dishevelment—cotton blouse stained and damp with perspiration, the skirt of her riding habit tucked into her boots. Her braided hair had come loose and now tumbled about her shoulders, the restraining ribbon lost somewhere in the woods.

Auntie May, who was fastidiousness itself, always eyed Avril with a kind but critical eye, automatically tucking back an unruly curl, straightening a collar, or retying a sash. The gestures were made lovingly, but Avril tried to look her best when she knew their neighbor was coming to call.

The decision was made. She would have to make a run for it. Taking off her boots, Avril started across the polished floor toward the stairway in her stocking feet. As she did, there was a peal of light laughter, followed by the mention of her name.

"You will not believe the change in Graham since Avril came, my dear. Remember how concerned we all were about him?" Auntie May was saying.

Ignoring the old adage Dilly often repeated—"Keyhole listeners doan never hear no good 'bout theyselves"—Avril waited very still, determined to discover why she and her guardian should be the topic of conversation.

"We thought he would never get over losing Lulie," May continued. "I mean, his grief went way beyond the bounds of reason. Of course, we expected him to observe the usual period of mourning, but after the first year we became worried. It went on, month after month, his staying here at Montclair, refusing all invitations, rebuffing all his friends' well-intentioned suggestions that he come out into society again. I do declare, it's a miracle how Avril's coming seems to have shaken him out of his self-imposed exile!"

Avril clapped her hand over her mouth to suppress a giggle. She—a "miracle"? Still she felt a small, smug sort of satisfaction at having brought such a welcome change to Graham's life.

Then she heard another voice with a musical, lilting tone. The speaker, obviously a woman, spoke so softly that Avril could not hear the question, only Auntie May's answer.

"Oh, still very much a child! And I'm afraid Graham has let her run fairly wild. But what could a man with no experience of children know about raising a little girl. Then she was a victim of such a cruel tragedy, both parents dying within a few days of each other, you see. Graham's sympathy has probably outweighed his judgment. Hugh has tried to offer guidance and I have done what little I could do. But I'm sure you're quite right, dear Clarice. Your suggestion is well-advised. We will, however, have to put it very diplomatically if Graham is to understand the need—"

Avril would have liked to linger long enough to learn just what Auntie May meant, but at that very moment she heard the clatter of horses' hooves on the shell drive and turned just in time to see Graham dismounting in front of the veranda. He handed the reins to a stable boy and headed for the house. In another minute he would come inside and catch her eavesdropping—and in this grubby attire! Scooping up her boots in one hand, her skirt in the other, she dashed up the stairs.

Reaching the top, Avril leaned over the banister and saw Graham stop in front of the round gold mirror with its sculptured eagle. He straightened his cravat and smoothed back his thick, dark hair. Then, placing his riding crop and gloves on the hall table, he made his way to the drawing room. At his entrance Avril heard the happy rise of the ladies' voices in greeting.

She made a little face. She hoped the company wouldn't spoil her evening with Graham. If they stayed—

"Where you been at, Missy?" demanded a sharp voice from behind, and Avril jumped and spun around to find Dilly, hands on hips, scowling disapprovingly. Dilly still treated her as if she were a baby, Avril thought, ready to defend herself.

But Dilly did not wait for an explanation. "Jes' look at you," she scolded. "You looks lak a fiel' hand—no shoes, dress all rumpled and dirty, and where is yo' hair ribbon? I declare, I doan know what we's goin' to do wid you! Runnin' all over de countryside lak one ob dem harum-scarum boys—dem Camerons! You gettin' way too old to be playin' wid nuthin' but boys. Now you come along wid me, missy. Missus Cameron and her lady friend are waitin' downstairs fo' you. Hurry! We's got some job to git you cleaned up and prettified 'fo you shame Mastuh Graham!"

Twenty minutes later Avril, wearing a lime-green cambric muslin dress, with her hair brushed and held back with a dark green velvet bandeau, passed Dilly's inspection and went down the stairs, curious to know the identity of Auntie May's "lady friend."

Peering around the drawing room door to take a look before she herself could be seen, Avril saw Auntie May pouring tea. Opposite her, on the sofa, sat Graham and a lady as lovely as any princess out of a storybook.

The lady's head was turned toward Graham and her profile was as clear and delicate as a cameo. She had a narrow, arched nose, sloping forehead, and long, slender neck. Rich brown hair was piled and looped into an elaborate coiffure, and she was wearing an exquisite gown of deep apricot silk with lace-edged ruffles outlining the bateau neckline and the long sleeves at the wrists. One graceful hand held a teacup while she listened in rapt attention to something Graham was saying.

Fascinated, Avril unconsciously stepped into view.

Seeing her, Auntie May called out, "Ah, here she is now! Come in, Avril. There's someone who wants to meet you."

Avril felt the other lady's eyes coolly appraising her as she took a few steps into the room. Suddenly she felt like an insect under a magnifying glass.

Auntie May's next words did nothing to relieve the tension. "How well Avril looks, Graham. All this country air and good food has done wonders for her. She's certainly not the scrawny little thing she was when she first arrived."

Avril flushed, feeling awkward. Why did grown-ups, even Auntie May, talk about children as if they weren't even there? Graham never did. She shot him a grateful glance, but he was looking at his other guest so did not see her silent plea for support.

"Avril, this is my dear friend, Lady Fontayne—"

"Oh, *please*, May, not so formal!" protested the other in mild dismay.

"Well, you *were* married to a member of the English nobility. We cannot forget *that!*"

"But I am an *American,* born in Virginia, remember? I only *married* a titled Englishman. But we spent so much time traveling on the Continent that we scarcely ever used it. However, that is all in the past, and now that I am a widow and living again in America, I wish only to be addressed as an American. After all, was not our War of Independence fought to free us all from the tyranny of *titles?*" Though the words were spoken lightly, there was no mistaking the determination in her tone.

"As you like, my dear," conceded Auntie May. To Avril, she explained, "Clarice and I were girlhood friends, and though she lived for many years abroad, she is back now—this time to stay, we hope!"

"Well, we shall see about that." This time Mrs. Fontayne's laugh was strangely grating to Avril's ears.

"Clarice is staying with us at Cameron Hall just now and we are trying to persuade Graham to come away with us for the evening. Hugh and I are having a few of her old friends in to greet her after her long absence. Do say you will come, Graham!" May pleaded.

Graham laughed and shook his head. "It's difficult to resist you, May, but not tonight."

"But why not?" This came from Mrs. Fontayne.

"Well—," began Graham, but Auntie May interrupted.

"Now, don't say we've given too short notice. If I sent you an invitation a week in advance, you'd have a hundred excuses by then. We must properly welcome Clarice home, mustn't we? Besides, my dear, you're in need of some lively adult company for a change, and I can promise you that!"

"And I happen to know that May always keeps her promises," purred Mrs. Fontayne. "May's parties were always the most delightful of any I attended in the old days. We lack only your presence to make the evening complete." Awaiting Graham's answer, she cocked her head in a way that irritated Avril.

"Graham, it would take a cold heart indeed to resist Clarice's charm," prodded May.

Again Mrs. Fontayne smiled, displaying dimples on either side of her round, rosy mouth. This time she rapped Graham's knuckles with her closed fan. "I simply will not take no for an answer. Do come!"

Graham threw up both hands in a gesture of helplessness. "All right! Very well, I surrender!"

With a swift dart of indignation, Avril realized that Graham was completely beguiled by Clarice Fontayne, or he would never have forgotten his promise of another lesson in chess this evening. When the ladies rose to leave, he accompanied them to the door without a backward glance at his bewildered ward.

Avril drew in her breath when she saw Mrs. Fontayne place her slender hand on Graham's arm and lean toward him. "Adieu, then, for a little while."

Looking on at the little scene, Avril felt an irrational anger toward the lovely intruder and toward Auntie May for bringing her to Montclair. When they said good-bye, Auntie May kissed Avril affectionately but Mrs. Fontayne held out her hand daintily, her fingertips barely touching Avril's, her eyes still seeking Graham. Nor did Graham seem to notice that Avril was standing there, forlorn and forgotten, as he extended his arm to escort the enchanting creature to her carriage.

Watching the carriage wind down the drive, Avril's hands balled into tight fists. She was feeling something she was to battle the rest of her life where Graham was concerned. Though too young to recognize it for what it was, she knew only that she felt somehow threatened and vaguely realized her feeling was connected with Clarice Fontayne's advent into their lives.

chapter
3

AN EAR-SHATTERING clap of thunder catapulted Avril out of a dreamless sleep. She sat bolt upright in bed as scissors of lightning slashed through the darkness lighting her whole bedroom. Clutching the sheet, she cowered as the crackling echo split the quiet summer night.

Trembling with fear, Avril was too frightened to call out. Then she realized she was alone anyway, since Dilly no longer slept in the trundle at the foot of her canopy bed.

For a moment she was immobilized, knowing more was likely to come, yet afraid to budge. When another crash reverberated through the house, she jumped out of bed and ran barefoot along the uncarpeted floor to the door. Flinging it open, she ran out into the hall looking for Graham, stumbling on the hem of her nightdress in her haste. Shivering, she reached the head of the stairs and saw that the glass-globed candles on the hall table were still burning. That meant he had not yet returned from the party at Cameron Hall.

A kind of helpless anger swept over Avril, momentarily quelling her fear. Another party! There had been so many parties this summer—at Cameron Hall and in Williamsburg as well, where Mrs. Fontayne had taken a house. Evening after evening Graham had changed his plans at the last minute to accept yet another social invitation, she thought with resentment, plopping down on the floor and gathering her gown around her knees.

She huddled on the top step—small, square chin on fists, elbows on nightgowned knees, bracing herself for the next roll of thunder. She wasn't going back to her room until this scary storm was over. Maybe Graham would be home soon—

Avril's face twisted fiercely at the thought of Mrs. Fontayne. Ever since Auntie May had brought her to Montclair, things had changed. There were fewer and fewer uninterrupted times with Graham. The long twilight walks, the evenings reading or playing chess had become rare occasions.

And it was all that woman's fault! Avril fumed. Clarice Fontayne, so dainty and beautiful, with her slender, graceful figure, her flirtatious manner! Being in the same room with her made Avril feel skinny, awkward, insecure. And the way Graham looked at her and laughed at every silly word . . . It was just too much to endure.

Another peal of thunder roared and Avril shuddered. She wished Graham were home so she could steal down the stairs, curl up with him in the big wing chair by the library fire, and feel his strong arms around her, fending off all her fears and doubts. All at once Avril felt very lonely and abandoned. A salty tear trickled down each cheek and she leaned her head against one of the banister posts.

Yet another rumble of distant thunder, this time farther away and not as frightening, but now she could hear the rattle of rain as it descended in torrents.

She would wait here until Graham returned, Avril decided. Make him sorry he had left her alone in this terrible storm. She shifted on the cold, hard steps, trying to find a more comfortable position. Gradually, as time passed, her eyes grew heavy. She nodded, yawning, and heard the grandfather clock in the downstairs hall striking the hour. As she counted the bongs, she drifted off. . . .

When Graham entered the house sometime later, a sudden gust of wind ripped the door from his hand and banged it sharply against the wall, waking Avril from her slumber. She was about to call his name when something stopped her.

She watched as Graham unfastened his cape and threw it across a chair. He stood there for a moment, his broad shoulders drooping under the elegant waistcoat. Avril knew instinctively that something was troubling him and longed to comfort him as he had so often comforted her, but she could not move.

From her perch, she watched him cross to the library and go inside. He did not bother to close the doors, so she had a clear view of the fireplace. Hector had left a small fire burning in the grate, and Graham crossed the room to stand before it, staring into the embers.

Graham felt his loneliness well up within. No amount of lively companionship or festive partying had yet eased that deep, unhealed wound. Tonight, riding back home to Montclair through the driving rain, thoughts of Lulie had flooded his mind.

Luella—his lovely, lost bride—though he always thought of her as Lulie. So young, the childish nickname had clung to her into glowing womanhood.

Remembering the first time he had seen her, a thousand memories moved across the screen of his mind—images of the impulsive young man who had loved riding, dancing, and pretty women. He had met Lulie while visiting a classmate in Charleston. She was a fragile beauty with enormous brown eyes and hair as black and silky as a raven's wing. Her demure charm was irresistible, and he had boldly scratched out every name but his from her dance card and spent the entire evening with her, entranced.

On the veranda of her parents' home, they had sipped punch and he had declared his intentions. "You may not believe it, but I am going to marry you," he had burst out, to her shocked surprise.

His courtship had been persistent, ardent. Her parents had finally given their consent and they had been married. Three months later she was dead, taken from him by a savage fever. And Graham had been left a widower at twenty.

For years he had mourned her. Three months did not make a marriage, nor warrant a lifetime of grief, his friends all said. He was urged to get on with his life, leave the past behind him—all the trite, easy phrases spoken by those who could not possibly understand what he had lost. They could not know that he was mourning the loss of something he had never fully possessed—a deepening relationship, growing devotion, a home, a family, loving companionship. All these had been stripped from him before they had ever been his.

He had brooded, drifting dangerously into melancholia. Gradually he had pulled himself through the worst of his depression. But it was not until the deaths of his friends, Paul and Eva Dumont, that he had been jolted from his self-imposed exile. Graham's new life had begun, he mused, when he had brought Avril to Montclair.

It was she who had brought the welcome diversion to his life that friends and family had failed to provide. This child who needed him so badly had in turn given him something to live for.

Graham's brow furrowed over his high-bridged aristocratic nose as he thought of the conversation he had had this evening with May Cameron and Clarice Fontayne.

His guardianship of his friend's daughter was well-known in the community and now, he was sure, had been widely discussed. Perhaps he himself should have foreseen some of the problems when he had first brought her here. Why had they not been obvious at the beginning, he wondered, and why had not the same people who warned him now, advised him then?

The question now was whether he should act upon this recent advice. He knew his reluctance to send her away to school was selfish. Avril was a delightful child, open, eager to learn, spontaneous in her affection, quick to laugh, easy to please. With her, he had recaptured some of his youthful zest, his enjoyment of simple games. There were fewer and fewer moments when he felt useless, with no purpose, no goals.

Graham sighed. He knew there was much truth in what both May Cameron and Clarice Fontayne had said when the subject of Avril had come up during dinner tonight.

"She is growing up with no contacts with girls of her own age.

You may be educating her mind with books you select, Graham," May had said, "but what about her spiritual training, the manners and social graces she should acquire before she can take her future position in society? What about matrimonial prospects? As her guardian you should be thinking of Avril's future."

"It is never too soon to prepare a girl for the place she will occupy in later life," nodded Clarice in agreement. "If Avril is the heiress May assures me she is, she must learn how to spot fortune hunters or others who would use her for their own gain. Only exposure to people from many different backgrounds in a variety of situations will give her that savoir-faire to be discriminating. I know that *my* days at boarding school were not only my happiest but also gave me my most valued and lasting friendships."

"But where would I send her?" Graham asked.

"Oh, there are any number of fine female academies," May said quickly. "There is Faith Academy in North Carolina, for instance, of which I have heard nothing but fine reports. Would you like me to get the necessary information for you to enroll Avril this fall?"

Graham had agreed gratefully. Now he was having second thoughts. On one hand, he knew May and Clarice were right. He was unhappily aware that he could not provide the instruction in deportment and etiquette that young ladies were supposed to have. Avril needed the atmosphere of a good boarding school. But even as he determined to abide by this decision, his real desire was to keep Avril here at Montclair. Already he knew that he would miss her greatly, that she had filled a terrible void in his life, that he had come to love her dearly. He felt a mixture of emotions: remorse over his lack of responsibility for her welfare, guilt because he selfishly wanted her near him.

But he knew what he must do—and without further delay. Unconsciously Graham straightened his shoulders.

As soon as May found out about this school in North Carolina, they would tell Avril. In the meantime—well, let the child enjoy her carefree existence at Montclair.

The driving rain slashed at the windows, and the sound of the wind was a long, keening wail around the eaves of the house.

Taking a taper from the box on the mantelpiece, Graham leaned down and relighted the dying fire. He put the candle into a brass holder, then left the library and walked down the hall toward the master bedroom he had occupied alone for the last eight years, unaware that his movements were being observed by the small shadowy figure crouched at the top of the stairs.

chapter

4

ALMOST FROM THE MINUTE she opened her eyes, Avril felt there was something different about this day. In the first place it was raining, a gentle, pattering sound rustling the leaves on the tree outside her open window, softening the morning light to a misty gray.

Next she had a kind of quivering in the pit of her stomach—half anticipation, half apprehension, as if something were about to happen.

Then the bedroom door opened quietly and Avril heard Dilly's felt-slippered feet on the polished floor as she came in and closed it behind her. Through slitted eyelids Avril saw her move to the armoire and take from it the white lawn dress embroidered with tiny sprigs of lilac that had been made by a Williamsburg seamstress for Avril at Mrs. Cameron's direction and declared by her to be "very apropos" for a child's half-mourning attire.

But why was Dilly laying out her best dress today? Avril wondered, her eyes now popping open in surprise as she watched Dilly take out starched petticoats from one of the bureau drawers, ruffled pantaloons and fresh white cotton stockings.

She sat up in bed and Dilly, alerted that her charge was now wide awake, turned around. "Time you wuz up, missy. Mr. Graham 'spectin' some genmun along wid de Jedge and Missus Cameron dis mawnin'. He tole me to hab you dressed and down in de parlor 'fo ten."

"But why? I was going riding. Logan and Marshall were going to meet me by the river and we were—"

"Doan know nuthin' 'bout dat. All I knows is what Mr. Graham tole me to do. Now, git on up. I axed Lonnie to bring up hot water for yo' bath and we's got to hurry."

Avril's lower lip thrust itself out in a pout. She hated to have her plans changed without warning. She had quickly become friends with the Cameron boys. Today they had agreed to meet at the river, build a raft, and play "shipwrecked pirates."

Marshall had accepted her more readily than Logan, who was older by a year and sometimes considered himself too old to play with a girl or to take part in the imaginative games Marshall was always suggesting. More often than not, he condescended to join them, as long as he was permitted to be the captain or king or whatever leader the game required. And because it was so much more fun to have him, the younger two usually allowed him to have his way.

Now her day was spoiled, Avril fretted.

"Why do I have to get all dressed up for company?" she pouted.

"Now, none of dat mule-headed actin'," Dilly ordered as she helped Avril out of her nightie. "How many times do Mr. Graham ever ax you to do somethin'? Think you could be sweet and pleasant when he do!" She sniffed indignantly.

Immediately Avril was conscience-stricken. Dilly was right. It must be important or Graham would never have requested her presence. He was kindness itself, and Avril adored him. More and more every day she lived at Montclair, she realized how lucky she was to have him as her guardian.

Subdued, Avril sat while Dilly applied the brush to her unruly mane, only grimacing once in awhile when the brush hit a snag of stubborn curls. Finally, smoothly brushed and bowed, and neatly buttoned into the becoming, high-waisted gown, Avril straightened her shoulders, awaiting Dilly's approval.

"Um-hum," it came as Dilly, head to one side, turned her around slowly, then gave a last adjustment to the lavender satin sash. "Yes'm, think you'll do jes' fine."

Coming down the steps, Avril had a clear view of a portion of the parlor. Besides the familiar figure of Auntie May Cameron, and her husband, two other gentlemen were seated on the damask-striped sofa opposite them. Graham was standing in front of the fireplace, where he could see her approach. He nodded as she drew near, then came to the doorway to usher her inside the room.

"Come, Avril, we've been waiting for you."

That funny little shiver passed over her again as she entered the room, aware of the eyes of all the adults upon her. Something very strange was going on, Avril was sure, and it had something to do with her.

Auntie May, looking beautiful in pink taffeta and a matching bonnet with plumes, its puckered lining framing her oval face with a delicate rosy tint, rose to greet Avril and cupped her cheek with her cool hand.

"Here, darling, sit beside me," she said as she arranged herself again on the sofa and patted the pillowed seat.

Gravely Graham introduced her. "Gentlemen, my ward, Avril Dumont."

The two men, who had risen at Avril's entrance, bowed in turn as Graham said, "Mr. Emory Fisher and Mr. Horton Daniels."

Avril nodded, acknowledging the introductions, then clasped her small hands together tightly on her lap, fastening her eyes on Graham as he continued speaking.

"Mr. Fisher and Mr. Daniels are lawyers, Avril. Lawyers are well versed in legal matters and are able to advise people on all matters pertaining to the law—what to do and what not to do under different circumstances. You understand that, don't you?"

Avril nodded again, still mystified by what all this was leading up to, and kept her gaze fixed upon Graham.

"As you also know, my dear, your father designated me as your guardian and entrusted me with your care if anything should happen to him and your mother. Of course, neither of us ever thought—" Graham paused. "They were both young and healthy, and he could not foresee anything other than living to see you grown, married, safe, and protected—" Here Graham paused as if emotion made it difficult for him to go on. There was an uneasy stir among the occupants of the room. At last Graham was able to finish. "So, because your father, being human as we all are, could not look into the future and imagine the untimely death he was to suffer, he made no provision for you. That is to say, your parents left no will, no written document to ensure that you, as their only child and heir, would inherit their combined goods and property—house, land, personal belongings, bank accounts. Do you understand what I'm telling you, Avril?" Graham asked.

Listening attentively, Avril came to the conclusion that her plight was not unlike those of heroines in some of the stories she had read.

"You mean that I am a penniless orphan?"

There was a ripple of suppressed laughter.

Graham smiled at Avril's question but replied with great seriousness. "No, my dear. Not at all. Quite the contrary, in fact. You are potentially an heiress to a sizable fortune. However, we have a problem that must be resolved in order to guarantee that you will be the beneficiary of all that your parents would have left you had they been able to make provision for that before their untimely deaths. As it is, there is a danger of your losing everything unless—"

Graham cleared his throat. "You see, my dear, the way the law stands, unless specific exceptions are made in a will or provisions made before the death of parents, only male children are eligible to inherit an estate. Your parents were both very wealthy and their combined property and individual wealth amount to an enormous fortune. Unfortunately such wealth breeds unscrupulous claimants, and greedy would-be inheritors often appear on the scene."

At this point Graham, hands clasped behind his back, began to pace back and forth. Then he halted in front of Avril and, holding her in a gaze both tender and concerned, continued, "In your case, a male claimant, a very distant relative, has come forth to claim the whole estate. That is what we want to discuss with you. You see, if a female child is the sole survivor—as you are—" Again Graham paused. "The inheritance is transferred into the keeping of her husband as her protector—if she marries."

Graham seemed to be casting about for support, looking first to the two lawyers, then to Judge Cameron. "On the advice of these two gentlemen and of my trusted friends, we have come up with a plan to save your fortune. We could safeguard your inheritance until you reach the age of twenty-one . . . if you would consent to a marriage."

"Marriage!" gasped Avril. "But who? Who would want to marry me?"

Graham's face flushed but he held her eyes steadily. "We have discussed this at length, and it is thought I would be the most logical person. I am already your legal guardian, since your father did leave a witnessed paper to that effect. This would be a marriage on paper only, secretly performed, and later quietly annulled—the purpose being only to protect your rightful inheritance and secure your future."

"But am I not too young to be married?" Avril looked bewildered.

For the first time Mr. Daniels spoke. "Not if you give your consent . . . since it has all been explained to you and since you were neither threatened nor persuaded against your will."

"If you fully understand the reasons we are suggesting this legal step be taken, only your consent is needed," Mr. Fisher added.

Numb, Avril turned to Auntie May for her reassurance and Mrs. Cameron patted her arm. "What Graham is suggesting, darling, is that you give your consent to a legal ceremony so that he can continue taking care of you until you are old enough to take care of yourself. At twenty-one, you will be a very wealthy young lady, and you can decide then what you want to do with the house, property, and valuable land your dear mama and papa owned and wanted you to have. Otherwise, strangers will get everything. So, you understand, this is for your own good."

Mr. Daniels then picked up the thread of explanation. "Miss Dumont, this measure will give your guardian greater authority to protect all that belongs to you. It is simply a matter of legality."

"As the law now reads," Mr. Fisher followed up, consulting a heavy volume, " 'a husband has custody of his wife's person; total, exclusive, sole ownership of her property—real estate, lands, jewelry, monies, and any other so designated items, chattel and the use thereof, unless previously settled on her by will or placed into a trusteeship if she is a minor.' In your case, Miss Dumont," he said, looking up over his spectacles, "this was not done. So, unless you marry immediately, everything that should have been yours to inherit upon your parents' deaths is in jeopardy."

"You see, darling, why this formality is necessary—and right away?" Auntie May leaned close to Avril and she was immersed in the scent of roses that always clung to Mrs. Cameron. "It is the only way Graham can do what your dear mama and papa trusted him to do in your behalf."

"Judge Cameron is legally qualified to perform the ceremony, so there is no need to wait," added Graham, who had been strangely silent since his introduction of the subject.

Avril focused her large gray-green eyes on Graham. "You? You would marry *me?*"

Graham's lean, handsome face reddened slightly. "Yes, but of course it would be understood by all of us that when you are twenty-one, this marriage, which will exist only on paper, can be easily put aside, leaving you free to marry anyone of your choice. It is only a legal guarantee that your home in Mississippi will remain yours as well as the income from the lands belonging to your estate. It will not in any way inhibit your girlhood, your education, or any future matrimonial plans."

Avril continued to stare wide-eyed at him and for a moment Graham seemed to be struggling for composure.

It was Judge Cameron who came to his rescue. "I'm certain that an intelligent young lady such as you seem to be should have no trouble grasping the importance of the situation. Are there any questions you would like to ask, my dear?"

Auntie May rushed in with an impatient little toss of her head that set the plumes of her bonnet dancing.

"Oh, come now, Hugh," she admonished her husband, "there's no need for Avril to understand every tiny detail as long as she knows Graham is doing this for her own good. Listen, darling, all you have to do is sign your name on the papers the lawyers have drawn up. Then we shall just go through the little ceremony in which you and Graham will repeat the words Hugh gives you to say and *voilà,* you can put it out of your mind. Isn't that right, Hugh?"

"Well, just about—," answered Mr. Cameron cautiously.

Avril did not understand at all, but it didn't really matter. The one thing of which she was certain was that she wanted to please Graham, whatever that might mean. If he wanted her to sign papers, then that's what she would do.

Within a few minutes the two of them were standing side by side in front of Judge Cameron, who had put on his spectacles and looked quite imposing. From the scent of roses and the rustle of taffeta, Avril knew that Auntie May was close behind her, flanked by the two lawyers.

Judge Cameron read some words from a small black book, and in a faint voice Avril repeated them after him: "I, Avril Dumont . . ." followed by the solemn promises that were echoed by Graham in his deep, steady baritone.

Afterwards she placed her wobbly, childish signature under his firm, bold-stroked one on the line Mr. Daniels pointed out after reading the following paragraph slowly aloud:

> On this tenth day of September, in the year of our Lord eighteen hundred and eight, in the county of Mayfield in Virginia, the marriage of Avril Dumont and Graham Montrose was legally solemnized and so witnessed.

chapter
5

"BUT I DON'T WANT to go away! I don't want to leave Montclair! I won't go! I won't!"

The three adults facing Avril reacted in stunned silence to the girl's outburst. The first to recover was Clarice Fontayne, who lifted her delicately arched eyebrows knowingly above her unfurled fan.

"Ah, a temper to match the hair," she remarked in an amused tone.

Auntie May quickly moved toward Avril, who stood quivering with emotion, hands balled into fists, huge gray-green eyes blazing with indignation.

"But, darling, don't you see it is for your own good? You are much too isolated here—with no young girls of your age for companions. School will be a wonderful experience. So many new things to see and do and learn."

"I don't need anything or anyone new! I am perfectly happy! And I'm learning all sorts of things right here at Montclair. We are just teaching Fancy to jump and I am getting much better. Please, Graham, don't make me go!"

Graham turned pale. He had not expected this violent reaction to the prospect of going away to school. Avril had never behaved in such a defiant manner.

"My dear—," he began, halted, then tried again, "I believe . . . we feel . . . it is thought—"

45

The eyes staring at him in disbelief suddenly grew bright with tears, and the stubborn little mouth trembled. Graham's heart wrenched within him. To hurt this dearly loved child was the last thing he wanted. Before he could say more, she gave a rebellious toss of red curls and stamped her foot.

"It's not fair! I don't want to go! I shall hate it! If you send me away, I shall never forgive you!"

And with that the tears spilled over and ran down her flushed cheeks. She wiped them away angrily. Then with one last furious look at each face staring at her in astonishment, Avril whirled around and ran out of the room, letting the double doors slam shut behind her.

"Well!" Auntie May let out her breath. "I never dreamed the child would take the idea of boarding school so negatively. I must admit I am more than a little surprised."

Clarice gave a little laugh, fanning herself. She glanced over at Graham. A lightly mocking smile touched her pretty mouth.

"Graham must have spoiled her extravagantly for her not to think of going away to boarding school as an exciting adventure."

Graham looked worried. "I hope not. I did not intend—"

"No, of course you did not. These things happen and before long you have 'l'enfant terrible' on your hands—unhappy herself, and certainly not a cause of joy to anyone around."

"I'm afraid Clarice may be right, Graham dear," May nodded. "Avril has had the run of the place since she came, with no real discipline, no duties expected of her, and most unfortunate of all, no formal studies. A girl with her breeding and background and her future position *must* be educated."

Graham did not bother to defend himself. How could he explain to the two ladies that Avril had not needed discipline, that anything he had asked she had done quite willingly, that instead of a problem she had been a pleasure, a cheerful, bright companion, an antidote to his loneliness. He had been more shocked by her outburst than either of them.

"Would you like me to follow her? See if I can talk some sense into her?" May asked anxiously.

Graham shook his head. "No. That is my responsibility. Perhaps we should have prepared her for this, not just sprung it upon her, expecting her to be delighted. I shall talk to her later. But first, I think she should be given time to compose herself."

"Well, then, we should be off"—Clarice rose and, picking up her gloves, beaded purse, and ivory-handled parasol, gave Graham an amused smile—"and leave Graham to his difficult task."

May darted an uncertain glance at Graham. "You're sure I cannot be of any help?"

"Quite sure. At least for now, May. Later, when we ready Avril for her departure, we shall probably need all the help we can get," he replied, opening the large double doors and allowing the ladies to precede him into the hall.

At the front door May turned back, anxiety puckering her brow. "Are you certain you don't want me to go up to Avril before we leave?"

Graham glanced toward the upstairs rooms where Avril had fled after the upsetting scene. The line of his jaw was set. "No, thank you, May," he insisted. "I'll attend to it."

"Maybe that would be better," sighed May. "It's clear the child adores you."

Clarice put a slender hand on Graham's arm and said in a low, teasing voice, "Don't take it so seriously, *mon cher*. A child Avril's age is given to such displays. Melodrama is a tool used to manipulate one like a puppet or a weapon to achieve certain demands. Do not give way. *You*, after all, are the adult." She gave him one of her most charming smiles and swept past him on a whiff of expensive perfume.

After his guests' carriage had rumbled down the driveway and out of sight, Graham remained deep in thought. Looking down, he was surprised to see that he was still holding the booklet on Faith Academy May had brought him. On the cover was a pen and ink sketch of a brick building. Flipping through the pages, he quickly scanned the contents—information as to the teaching staff, boarding accommodations, eligibility for admission, curriculum offered, and fees.

Tapping the booklet on his open palm, Graham glanced again toward the second floor. Then he mounted the steps and strode down the hall to Avril's bedroom, where he paused before rapping softly on the door.

"Avril," he called. "When you are quite ready to discuss this matter, I will be in the library." Then he stooped and slid the little brochure under the doorway.

At his knock and familiar voice Avril raised her head. Leaning on her elbow she saw the brown pamphlet appear on the floor as Graham pushed it through the crack of the door. She guessed what it was but made no move to retrieve it.

She squeezed her eyes tight shut, wishing she could blot out the terrible scene. She knew she had behaved horribly. The minute she had heard the library door bang shut behind her she had stopped, expecting it to be yanked open again by an angry adult. Certainly she had expected instant punishment, for she knew she deserved it.

But the thought of going away to school, leaving Montclair, had come as such a shock that she had lost her head.

Standing outside the library door, frozen with guilt, she could not help overhearing the discussion about her that had followed her exit.

Clarice's comments had been particularly humiliating. "A temper to match the hair." Sometimes the Cameron boys had teased her about her red hair, but she had been crushed by the contempt with which the lady uttered the words.

She had not waited to hear more and had run upstairs, but just as she reached the landing, the adults came out of the room into the hallway. To avoid being seen, Avril had hunched down, hidden from view. It was then she had heard Clarice's warning to Graham. Cheeks flaming, Avril had scurried to her bedroom and there flung herself face down on the bed in a torrent of tears.

She was furious with herself for what she had done, but angrier still at what had been done to her. It was all that woman's fault, Avril was sure. Graham would never have thought of sending her away if she had not suggested it! But why would Graham want her to go when they were so happy together? And he was happy, she could tell. They had such good times together. Riding, walking, reading, talking . . .

Avril pounded her fists into the mattress. Seething inside, fury like quicksilver raced through her slight frame. But it was an impotent kind of fury. She would, in the end, have no choice. Children never did. Adults ran the world—in this case, strangely enough, the ladies. And no matter how Graham really felt about it, he would pay attention to their advice.

She didn't blame Auntie May. Avril knew that *she* truly believed this was the wisest course and desired it only because she loved Avril. It was Mrs. Fontayne she didn't like, could not trust.

Avril had noticed the way Clarice Fontayne made everything seem amusing with her honey-sweet voice, making comments about people that grown-ups thought clever and witty, but were actually cruel and cutting. How strange that no one else seemed to notice. Not even Graham.

Sighing, Avril swung her legs over the edge of the bed, jumped down and went over to the door to pick up the slim book. She took it back to the bed and, sitting cross-legged, began to read.

After a long while, she tossed it aside and got up to pour fresh water from the rose-patterned pitcher into the porcelain bowl on the washstand, splashing her swollen eyes and warm face with the cooling liquid.

She brushed her hair, tugging viciously at the tangles almost as if to punish herself. Then she made a face in the mirror and, smoothing her wrinkled pinafore, picked up the pamphlet from Faith Academy and started downstairs.

At the library door she knocked tentatively until she heard Graham's gentle "Come in" before pushing it open and going inside.

"I'm sorry, Graham. Very sorry," she whispered meekly.

"I'm sorry, too, Avril. It was a mistake not to talk it over with you first. That was my fault. I apologize." His gaze on the abject little figure before him was tender.

She raised her chin then rather defensively and said in a firmer voice, "But I still don't want to go."

Graham was silent for a minute, as if giving her words full consideration, then he spoke to her very directly.

"Do you believe, Avril, that any decision I make regarding you is, in my judgment, in your best interest and ultimately for your happiness?"

Never taking her eyes from his face, she nodded solemnly.

"Well, then, you must trust me this time as well." There was firm conviction in his next words. "It is settled, Avril. You have been enrolled in Faith Academy, which I am convinced is a very fine school in every respect."

Avril caught her lower lip between her teeth to keep it from quivering and tightened her hands clasped behind her back.

"I'll go then, if that's what you want me to do," she said, but her tone was plaintive.

"Thank you, my dear. I counted on you to understand my decision in this matter." A smile lifted the corners of his mouth as he continued to look at her. She was being dramatic, he thought, with some inner amusement. "I feel sure once you are at the Academy with girls your own age, you will wonder why you ever made such a fuss. Mrs. Fontayne tells me her days at boarding school were among the happiest of her life."

Avril dug her nails into the palms of her hands to suppress the angry protest that rose to her lips. She certainly did not care to hear about Clarice's school days!

"I *am* happy, *here* with *you!*" Avril cried stubbornly. "Girls my own age are probably silly, giggling creatures. And what shall I do without Fancy?" Now the voice quavered.

"Fancy will be here waiting for you when you come back for vacations and holidays. In the meantime she will receive the best of care, have no fear."

"I shall still miss her—and you, Graham—most awfully!" Avril moved closer to his chair, her eyes luminous, pleading.

Graham put out his arm and pulled her close.

"And I shall miss you, too, Avril. But children need companions their own age. Aren't you ever lonely here?"

She shook her head emphatically.

Her body had stiffened and Graham felt the tangible obstinacy in her rigid bearing. What a determined little thing she was, he thought. Was she playing on his sympathies, trying to get her own way as Clarice had suggested? He must not waver, for her own good, he reminded himself sternly. So when he saw the silent pleas in the gray-green depths of her eyes, he forced himself to strengthen his resolve.

A silence, taut with the conflicting emotions of these two who had grown so close, stretched for a full minute.

Then cocking her head to one side, Avril demanded belligerently, "Where *is* North Carolina anyway?"

Graham threw back his head and laughed heartily, then gave Avril a hug. "And *that* very question tells me there is a very real reason—a need, in fact—for you to go to school and learn your geography, my little 'know-nothing'!"

Avril knew she was defeated. The argument was at an end. Outwardly resigned and submissive to the decision, Avril told herself that someday when she was older and could decide for herself, she would live here at Montclair with Graham . . . and no one could send her away!

For the next few weeks there was a flurry of activity in preparation for Avril's departure. Mrs. Cameron would see her safely to the Academy, as she had relatives in North Carolina she could visit along the way. There was much sewing, shopping, and packing to be done, and Auntie May took over all the details that were so foreign to a bachelor such as Graham.

Faith Academy students were required to adhere to a rigid dress code and were issued regulation uniforms. Dresses for Sunday and other special occasions, however, were permitted in the girls' wardrobe, so Auntie May, hoping to awaken some interest in Avril, took her to her seamstress in Williamsburg for the fittings.

Avril, still quietly resentful of Auntie May's part in the plan to send her away, did not feign enthusiasm for the tiresome ordeal. In these last days at Montclair, she wanted nothing more than to ride Fancy along the now familiar trails and to spend time with Graham.

Auntie May put down Avril's indifference to childish stubbornness. Not unsympathetic to what she assumed was a natural fear of such a change, she did not suspect the depth of Avril's bond to Graham. If she *had,* May might have congratulated herself on this strategic move to put distance between them before the child's devotion became obsessive.

The week of departure came at last. In Avril's bedroom her trunk stood open. On the bed neat stacks of lace-edged cotton chemises, petticoats, and pantaloons waited to be packed at the last possible moment to avoid excessive wrinkling.

Inexorably the hours flew past, and, on the night before she was to leave, Avril knew that everything had been done to make the occasion a festive one. All her favorite dishes were served at supper. Cookie had even baked a lemon sponge cake for dessert. Afterward, Graham presented her with a going-away gift of a lovely leather writing case.

"So you can practice your penmanship," he said, striving for a casual tone, "and keep me informed with regular letters of your progress, as well as all the good times you'll be having."

There was much more each longed to say to the other. But one could not find the words, and the other dared not.

The next day Auntie May arrived from Cameron Hall with all her baggage and hatboxes and hampers to be transferred to the Montrose carriage already laden with Avril's belongings.

There was so much last-minute bustle that Avril had just the barest moment for a last good-bye as Graham took her face in both his hands, kissed her lightly on each cheek, then handed her carefully into the carriage, where Auntie May was settling herself. The two adults exchanged a few remarks, assurances, and farewells, then the coachman clicked his reins, the wheels began to move, and they were off. Avril poked her head out the window, gazing wistfully back at Montclair for as long as she could see it, waving her hand frantically to Graham, who stood on the porch steps waving in return. Then they passed the bend of the drive, and the house was lost to view.

In all the business of preparation and departure, no one had seemed to recall the significance of this day—September tenth.

Part II

Faith Academy
New Hope, North Carolina 1809

Train up a child in the way he should go: and when he is old, he will not depart from it.

Proverbs 22:6

chapter
6

COLD DAWN seeped through the narrow windows of the Girls Dormitory with thin fingers of light. Avril shivered, pulled the covers around her shoulders, and shut her eyes tighter, dreading the bell that would soon ring through the upper hall, signaling the start of another day at the Academy.

Snuggling deeper, she thought longingly of how it would have been at Montclair on such a morning. A fire would already be crackling into flaming warmth on the hearth of her bedroom, Dilly might wake her crooning her name softly, and then there would be a lovely breakfast downstairs with Graham and the prospect of a brisk ride on Fancy.

Avril tried to escape back into sleep, knowing the dull ache of homesickness was waiting for her as soon as she came fully awake. She had tried hard to adjust to the new and different regimen of life at the Academy, but it was very difficult. Here there were rules, regulations, and set times for every activity, a far cry from the easygoing way of life she had known at Montclair. She missed the freedom more than anything—except of course, Graham.

The clanging sound of the rising bell shattered the quiet and a little moan from the next bed alerted Avril that Becky was awake. Rebecca Buchanan had become Avril's closest friend at the Academy, and this friendship had assuaged somewhat her constant longing for home.

Rebecca came from nearby Pleasant Valley, where she lived on her family's plantation, Woodlawn.

In fact, Becky had been the first girl Avril had met upon her arrival at the austere boarding school. They had liked each other at once, despite the fact that they were opposites in both physical appearance and personality.

Becky was small and plump with rosy cheeks, bright blue eyes, and dark hair. In contrast to Avril's reserve, bordering on shyness with strangers, Becky was vivacious and outgoing, perhaps due in part to the large and lively family in which she was the only girl among three older brothers.

"Mama and Papa thought I was growing up too much a tomboy. That's why they sent me here—to become a lady!" she confided to Avril, laughing merrily. "At least that's what they hope!"

Becky had an assortment of relatives—aunts, uncles, and cousins—besides her immediate family about whom she talked so continually that Avril began to feel she knew them all intimately.

But Becky spoke most of her brother Jamison, who was closest to her own age and, in her opinion, the brightest, wittiest, kindest boy in the world. And as if these qualities were not enough, she declared him to be also the best top spinner, the best horseman, and the best square dancer in the entire county.

"Just wait until you meet him, Avril! You'll know every word I've said is true!" Dimpling, Becky added, "And wait until he meets *you!* I've already written him all about you!"

Avril could not help wondering what Becky had chosen to say about her.

"You must come visit us!" Her roommate had extracted a pledge to do so at the first opportune time.

Now as Becky began to stir, Avril sat up and leaned across the small space between their beds, tugging at her covers.

"Becky! Today we're going to buy Christmas presents, remember?" Avril called softly.

On Fridays the older students were allowed a visit to the New Hope shops as an extra privilege of their age and rank. Although these excursions were always chaperoned by one of the teachers, the shopping forays allowed the girls to wander, two by two, within the confines of the small square.

At this reminder of the exciting break in their usual daily routine, Becky's eyes popped open and she was out of bed in a flash.

The girls chatted happily as they dressed, helping each other with the back buttons of their simple gray dresses and blue cotton pinafore ties. They took turns brushing each other's hair and stuffing it under their white bobbinet caps with cherry-colored ribbons signifying their status as "upper-form" pupils. The younger girls wore pink.

As they clattered down the uncarpeted steps to the dining hall, they continued discussing the purchases they hoped to make that day. Of course, with so many to buy for in her family, Becky's list was much longer than Avril's.

Arriving late at the dining hall, they received a look of admonition from the tutoress at the head of the table. Hurriedly the two took their places and bowed their heads for grace along with the others.

> "Come Lord Jesus, our Guest to be
> At this feast bestowed by Thee."

Avril and Becky always avoided looking at each other during this traditional blessing for fear they would burst into giggles. The usual breakfast of oatmeal porridge, thick slices of whole wheat bread, and tea laced with milk hardly seemed much of a "feast" to the two girls.

After grace, there was noisy scraping on the bare pine floors as chairs were pushed back and everyone sat down to eat.

The daily schedule at the Academy rarely changed. Following breakfast the students gathered for Bible reading and morning prayers, after which they were expected to make their beds and tidy up their cubicles in the dormitories, gather their school textbooks and slates, and report to their first class by eight.

At eleven the classes broke for a midday snack of hot cocoa and bread and butter. If the weather was pleasant, they went outside for a play period. This was a welcome release for both Avril and Becky—perhaps more than for some of the other girls unaccustomed to fresh air and vigorous exercise. But Avril, whose companions for the past year had been the Cameron boys, and Becky, who had always played with her brothers, looked forward to this recess with keen anticipation.

Today it was even more difficult for them to settle down to their history lesson. Friday afternoon freedom beckoned, distracting their thoughts from the dreary lecture on ancient Greece and Rome.

Hard as she tried to concentrate on the map to which Dame Finley was pointing with her long ruler, Avril kept glancing at the clock. The hands inched forward toward the hour.

Avril and Becky kept casting hopeful looks at one another and finally, when the bell rang for the end of class, they were the first on their feet to be dismissed.

Rushing upstairs, nearly tripping over each other in their haste, the girls put on their bonnets and gloves required for going "downtown," threw their short, dark blue capes lined in bright red flannel around their shoulders, and flew down the steps almost as fast as they had run up. They waited impatiently for the rest of their group to assemble and then marched in a decorous double line behind the austere figure of Dame Whitman, who was their chaperone for the outing.

The pace of the group quickened when they reached the town square, and a ripple of anticipation moved through the throng of eager little shoppers. The stores were filled with things to delight the eye as well as tempt the pocketbook. Avril and Becky, each with her own carefully prepared list, moved through the shops with deliberate care, choosing gifts for loved ones at home.

While Becky filled her shopping bag, Avril decided on some beeswax candles tied with red and green ribbons for Graham's elderly Aunt Laura Barnwell, with whom Avril had spent the night in Williamsburg on her journey to the Academy in the fall, and a pair of warm knitted wristlets for Dilly, whose arthritis had worsened in the harsher Virginia climate.

But Graham's gift took more thought. It must be something very special, something no one else would give him. She considered a hand-tooled leather box for his desk, but the asking price was more than the amount of money she had saved from the "pin money" allowed by the Academy for families to send to the students. She wished she had become more proficient in knitting so she might make him a scarf as some of the other girls were doing for their fathers. It was time to go before Avril had made a final decision. She would have to make up her mind before next Friday.

On the way back to school they were allowed to stop at the Village Bakery for molasses cookies. Upon emerging from the fragrant warmth of the shop, the girls were met with a happy surprise. Floating down from the leaden skies were large, lazy snowflakes, and by the time the little expedition had reached the Academy the whole world seemed cloaked in white ermine.

Passing through the arched front door over which were carved the words, "THIS IS A PLACE OF PEACE, A DWELLING OF BLESSINGS," they hurried to spread the news to the younger students who had remained inside during the afternoon for lessons in knitting, embroidery, music, or painting. There was a dash to the windows to verify the state of the weather, and by the time the girls had assembled for supper, whispered plans for sledding and toboggan-ing tomorrow had circulated throughout the entire dining hall. Even the prospect of this change in routine lent its own special seasoning to the evening meal of pumpkin soup, ladled into bowls passed down from steaming tureens at the head of each table.

It was still snowing at bedtime. Settling under their quilts, Avril and Becky whispered long after the lamps were blown out, both hoping the weather would hold.

Hearing the nightwatchman making his rounds, Avril slipped from her cot to look out the window. The man was blowing on his conch shell, crying the hour: "Hear, brethren, hear! The hour of nine has come. Keep pure each heart, and chasten every home."

As he passed, he left footprints in the deepening snow.

The ecstatic delight with which the first snowfall had been greeted was soon replaced by anxiety, as all the next day it continued. A strong wind blew drifts along the paths and obscured the roadway in front of the Academy. Temperatures dropped, as did the girls' expectations of fun and frolic. Word came that all over the county the snow had reached blizzard proportions, and as it froze in the icy air a thick crust formed, closing whole households in snow-locked captivity.

With only a few weeks until the Christmas holidays, it was apparent that the roads to and from New Hope were now virtually impassable. Except for the few students who lived nearby, it appeared that most of the girls would not be able to go home for their midyear vacation.

For Avril, who had been counting the days until her return to Montclair, the blow was devastating. Even the fact that Becky would not be able to go to her home either did nothing to subdue her own disappointment. She was inconsolable, and tears of frustration dampened her pillow night after night, no matter how Becky tried to comfort her.

Faced with a school full of homesick girls, the faculty was hard put to combat the combined depression that swept through the Academy. But something had to be done to stem the tide of misery and make the students' enforced stay both festive and meaningful. Someone suggested a Christmas pageant in which everyone would participate, and it was after breakfast and devotions one morning that Dame Nesbitt, the headmistress, made the announcement.

This proved to be a stroke of genius! Soon every girl, from the youngest and smallest, who took the part of a shepherd boy, to the tallest and oldest, who was given the choice role of the archangel, was involved in rehearsals, with the heady prospect of performing before an audience made up of New Hope residents.

The play was to be held in the school just prior to the Christmas Eve service at the nearby church with which the Academy was affiliated.

Avril and Becky, both of whom had sweet, true voices, were chosen to be in the heavenly chorus and thus excused from the knitting and sewing classes, in which neither particularly excelled, to practice carols with Dame Francis, the music teacher.

Avril found herself enchanted by the beautiful Nativity story and the lovely hymns accompanying the narration. Her religious training had been sadly neglected, she learned, for she had never heard anything like this. As a small child she had spent most of her time with Dilly, who, though devoted to her young charge, was ignorant of spiritual matters and had no ability to instruct her in any but the most obvious "shoulds" and "should nots."

Nor had Avril's parents given her any such training. The young Dumonts belonged to the planter class of Natchez and, given the circles in which they moved, saw nothing unusual about the way in which they were bringing up their daughter. Following the pattern of social life dictated by their position, their time was taken up with visits, parties, and travel. There was little time to spend with Avril, though they saw that her every need was met and left her in the care of only the most trusted servants. Nevertheless, it was not surprising that by the time Avril arrived at Montclair, she knew practically nothing of basic Christian principles.

And despite her deep regard for her guardian, she had not gleaned anything profoundly meaningful from Graham's personal ritual. Since no church was less than a day's ride from the plantation by horseback or carriage, he never attended services except when visiting in Williamsburg. Grace at mealtime and a Scripture verse dutifully read to Avril at breakfast each day were the extent of her spiritual "lessons," for with his natural reserve, Graham had never talked freely of his own beliefs.

Still, at some unremembered time in the past, someone must have taught Avril the little verse she recited hurriedly before hopping into bed at night:

> Matthew, Mark, Luke and John,
> The bed be blest that I lie on.
> Four posters to my bed—

Four angels round my head—
One to watch and one to pray.
Two to bear my soul away.

To be truthful, Avril hadn't even known who Matthew, Mark, Luke, and John were until coming to the Academy and learning they were disciples of Jesus. Now she wasn't at all sure that Dame Francis would even consider her hastily said ditty a real bedtime prayer.

For all her disappointment in not being able to spend the holidays with Graham at Montclair, Avril would look back on this Christmas at the Academy as the beginning of what was to be a lifelong quest.

chapter
7

WITH THE SOUND of enthusiastic applause still ringing in their ears, Avril, Becky, and the other upper-form students pounded up the stairs to the dormitory to get out of their pageant costumes and dress for the service at the church.

"Wasn't it fun?" asked Becky, breathless as she tossed her gilt-paper halo on the bed and struggled out of her white, gauzy, cotton angel's robe.

"Oh, it was beautiful!" sighed Avril, still in awed wonder of the final scene of the tableau when all had knelt in adoration at the stable crib, presided over by Mary and Joseph and attended by the lavishly costumed three kings.

Avril had become so enthralled with the unfolding drama, so new to her, that she had forgotten to sing with the angelic chorus a number of times. The fact that this story was true, that it had actually taken place many hundreds of years ago, stunned her imagination. It was far more interesting than any of the fairy stories she had read. Baby Jesus was *real*, and that this same infant was also the God who had created the world was staggering information.

"Come, Avril! Hurry, or we'll be late!" urged Becky. "Here, let me help you get those wings off!"

Avril did not really want to take off her wings made of triangles of white paper, overlapped and pasted on cardboard. She had loved being an "angel," loved being part of this incredible story.

But Becky was already tugging at the strings attaching them to Avril's shoulders. Waiting for her was the pretty emerald green bombazine dress that Auntie May had had made for her, with its corded banding around the hem and the ecru lace edging the high collar and long sleeves. There had not yet been an occasion to wear it.

As soon as they were dressed both girls ran back downstairs, joining the lines forming at the entrance to walk over to the church.

Looking up, Avril saw that the night sky was sprinkled with thousands of stars while her boots crunched on the ice-crusted snow underfoot. She drew in a lungful of the frigid air, and her whole body tingled with anticipation. She had never been out this late in her entire life! Climbing the steps into the church, she sensed she was on the brink of some momentous event.

As she entered the darkened church she was handed a long, beeswax candle. In hushed expectancy, she took her place with the other Academy students in one of the special pews reserved for them.

Silently, ushers with lighted tapers approached the end of the pews and lit the candles of the first worshipers in each row until the whole church came alive with light. Avril felt as if her heart would stop, so breathless was the moment. When at some unseen signal, the entire congregation stood, their candles flickering like the stars she had seen in the night sky, she gave a little gasp.

Suddenly the organ struck a chord, and joyful voices rang out:

> Praise the Lord, whose saving splendor
> Shines into darkest night!
> Born this night of Glory, to Him render
> Praises, for this never-ceasing Light!

The organ continued to play softly in the background as a group of young men carrying bells entered from the side door and formed a half-circle in front. Soon the place reverberated with the glorious ringing of the bells accompanied by the organ. Then came the voice of a boy soprano, rising above the instruments in unwavering purity:

Morning Star, O cheering sight!
Ere Thou cam'st, how dark earth's night!

Avril felt prickles along her scalp and a shivery sensation rippled down her spine. Unexpected tears stung her eyes and she had to swallow very hard over the lump that rose in her throat.

Caught up in the miracle of the moment, she was still in a daze when the minister stepped to the middle of the wooden railing in front of the pews.

"And now we will join in our traditional celebration of the 'Lovefeast.' As in the early days, when Christians met and broke bread together as a symbol of their fellowship and love, it is our custom in this church to partake of a simple meal on certain occasions of particular spiritual significance. The name we have given this time of communion is derived from the Greek word *agape*.

"This sharing does not in any way supplant the observance of the Lord's Supper. We simply seek to foster the spirit of unity and good will among men to remind each of us that Christ is present within you as with your neighbor who knows Him as personal Savior.

"As you share, make the commitment within your heart to live more worthily and obey more carefully all the commands that Jesus, our Savior, has given and to strive to follow Him more closely in all your daily activities."

Avril was leaning forward in her seat, listening to every word, feeling her heart thud. With every fiber of her being, she wanted to believe what the minister was saying.

Could Christ really be within *her*?

From both sides of the aisle women were passing huge, round trays containing mugs of steaming coffee and baskets of warm sweet rolls. Avril took hers with hands that trembled slightly, feeling the warmth spread through her as she sipped the delicious creamy coffee and nibbled on the bun. Never had anything tasted so good. Eyes shining, she smiled at the girl beside her and at Becky. A lovefeast, indeed! Becky was her dearest friend, and if Avril couldn't be at Montclair with Graham this Christmas, she was glad to be here with Becky.

As the girls trooped wearily back to their dormitories at the close of the service, Avril felt lightheaded. Something strange and wonderful and completely new had touched her. She was not sure exactly what, but it warmed and comforted her in an indefinable way.

On Christmas morning the girls awoke later than usual and, shivering with cold, scurried downstairs to the dining hall, toasty from the heat of the big porcelain tile stove, a product of the church-owned pottery plant. At each place they found small gifts, sweets, nuts, and individual fruitcakes. The teachers, it seemed, had risen long before daylight to decorate the room with candles and evergreens and to arrange festive centerpieces of pinecones, berries, and fruit on the tables, hoping to make this holiday a special time for the snowbound students.

Ordinarily mail was brought to New Hope every two weeks. But with the inclement weather and the condition of the roads throughout the South, it was not until late in January that the girls at the Academy received their Christmas packages and letters from home. For Avril, there were letters from both Graham and Auntie May as well as from Great-Aunt Laura Barnwell. She tore open Graham's first, her eyes racing down the pages of bold, slanted handwriting as she devoured his news.

My dear Avril,

When I learned you would be unable to come home to Montclair for the holidays, my heart was heavy. The prospect of staying here alone was very dreary indeed. In fact, it was "out of the question" in the minds of my relatives and friends.

First, May Cameron braved the snowstorm to insist that I ride with them by sleigh to Williamsburg and enjoy the holiday festivities there from the sixteenth of December through the sixth of January. Williamsburg is always the scene of much merriment during that time.

I did not hesitate to give my answer. I knew that Aunt Laura's younger sister, Sally, would also be spending the holidays in her old homeplace and would be bringing her grandchildren. It seemed a good idea all around. I'm only sorry you could not be with us. Of course, there will be other Christmases, but since you have never experienced a Williamsburg Christmas, I shall do my best to acquaint you with some of the special events marking the season.

One of the highlights is the parade of the militia. Bonfires on every street corner glow brightly in the chilly dark as the men assemble, dipping their torches to set them aflame. From afar comes the sound of the rousing music of the Fife and Drum Corps. The streets are lined with people shivering as much from anticipation as from cold, I suspect. In the windows of every house, candles are burning and the street lanterns also lend their light. The music becomes louder as the marchers progress down the street, the crowd picks up the melody, and the very air vibrates with the happy voices of carolers singing "Joy to the World"—an auspicious beginning to the week commemorating our Savior's birth.

Reading these words expressing Graham's enthusiasm for celebrating the birthday of the Christ she was just learning about sent a thrill of hope through Avril, bonding her closer than ever to Graham.

Aunt Laura's letter was a newsy account of the family celebration:

The children were too excited by Christmas Eve to attend the candlelight service at Bruton Church, but we all went on Christmas morning. It was a lovely, quiet service. The church looked beautiful and I was so pleased to see that the nandina, pyracantha, and holly I had sent over earlier had been used effectively in the decorations. I am so grateful our ancestors chose to come to Virgina to settle rather than to the stricter Puritan Massachusetts colony, where they are forbidden to celebrate Christmas. Decorating the churches is a long-held English tradition as the old rhyme admonishes:

> *Holly and ivy, box and bay,*
> *Put in the church on Christmas Day.*

What better way to give thanks for the miracle of the Holy Child's birth than to celebrate it at least as festively as we do family birthdays?

I praised the Lord for another year of worship as the family went up and took the sacrament together, sipping from the silver communion cup that was passed among us.

Again Avril was touched, visualizing Graham's dark head bowed as he knelt at the altar. Avril was firmly convinced that he would not have participated unless he was a true believer—not even to please Aunt Laura. She felt warmed by the thought of yet another thing they shared.

Auntie May's letter was more frivolous, full of descriptions of the parties and other festivities. She wrote in her fun-loving way:

I just wish you could have been with us, dear Avril, as we went from house to house on Christmas Day. Such abundance everywhere, so much laughter and merriment. We dined at your dear little aunt's at midday. As usual, she outdid herself—roast wild turkey, scalloped oysters, cranberry relish, and petit pois in rings of acorn squash, as well as three kinds of pies—mince, pecan, and sweet potato!

There have been many parties and balls all the week, and none more elegant than the New Year's Eve fete given by Clarice Fontayne in her newly acquired townhouse. She has brought so many interesting customs from her years abroad and every room was gaily decorated, with hundreds of candles complementing the ladies' complexions.

All during the evening music was played, fiddlers and minstrels strolling among the guests, singing ballads and Christmas songs.

Her menu matched the beauty of the decor. A buffet supper to please a king's taste, I would say, if we had not already declared our Independence— pheasant, fresh mushrooms in a wine sauce, baked ham, fruit aspic, rum cream pie, served along with a punch of mulled cider, potent enough to curl a wig! I might add that, in some cases, indeed it did!

Afterward there was much dancing: reels, square dances, and a new French rondelé Clarice tried to teach us all, resulting in much hilarity as we attempted to master the intricate steps.

When midnight approached, Clarice bade us each to follow the old tradition of tossing a sprig of holly on the blazing yule log to burn all our troubles of the past year.

Mrs. Fontayne asked about you and if you were enjoying your days at school. Graham and I both assured her that although you were probably unhappy about the unfortunate weather that has prevented your coming home for the holidays, you were most happy otherwise. I am right, am I not, dear?

At the mention of Clarice Fontayne, Avril's nose wrinkled unconsciously. She could not bring herself to like the woman even though she felt guilty for her unkind thoughts.

Avril picked up Graham's letter again and read it through for the second time, cherishing each word.

Yes! There would be "other Christmases" to spend together. And before that, the summer ahead—a long, lovely summer at Montclair. Maybe Graham would then realize they had both been too lonely apart and she could convince him not to send her back to the Academy in the fall.

A tap at her door broke into her daydream, and one of the younger girls poked in her head. "Avril, you have company in the parlor. Dame Fenton says you are to come down at once."

Company! Avril jumped to her feet. Students at the Academy were allowed visitors only if they were relatives or were specified on an approved list forwarded to the headmistress by the girls' families. Who could possibly be coming here to see her?

chapter
8

DAME FENTON was waiting at the bottom of the staircase as Avril ran down the steps.

"Your cousin is in the front parlor, Avril." She frowned as she began to smooth back Avril's flyaway curls, straighten her bonnet, and retie its strings. "Do conduct yourself properly and credit the Academy with your decorum," she admonished.

The headmistress was so busy attending to Avril's appearance that she failed to hear or to respond to Avril's surprised exclamation, "Cousin?!"

"Now run along, dear." With a final brush of Avril's collar, Dame Fenton gave her a gentle push toward the parlor door.

Avril entered the room cautiously. A dark-haired man in a swallow-tailed black waistcoat was warming his hands in front of the tall porcelain stove in the corner.

At her entrance he turned and she could see that his features were sharp, his nose aquiline, his skin olive, his eyes black as coal. A smile only briefly touched his thin lips.

"*Bonjour,* Avril. I am happy to see you at last. I have been trying to accomplish that feat for a long time now, since shortly after your parents' deaths, as a matter of fact. But your guardian, Mr. Montrose, has—" Here he hesitated, as if searching for words— "made it most difficult, to say the least. I am your dear mother's cousin, Claude Duchampes." He made a slight bow.

"Please sit down, so we can talk." He motioned to one of the few chairs. Avril crossed the room and sat stiffly, her back rigid, as he took a chair opposite her. "You are puzzled, n'est ce pas? So, I explain." He proceeded.

"I practically grew up in your mother's home. You see, I was orphaned when I was very young and Tante Evangeline, your grandmére and your mother's mama, took me in. I was a few years younger than Eva. She was already quite a beautiful young lady, and I loved her dearly."

Avril stared at this stranger. How was it she had never heard of him? Never seen him before?

"You look mystified. I understand. You have not seen me since you were a tiny little girl. You could not remember. I was sent to France to school and, sadly, when I returned—your *pauvre mére—trés triste*."

He gave a sympathetic shrug before continuing. "When I came again to Natchez and discovered my cousins both dead and the place deserted . . . well, it was only then that I learned that a friend of Paul's had come and taken their only child to Virginia. Naturally I was concerned. Not only for my little cousin's welfare, but also because I knew nothing of this person who had declared himself her guardian."

"He and Papa were in school together . . . ," Avril ventured, sensing some implied criticism of Graham.

There was a slight pause, a lift of a jet black brow. Monsieur Duchampes went on. "So he says." Another little shrug. "But, wishing to make sure of the conditions of my—of you—I traveled to Virginia to see for myself." At this point his expression altered; something hardened in the soft dark eyes. "Unfortunately, Mr. Montrose took affront, misconstruing my concern for criticism. When I tried to assure him of my motives, he became angry. When I asked to see you, he refused, ordering me off his property." Again the shrug, the shake of the head.

Avril's brow puckered. None of what this man was saying seemed at all like Graham. Yet a shadowy scene from the past drifted into her mind, though she could not quite recapture the details.

Then Monsieur Duchampes was speaking again. "I chanced to be in this part of the country on business, so near to the place where you had been sent to boarding school, and could not resist making another attempt to see my cousin's beloved child . . . especially when I have something very precious to give her."

He drew a slim, leather box from his waistcoat pocket and presented it to Avril.

"This belonged to your mother."

Avril took the box, opened it, and found a narrow gold bracelet with three tiny moonstones embedded in its circlet. It was fragile and dainty and slipped easily over her wrist.

"Oh, thank you," she breathed. "But you shouldn't . . . I shouldn't—"

"*Mais non,* it is nothing." He waved aside her protests. "Your dear mama would have wanted it so. But I am happiest of all to see you again. Soon you will be a young lady yourself and able to make your own decisions. No one can then prevent you from seeing whom you wish or going where you will."

The sound of a bell pealing through the hallway alerted Avril. She stood. "I'm sorry, but I must go now. That was our study bell."

Monsieur Duchampes rose also. "Of course, Avril. I must leave, too. But before I do, I must warn you—. " He paused dramatically. "I do not wish to malign anyone, you understand. Still, it is important for you to know that you are not totally dependent on the kindness of strangers. You do have relatives of your own—your own blood. As they say, 'Blood is thicker than water', and in the end, family, one's *own* family, no matter how distantly related, is what really matters."

Avril felt increasingly uneasy. What was this man trying to say? He was holding her hands too tightly. She wanted only to get away, but dared not appear rude.

"Mr. Montrose has made it clear that I am not welcome at Montclair. So I cannot come there to see you as much as I regret that, as I'm sure your dear mama would, too. But when you are twenty-one, Avril, all will be different, all will change. You will be free. You understand?"

She nodded uncertainly.

"You will be in charge of your property, able to say what happens to the beautiful house, the jewels, the productive rice lands. All that should stay in the family—*our* family—the Duchampes. You would not wish these things to go to strangers, would you?"

"I suppose not—" Avril said hesitantly.

"Good! Then we agree! We are friends, eh, little cousin? There is really not that much difference in our ages. Eva was ten years older than I and merely seventeen years older than you! So! We have much in common, eh? Both orphans, both Duchampes!"

He leaned down suddenly and kissed Avril on both cheeks. "*Eh bien! Au revoir* for now. Every time you look at the bracelet, remember me and how close your mama and I were."

Avril began backing toward the parlor door.

"Oh, one thing more." Monsieur Duchampes held up a restraining hand. "I wouldn't mention our little visit to Mr. Montrose. For some reason he has a grudge against me. He might not approve of our little rendezvous. Agreed, little cousin? He smiled at her, giving her a furtive wink.

Avril nodded, not knowing what else to say, and dropping a short curtsy, turned and fled from the room. Running up the stairs, she almost bumped into some of the other girls hurtling down to the study hall. Becky was among them.

"Where have you been, Avril?"

"I'll tell you later!" promised Avril, brushing by her friend and hurrying back to her room. She felt upset. Claude Duchampes' unexpected visit had been most disturbing. She knew instinctively that Graham would be very angry if he knew about it. That very fact made it easier to comply with Monsieur Duchampes' request, though she disliked keeping anything from Graham.

She looked again at the bracelet. On impulse she removed it, put it back in the box, opened her bureau drawer, and shoved it beneath some of her chemises. Somehow she did not want to wear it even if it *had* belonged to her mother.

She banged the drawer shut and started back down to study period. She wished she could put out of her mind the entire afternoon's episode. One thing she knew positively—she would never tell Graham about it.

Part III

Montclair
Spring and Summer 1810

Now the God of hope fill you with all joy and peace in believing, that ye may abound in hope, through the power of the Holy Ghost.
Romans 15:13

chapter
9

THE CARRIAGE rolled nearer Montclair, and Avril leaned forward eagerly. With every familiar landmark her heart leaped higher. The elms along the driveway would be all leafy green by now and the fields around the house golden with daffodils.

Would Graham be on the veranda awaiting her arrival? Oh, she hoped so, though he might well be making his plantation rounds, since he was not expecting her until after midday.

But Avril had risen early, too excited to sleep any longer. She had arrived in Williamsburg by stage, accompanied by one of the Academy teachers who had relatives in town. Avril had spent the night at the Barnwells, where Graham had sent the Montrose carriage for her the night before, since it was planting time and his presence was required on the plantation. She understood all that, of course, but the delay in seeing him only intensified her desire.

At last the carriage rounded the last bend, and the stately brick and clapboard mansion came into view. It was just as Avril remembered it from the first time she saw it nearly four years ago.

When the driver drew to a stop in front of the porch steps, Avril did not get down at once. She sat there for a full minute trying to compose herself. She hoped to appear poised and ladylike to Graham, a product of all the deportment training at the Academy, proof that the year had been worthwhile. She did not want to seem a harum-scarum child, scrambling out to fling herself into his arms, though it would take all the discipline she could muster not to do just that.

So she waited, trembling with excitement, as the front door opened and his tall figure stepped out onto the shaded veranda. Drawing a deep breath, she took hold of the brocaded strap by the carriage door and, when it was opened for her, sprang lightly down.

"My dear! My dear child! How good it is to have you home!" Graham was holding her at arm's length now and his whole face was alight with pleasure.

Avril had added at least three inches to her height, and the carrot color of her hair had darkened to a rich, deep russet, the color of autumn leaves. But the eyes were still the eyes of a child—clear, innocent, and now shining with delight.

"Oh, Graham, I'm so happy to be home! I've missed it so! And you!" she exclaimed and, forgetting her resolution, hugged him impetuously.

He laughed, caught her about the waist, and swung her in a wide circle. As he did so, Avril looked up onto the porch and felt her heart sink. Two other figures had emerged from the great house. One of them was Auntie May Cameron and the other—Clarice Fontayne!

"Welcome home, Avril!" sang out Auntie May in her high, sweet voice, and picking up her skirts daintily, she came to the edge of the porch and held out her arms to Avril. "How you've grown and how pretty you look in that bonnet. That shade of blue is just right for your coloring. Come, darling, let me have a good look at you!"

Avril concealed her disappointment with an effort. She had been anticipating her homecoming for weeks, and all the way from Williamsburg had planned what she would say to Graham, what they'd do, how they would spend their first evening together after their long separation. Perhaps they would even go riding before dusk. She was anxious to see her mare, Fancy, too. Oh, there was so much to tell and hear about, and she had so wanted Graham all to herself.

Now she knew she would have to sit for tea and make polite

conversation, giving Auntie May a report on life at the Academy. Worst of all, she must grit her teeth and endure Clarice Fontayne's posturing and preening.

After she reached the top of the steps and had been enveloped in Auntie May's scented embrace, she turned to greet Mrs. Fontayne courteously.

"*Cherie!* What a young lady you've become, a credit to your guardian's wisdom in sending you off to school, *n'est ce pas?*" Clarice's amused glance slid over Avril's head to Graham and lingered there fetchingly.

Her condescending tone, the kind one would use with a child, infuriated Avril and she could not refrain from giving a mild retort, "Oh, it wasn't the school or being away from Montclair! It's just that I'm fourteen nearly fifteen. People *do* grow up."

Clarice regarded Avril, appraising her anew. "Oh, but you have learned the art of repartee, haven't you?" she laughed and shrugged her slender shoulders.

To Avril, her laughter sounded affected and there was none in her cool blue eyes when they touched Avril briefly again. It was clear she was not really amused.

"Graham, I must go and leave you to your reunion *en famille*," she said, thrusting open her yellow silk parasol, the ruffled edges casting delightful shadows on her perfectly contoured face. "If you will have my carriage brought around?"

"Of course." Graham called for Hector to alert the Fontayne driver, who was enjoying the shade of one of the large elms.

Auntie May's chatter covered the awkwardness Avril felt keenly between herself and Mrs. Fontayne. Then Graham was back and soon the carriage with blue painted trim rolled around the side of the house, coachman and footman in matching livery.

"So, we shall see you at the supper party this weekend?" Clarice asked. The two adults nodded. To Avril, Clarice merely said, "A party for grown-ups, *cherie*. I fear you would be bored." With that she touched Avril's cheek with the tips of her silk-gloved fingers in a gesture that appeared affectionate. But Avril had the distinct impression that the lady would much rather have pinched it.

Graham escorted Clarice to her carriage and handed her graciously into it. Then she leaned forward and whispered something that made him laugh. Avril's cheeks flamed, imagining that she herself was the butt of some form of ridicule made to sound clever. Quickly, Avril turned her back. She hated seeing Graham and Clarice together. She linked arms with Auntie May and they went into the house together.

After her disappointing homecoming, Avril's first few weeks back at Montclair were idyllic. She awoke every morning eager for the day to begin. Sometimes she could scarcely believe she was really here, with a long summer of lovely days to be strung together like a daisy chain.

Adding to her enjoyment of her freedom from the restrictive atmosphere of the Academy was her secret decision not to return to school in September. Avril had formulated a plan that she was sure would guarantee her remaining at Montclair. She would make herself so indispensable to Graham that he would not be able to part with her. While this would take a great deal of effort on her part, Avril had no doubt that she could accomplish her purpose.

Their days together took on a pleasant pattern. Avril made sure she was down for breakfast neatly groomed, every hair smoothly brushed and bowed, at her place when Graham appeared. The minute she heard his footsteps on the stairs, she poured his coffee, and had it sugared and creamed to his liking, and ready for him even before he entered the dining room.

She always tried to have some fact, some bit of information to give her conversation sparkle and impress him with an intelligence that he would find both interesting and remarkable in a girl her age. Her purpose was twofold—to prove to Graham that the year at the Academy had not been wasted but had been sufficient, giving her incentive to pursue good literature, history, and geography on her own.

When Graham had finished his daily consultation with his overseer, Avril would sometimes have Fancy saddled and herself attired in riding habit, ready to accompany him on his rounds of the sprawling plantation.

At other times they would ride more leisurely, in sun-dappled woods, just as the purple dusk descended. Occasionally they would ride over to Cameron Hall to accept the frequent invitations extended by Auntie May for an evening with friends from neighboring plantations. On such occasions Avril especially loved the moonlit ride home—alone with Graham.

At home, they read books together. Graham, an avid reader, had a standing order with a New York firm to receive the latest publications. When these boxes arrived, they both delighted in opening and examining the volumes. Then they chose one of the more promising and took turns reading aloud, sometimes late into the evening. Then, when eyes and voices grew weary, they would sometimes walk through the garden before saying their good-nights.

That summer, the days were a series of cloudless blue skies. Nothing marred Avril's happiness.

Even Avril's hidden resentment of the lovely widow, Clarice Fontayne, had no reason to surface. From Auntie May, Avril had learned that the lady in question was visiting friends in the cool mountains and would not return until later in the season.

With that irritant safely out of the way, Avril almost forgot about her. It made her even happier to note that Graham did not seem to miss her, either, for he never mentioned her name. Besides, there were far more interesting things on the horizon: The Cameron boys returned from school in England.

Avril learned of their arrival one day when she was curled in the window seat of the library, waiting for Graham to finish going over the ledgers so they could take their afternoon ride. Acknowledging Hector's discreet tap on the door, she admitted him and listened as he announced a visitor to see her.

Puzzled, Avril went into the hall and saw a tall, vaguely familiar figure standing at the open door. She stood uncertainly for a moment, trying to grasp his identity before proceeding to greet him.

"Marshall! Marshall Cameron!" she gasped. "When did you get back?"

Marshall grinned sheepishly. "Yes, it's me," he said, conscious of his new height, the gangly limbs he had not quite tamed. "We—Logan and I"—he jerked his head toward the driveway where Logan was rather impatiently pacing his horse back and forth—"rode over. Mama wants to know if you and Graham can come for supper—a sort of homecoming celebration."

Avril looked past him at the young man still seated astride his horse. Logan seemed taller, too, broader through the shoulders, his thick, golden hair glinting in the sunlight, his boyish face now taking on the handsome planes of manhood.

Her temporary admiration vanished at the fact that he had not dismounted and come to greet her. How arrogant! Still felt he was too old to be bothered with a mere girl, probably. Avril lifted her chin defensively. *So much for him,* she thought. *I'll ignore him.*

She smiled sweetly at Marshall. "I'll ask Graham. I'm sure he would like to, since I don't know of any other plans."

"You can send word over later. Or for that matter, just come!" Marshall suggested, shrugging. "Well, then, we'll see you. Maybe we could go riding tomorrow." He hesitated a second before bounding back down the porch steps and leaping onto his horse.

As Avril watched the two gallop down the driveway, take the fence at the edge of the meadow, and disappear into the woods, she smiled, secretly amused that they were conscious of her eyes upon them. They were still just little boys, she thought. The brothers had grown taller and older perhaps, but neither had ever been willing to concede defeat to the other and were still enjoying a friendly rivalry. And though Logan had not paid her the courtesy due a young lady, she would show him a thing or two, Avril decided then and there.

Assuming Graham would accept any invitation forthcoming from his close friends at Cameron Hall, Avril raced upstairs, pausing only long enough to ask Polly, the maid who was just coming down from doing the bedrooms, to bring her up some rainwater so she could wash her hair.

With her chief motive that of showing Logan Cameron that she was someone to be reckoned with, not ignored, Avril spent the rest of the afternoon preparing herself for the evening at Cameron Hall.

The evening was successful beyond Avril's fondest hopes. Entering the Camerons' drawing room on Graham's arm later, she was gratified to see the startled look in Logan's eyes. She had selected her gown with care—a lemon yellow mull—a fine, delicate muslin—trimmed at the neck with bands of lace threaded with yellow satin ribbons, and embroidered all over with tiny butterflies. With Dilly's help, she had tamed her masses of dark red curls into two bunches on either side of her head, banding them with bows of yellow ribbons that matched those on her dress.

Marshall had lost his initial self-consciousness at being back with his former playmate and was soon chattering away with Avril, pointing out the differences between Americans and his English schoolmates. All the while Logan looked on, keeping his distance.

When at last it was time to leave, he ambled over to Avril and said in an offhanded manner, "When Marshall and I go riding tomorrow, would you care to join us?"

Avril felt a glow of triumph. She had won, but she did not think it wise to flaunt her victory by refusing. Instead, she smiled a slow, sweet smile and replied demurely, "Yes, thank you. That would be very nice."

Later, when she reflected on that night, Avril remembered she had been so happy thinking it would be like old times.

And, indeed, it seemed so for a time. The three of them rode out together almost every day. Though there were no longer the rowdy games of pirates and Indians, chasing each other through the woods or wading in the river, a new camaraderie developed between them and Avril was satisfied that now at last Logan accepted her as an equal. He still tried to best both Marshall and her by galloping faster, jumping higher fences or hedges, and generally proving his superior horsemanship. But his appreciation of her was evident.

Avril would never forget when it all changed.

It was nothing any of them did, but later she would think back and realize that if she had not heard of it through Logan and Marshall, things would have been different, her lovely summer left unspoiled.

chapter
10

AVRIL GAVE a sigh of pure happiness as she leaned on the sill of her bedroom window overlooking her favorite view of Montclair. Beyond the velvety green expanse of lawn and magnificent elms, the river shimmered in the early morning sunlight.

The dewy scent of newly mown grass was better than the most expensive perfume, she thought, closing her eyes and sniffing appreciatively. She whispered a little prayer of thanksgiving for life, for this glorious day, for Montclair—the place she had come to love most in the world.

Turning from the sight she treasured, she dressed hurriedly in a dark blue riding skirt, for she was meeting the Cameron boys at their usual place, the path in the woods where the borders of the Montrose and Cameron lands met. She pulled on her boots, bundled her hair up in a twist and secured it with the nearest ribbon, then rushed down the back stairway into the kitchen. There she cajoled Cookie to part with some fresh gingerbread she had baked for dinner dessert, along with some ripe peaches, to carry in her saddle bags for the picnic they had planned.

Humming happily, Avril ran out to the stables under a clear sky, never dreaming that soon the day would seem heavy and dark.

Mounting Fancy, Avril lifted her head, feeling the soft breeze on her face as the mare moved into a gentle canter. She never felt freer than when she was riding Fancy, and in a surge of exquisite joy,

Avril gave her free rein to take the trail at a gallop, losing her hair ribbon somewhere along the way. Her red-gold hair caught fiery lights from the sun that filtered through the trees.

The day ahead held the promise of fun, comradeship, and also a tenuous new undercurrent of excitement that surpassed anything she had ever experienced with the girls at the Academy on some school outing. Avril was not sure exactly what caused it, but she was keenly aware of Logan's altered manner toward her. Sometimes he held her horse's head for her when she dismounted or gave her a hand up when she mounted. He did not join in the competitive kind of teasing debates she and Marshall enjoyed, but kept himself a little aloof from them, listening, at times laughing at them.

Whatever it was that was different in his attitude toward her, Avril rather liked it even if she did not understand it.

The boys were waiting for her when she approached the clearing.

"What have you got there, Avril?" Marshall asked, grinning. "We've been up and riding a full hour and we're starved!"

She jumped down and fetched her contributions to the picnic, placing them beside the ham, biscuits, and apples Marshall had spread out on a rock.

While they sunned themselves and ate heartily, the horses wandered freely, munching on the sweet grasses and ferns. Avril, having skipped breakfast, helped herself generously until Logan made a chance remark.

"Ah, this is really living. We have company at the house and Mama has gone all elegant and Frenchified, even for breakfast. It was good to escape." He took a bite of a peach, let the juice drip off his chin, then wiped his sticky fingers on the turf.

"Ugh!" Marshall gave a disgusted grimace. "We're supposed to act like perfect little English gentlemen whenever her friend Madame Clarice is visiting." He mimicked a la-de-dah tone of voice that under other circumstances Avril would have found humorous.

But with the mention of that name, Avril suddenly lost her appetite, nearly choking on a biscuit. *Oh no!* she thought. *Clarice back so soon?*

"By the way, Avril, Mama is having a party in Mrs. Fontayne's honor this week. I'm, sure Graham will get his invitation, as she sent them out by hand this morning. It's only for Mama's and Father's friends and some of Mrs. Fontayne's from Williamsburg, too. But Mama says you can come along when Graham does and we can have our own party in the gazebo. Do come! The food is going to be very special. Our cook and her helpers have been baking for days!" Marshall went on, totally oblivious of the effect of his news on Avril.

"Did you know Mama is matchmaking, Avril?" asked Logan, regarding Avril with raised eyebrows.

"She is, Avril," chimed in Marshall. "She thinks Mrs. Fontayne would make a perfect wife for Graham."

Avril's stomach gave a sickening lurch at the thought of Clarice Fontayne as Mistress of Montclair. Surely they were mistaken. How could Auntie May even suggest such a thing?

The sound of the river below, rushing over rocks, the buzz of insects in the wildflowers, the rustle of leaves in the overhanging trees suddenly grew very loud in Avril's ears, mercifully shutting out the rest of their discussion.

Avril felt hot and faint. Shakily she got to her feet. "I must go," she said without explanation.

The boys registered surprise. "But we were going to ride over to—" began Marshall.

"I can't. I forgot something I was supposed to do," fibbed Avril and went to get Fancy, who reluctantly turned from the delicious greenery she was enjoying as Avril tugged on the reins.

Without a backward look at her astonished companions, Avril swung herself up on the mare's back, roughly pulled her around and started off at a trot back toward Montclair.

The minute they were down the small, winding cliff overlooking the river Avril leaned forward, giving Fancy her head; the mare twitched her ears, then laid them back, and took off. Avril clutched the reins, bent her head low and felt the thrust of the horse beneath her. The violence of the emotions she felt both shocked and frightened her. Somehow, hurtling along the pine-needled bridle path faster than she had ever ridden before was healing.

At the stable one of the grooms ran out, a look of amazement on his face as Avril brought Fancy to a wheeling halt. She slid out of her saddle, tossed the reins to him, then ran into the house and up the stairway to her bedroom.

Her cotton blouse clung damply to her back; her hair, wet with perspiration, stuck to her forehead and neck in little ringlets; her face was streaked with dust; and her legs trembled. She held out shaky hands rubbed almost raw from the leather reins, belatedly remembering she had left her riding gloves by the picnic spot.

She stripped off her rumpled, dirty clothes and then poured water into the wash basin and began to sponge off the sweat and grime. The cool, refreshing wash had a calming as well as cleansing effect. The knot of tension she had felt in her chest began to subside. She slowly dressed in fresh clothing and then went downstairs in search of something to soothe her throat, parched by the fast ride through the heat of the day.

There was a pitcher of lemonade in the kitchen Cookie had made to take to the spring house for later, but she poured Avril a tall glass while eyeing the girl anxiously.

"Somethin' de matter, sweetness?" she asked.

"Just hot and tired," answered Avril over her shoulder as she took the glass with her and wandered out into the hall. On the drop leaf mahogany table she saw a large, pale blue envelope in a silver tray. She stopped to examine it. Avril recognized the handwriting at once. It was from Auntie May, who had written her frequent little notes while she was away at the Academy. Avril picked it up and held it for a long, tempting moment. It would be easy to destroy it. Graham would never know why he had not received an invitation to the party honoring that spiteful Clarice Fontayne.

The thought lingered tantalizingly. Then the teaching at the Academy as well as her own reading of the Scriptures overwhelmed her with the deceitful thing she had almost done. *Thou shalt not steal. Thou shalt not lie*—She quickly replaced the little square of blue.

Standing there, Avril lifted her head and studied her reflection in the hall mirror. She was only a girl, even though she would soon be fifteen. There was nothing she could do to prevent Graham's seeing Mrs. Fontayne if he chose to do so, nothing she could do to keep Auntie May from bringing them together socially. A tide of helplessness engulfed her.

Outside, the summer afternoon, golden with sunshine, darkened. Avril left the hall and went into the library. Even when Graham was not here, this room seemed to hold his essence. Everything in it— the books, his chair, the hassock where she often sat at his knee while he read, the desk with its brass inkwell, the pen holder, the globed lamp—was a tangible reminder of him, Avril thought, as she touched the objects one by one.

She moved behind the desk and sat down on the leather upholstered chair, spinning around a couple of times. Then, playing with the drawer pulls absently, she opened one.

She had not intended to look through the papers Graham kept there or in any way invade his privacy. It was just that the folder at the top of the stack caught her eye immediately. It bore her name.

Almost without thinking Avril opened the cover. The first paper was crinkled and the ink rather faded. Her eyes roamed the sheet and she saw her father's signature and then Graham's. It was not a legal document in the strict sense, but an amateurish imitation. It was the "covenant agreement" made by two young men, promising forever friendship and a solemn vow to protect, cherish, and care for the family of the other if one survived the other's death. This was the signed exchange that had made Graham her guardian.

It was the first time Avril had seen it. But as she lifted it from the rest of the papers in the folder for closer examination, her eyes fell on the next document.

The marriage certificate. At the time she had not fully understood the explanations offered for its necessity. She knew only that Graham felt that it was important. Now, from the Academy's teachings on marriage as a "holy estate," Avril knew that marriage was far more than a contractual agreement between two people. It was a binding state, recognized in heaven.

She remembered Graham's telling her that the marriage, on paper only, was to protect her great fortune until she came of age. It still seemed a strange precaution for him to take. How had she been threatened that he should take so serious a step?

Avril heard voices outside the open windows and realized Graham had come in from his plantation rounds and was talking with Hector in the hall. Hastily she returned the folder to the drawer and shoved it closed.

In another minute Graham came into the room, saw her, and smiled. Holding up the blue envelope, he said, "Well, my dear, how would you like to go with me to Cameron Hall next Friday? It seems May is having a party, and you are invited to dine with the boys."

Avril arranged a smile on her face. It was not too difficult. After all, why should she fear Clarice Fontayne, or any of Auntie May's plans, for that matter? Graham couldn't marry anyone else— because he was already married—to *her*.

Avril dressed with special care on the evening of the Cameron party. Even though she was not to participate in the real event, she wanted to look her very best, if only to please Graham.

As she experimented with several hairstyles, Avril pretended she was preparing for a great ball with Graham as her escort. But most of the styles she tried were failures. In the end she simply plaited part of her hair and let the rest fall in natural curls about her shoulders, then fashioned a garland of tiny yellow roses from the garden and pinned a wreath of them around the coiled braid.

Her dress was of crepe-lisse, a silky gauze over a yellow undergarment, with short puffed sleeves and a wide satin sash. It was quite the most sophisticated gown Avril owned, and she sent a mental thank-you to Auntie May for insisting she have some new dresses made at the beginning of the summer.

Cameron Hall was ablaze with light as Graham and Avril arrived just after dark. Liveried servants waited in the drive to lead away the fine coaches after the elegantly gowned occupants alighted and ascended the "welcoming arms" stairway to the pillared porch where Judge and Mrs. Cameron stood to receive their guests.

Auntie May, looking lovely in blue satin with fluted ruffles and wearing the famous Cameron sapphires, exclaimed over Avril's dress and charming hairstyle. To Graham she confided, "There is someone here who has been most eager to see *you*!" She squeezed his arm and her eyes twinkled merrily.

Avril felt a sickening chill even on this warm, balmy evening. She knew Auntie May meant Clarice, and glancing into the lighted foyer, she saw her. What man could fail to appreciate such beauty? She was enchanting.

Clarice was surrounded by a small group of gentlemen who appeared to be hanging on her every word. She wore a rose satin creation with an overlay of white lace. The low-cut bodice was draped with lace and satin roses, ornamented with tiny pearls like dewdrops. Her hair was arranged in ringlets that fell on either side of her exquisite face. She carried an ivory fan, which she was fluttering flirtatiously as she chatted.

"Logan and Marshall are waiting for you, darling," said Auntie May, snapping Avril out of her reverie. "You three will have supper on the upper balcony. Go along, dear. You know the way."

A rebellious protest rose to Avril's lips. She did not want to be relegated to a "children's party." She wanted to stay downstairs with the grown-ups—and keep an eye on Graham and that woman! But Graham was already moving away from her, speaking to some friends who had hailed him. So there was nothing Avril could do but make her way through the throng of adults, who took scant notice of her, and reluctantly mount the steps to the balcony, where Marshall and Logan waited impatiently.

"Come on, slowpoke!" Marshall exclaimed when she reached the top of the stairs. "Our supper is served and we're famished. Do hurry!"

Auntie May had planned a wonderful feast for them, Avril had to give her that—all kinds of delicious dishes and an assortment of desserts as well. If she had not been so resentful of being excluded from the more sophisticated gathering downstairs, Avril would have enjoyed herself thoroughly.

After they had eaten, they got out the dominoes and played several games until the sound of music from below distracted Avril. She looked up from the small black rectangle she was attempting to place and listened.

"They've started the dancing!" she said to the boys, who seemed not the slightest bit interested. "Let's go and watch!" she suggested, getting up from her chair.

"But we haven't finished the game—and I'm winning!" objected Marshall, but Logan was already on his feet.

Resigned, Marshall followed the other two out to the upstairs hall. From their vantage point at the balcony rail, they had an unobstructed view of the center hall and a portion of the drawing room. Both areas had been cleared of furniture and the floors polished. Intrigued by the intricacies of the dance steps, the three hung over the banister, unseen observers of the colorful panorama below.

Avril immediately sought out Graham. His tall, handsome figure was easy to spot. He moved with unexpected grace for such a big man, she thought, her heart swelling with pride and admiration. Then seeing his partner, her worst fears were realized. Graham was leading the lovely Clarice, giving her his rapt attention.

Mesmerized, Avril's eyes followed them as they bowed, twirled, came together, and sidestepped through the arch created by the uplifted arms of the other couples. Graham was laughing at some comment Clarice had made. Avril's heart twisted with envy. If only she could be his partner, sharing this lighthearted pastime!

"Would you like to try?" A voice beside her cut into her absorption. She turned her head quickly. It was Logan, blushing a little as he explained. "I learned last year. One of the chaps at school invited me down to his family's country house for the holidays.

There was a ball for his older sister, and his mother employed an instructor to teach us."

"Well, yes—," Avril replied hesitantly. "If you think I can—"

"It's very simple, actually. Just a few steps to learn, then you repeat. See, I'll show you," he offered and took her hand.

While Marshall looked on sullenly, miffed at being left out, Logan led Avril through a few basics and then they began to move together quite fluidly to the rhythm of the music floating up to them from downstairs.

"You caught on very quickly!" Logan said and Avril felt pleased, nearly forgetting her futile wish that she could be part of the crowd downstairs.

"You look very pretty tonight, Avril," Logan said, then blushed furiously, as if he had paid her this rare compliment by accident.

"Thank you, Logan!" she replied, as surprised as he seemed to be.

But in that moment a curious confidence flowed through Avril. The potential of the future flashed through her mind as swiftly as a bird in flight. Maybe she was growing up.

Someday she would dance at a real party and someone else would think her pretty and clever, would look at her the way gentlemen looked at Clarice Fontayne—the way *Graham* looked at Clarice Fontayne. A sense of anticipation tingled along her spine and she smiled up at Logan.

Logan smiled back, having overcome his initial diffidence, never suspecting that Avril was practicing on him while dreaming of someone else.

chapter

11

LATE IN AUGUST Avril began in earnest her campaign to convince Graham that she should not return to the Academy. With her birthday only a few days away, Avril launched the first stage of her strategy.

It was nearly dusk after a late afternoon horseback ride when Avril and Graham turned their mounts back toward Montclair, proceeding by a different route than they had taken before. Suddenly spying something through the dense foliage, Avril reined in her mare and pointed.

"What is that, Graham? It looks like a little house."

He had pulled up alongside her, and as she turned to him for an answer, she saw a shadow of inexpressible sorrow cross his face before he masked it with a smile. In her enthusiasm Avril did not attach any significance to this glimpse of pain nor did she connect it with the small building a short distance away, obscured by a leafy screen of verdant foliage.

Not waiting for Graham's reply, Avril gave Fancy a light flick with her crop. "Let's do go take a look!" she called over her shoulder, ducking her head to avoid a low-hanging bough and moving forward through the underbrush. "Why, it's a cottage—a dear little cottage! Graham, it looks like a miniature Montclair!"

Excited by her discovery, she jumped down and tethered Fancy to a nearby limb and whirled around just as Graham on his gray Gallant came up behind her.

Avril ran up on the small porch and tried the handle of the fanlighted front door. It was locked. She ran to look in the windows but the shutters were closed. Disappointed, she turned to Graham, who had dismounted and was standing by his horse, making no move to join her.

"Oh, it's all shut and boarded up! I wonder who lived here. Did you know about this place, Graham?"

His hesitance piqued her curiosity. At the look on his face, she halted in her attempt to see inside the quaint replica of the larger mansion.

"What is it, Graham? Is something wrong?"

He shook his head. "No, not really. It's just that this place brings back some sad memories. This is 'Eden Cottage.' It was the architect's model for Montclair," Graham told her. "Grandfather Duncan Montrose designed it before the big house was built. It became a tradition for Montrose men to bring their brides here to live the first year of their marriage. It was a 'honeymoon house.'"

Avril's heart sank with pity. Auntie May had told her of Graham's tragically brief marriage.

"Oh, Graham, I'm so sorry! I never knew, I never thought—" she blurted out, feeling wretched to have opened old wounds.

He waved his hand, dismissing her apology. "It's not your fault, Avril. We—I—Lulie and I never came here. You see, she became ill on our wedding journey. Although the cottage was made ready and waiting for our return to Montclair—we never lived here." He paused. "After she died, the cottage remained unused. Eventually it was boarded up . . ."

Tears welled up in Avril's eyes. Impulsively she went over to Graham and embraced him tenderly. She felt his hand upon her hair, smoothing it gently, comforting her. She should be comforting *him*. Oh, how good he was! How kind and understanding. How she loved him!

It was then that a kind of revelation stole over Avril—a kind of clarification of that love. It had been there all the time, changing, growing into a different kind of love. Though Graham still thought of her as a child, his ward, his sacred responsibility—and that notion momentarily dismayed her—in time, perhaps, who knew what the future held? Only God.

With gentle fingers he lifted her chin, wiped her wet cheeks. "Come, it's too pretty a day for tears. Let's ride back to the house and try not to dwell on sad things."

That incident strengthened Avril's resolve. How lonely Graham must be—how much lonelier if she left for another long school term. If she were here, she knew she could make him forget all his past sorrows. She dreaded the thought of returning to the Academy and leaving Graham here in the big, empty house through all the bleak, winter days to come.

She must make him see that.

For her birthday Graham had invited the Camerons to dinner for a small celebration. Avril thought this the perfect opportunity to prove to Graham that she was now grown up enough to host a dinner party. She would dazzle him with her brilliant conversation, bringing up topics to show how much she had learned. She would be witty and charming and Graham would soon see she had no need of further education or "finishing."

That evening the high-ceilinged dining room was mellow with candlelight. Avril had gathered a bouquet of beautiful flowers and arranged an artistic centerpiece. She had received permission to use the best china and helped polish the ornate silverware. The weather had cooperated with all her plans, presenting a lovely sunset and soft breezes to cool the late summer air.

There were presents for Avril to open afterward. Her delight would have been complete as she admired the small ivory fan Auntie May had given her, the wooden pencil case from Marshall, chamois riding gloves from Logan, and a gold locket containing her parents' miniatures from Graham—except for an exchange she happened to overhear between her guardian and Auntie May.

"They have such an excellent music program that I think Avril should have harp lessons this term," she heard Graham say.

"Oh, that would be quite appropriate. Such a ladylike instrument. And then there is the clavichord. My own dear mother played beautifully . . ."

But Avril did not hear the rest of the conversation. All that registered was the firm note in Graham's voice, ruling out any idea that Avril would not be returning to the Academy.

She knew this was not the opportune moment to protest. She would wait until they were alone before bringing to bear all her finely honed powers of persuasion.

But as it turned out, her pleas were to no avail.

The scene that took place the next morning was the occasion of the sharpest clash of wills she and Graham had ever had. When she had first broached the subject, there had been a point where she had sensed possible victory. For a few seconds his eyes, regarding her, were clouded with doubt. She heightened her arguments, but his moment of indecision was short-lived. When he spoke his tone brooked no argument.

"Avril, you are already enrolled for another semester. You must go back."

"But why must I go back?" she demanded.

"Because, my dear, your education is not complete. You need training in a variety of subjects and social graces needed by a lady of quality—things that you cannot possibly acquire here. Montclair is isolated, as you know. Even the Camerons will soon be leaving again. Winters here are lonely—"

"But *you* are here, Graham! You could teach me! You are ten times smarter than any of the women teachers at the Academy."

Graham could not help laughing at this lovely, irrepressible, unreasonable child. He shook his head, holding up his hand as if to ward off any more outrageous suggestions.

"But I don't see why not!" persisted Avril. "And if the truth were known, I don't think you do either! We could be so cozy and happy here. It wouldn't seem at all lonely. And we could read. Just look at all these books, many more than the Academy has in its library. Give me one good reason why I must go back to school."

Of course, in the end, she knew it was useless. Graham had spoken and there was no recourse. Avril struggled to be calm and cheerful as the day of leavetaking approached. But inside there was a great aching void. Outwardly resigned, inwardly despairing, she dreaded her departure.

Avril managed a smile. She did not want to make Graham uncomfortable with her own unhappiness. He was doing what he believed was his duty. For now, her way was clear. Compromise, perhaps, but not capitulation.

But for all her brave resolutions, the morning Avril left she looked back through the carriage window as she drove off and felt a wrenching pang. It was always like that whenever she went away. It was as if she and Montclair were one—as if she and Graham—but she shook her head, refusing the thought.

It would have been even harder if Avril had known the long separation that lay ahead. But when they said good-bye, neither she nor Graham knew it would be years before her return to Montclair.

chapter
12

OF COURSE, Avril could not have known the series of unforeseen events that would prevent her seeing Graham or Montclair for such a long time. If she had, her return to the Academy and her reunion with Becky might not have been so joyous. As it was, except for rare moments of homesickness, Avril quickly settled back into the familiar routine of school and study.

This year, since their class category had changed, the two girls were moved from the dormitory to share a room on the third floor of the school building.

Over the next months the little room with its slanted ceiling and dormer windows was the scene of whispered confidences, smothered giggles, as well as midnight feasts with food foraged from the kitchen and spread out on the small table between the two narrow spool beds.

The friendship thrived, the two girls becoming more like sisters than roommates.

Avril wrote to Graham regularly, the twice-monthly letter to parents or guardians required by the Academy. But since all correspondence was subject to the inspection of the teachers, it was into her journal that Avril poured her deepest thoughts and feelings.

It was here she wrote freely of her growing love for Graham, a love that was more than she could fully comprehend and more intense than anyone guessed.

Graham's picture resided on her bedside table, beside the small double silver frame containing those of her parents. One day as she sat gazing at it, her pen poised above her open journal, Becky came into the room.

Casting an observant look at her dreamy-eyed roommate, Becky, who often displayed a wisdom beyond her years, remarked, "He *is* very handsome, Avril, but if he's your guardian, he must be frightfully old."

Avril rose instantly to his defense. "Not really," she replied crossly. What was fifteen years, or even twenty? she thought. Love spanned all bridges of age, time, separation. Love knew no barriers. At least, that's what Avril had come to believe. The longer she was separated from him, the more she knew her love for Graham was something special, apart.

"Wasn't he your father's age?" Becky persisted, curious.

"No, younger. He and my father were friends. Both attended the same preparatory school, lived in the same house for students, and became very close, but Graham was several years younger."

With this, Avril promptly shut her journal, closing out any further discussion as well. There were some things she wasn't willing to talk about—not even with her best friend.

Ever since she had found the documents in his desk drawer, Avril had become newly aware of her relationship with Graham. To strengthen her growing conviction that theirs was a unique bond was her awakening interest in spiritual things. Since the Christmas before, when she had participated in the pageant and attended the midnight service on Christmas Eve, Avril had felt a need to learn more about the "indwelling Christ" the minister had spoken about so movingly.

Avril had bought her own small Bible and had begun to read it. She did not understand much of it but loved the poetic beauty of the Psalms. She memorized some of her favorite ones and found comfort and a sense of peace when repeating them to herself.

During those times when the longing to see Graham or to be at

Montclair overtook her, she would turn to them, often finding a new perspective. She was particularly drawn to those that expressed her recurrent feelings of loneliness, of being without any real family, of uncertainty about her future. As she grew older, she thought a great deal about her parents.

What had they been like? How strange it was not to have any clear memories of them as people, merely shadows. She found herself envying Becky, who had so many caring, loving relatives and was always receiving letters and packages from home.

At times like that, when Avril felt sad and lonely, she would repeat over and over the verses she had learned. "Be of good courage, and he shall strengthen thine heart," and "When my father and my mother forsake me, then the Lord will take me up."

She did not really know how the Lord would do this. He was still vague in her mind, mixed up somehow with Graham and the teachers at the Academy who did see to all her worldly needs. It was this other nagging void, this little spot like a stone bruise in her heart that she somehow trusted the Lord to heal.

When winter road conditions again prevented Avril from spending the holidays with Graham at Montclair, she was invited to Becky's home for Christmas. Her initial disappointment was soon replaced by excitement at the prospect of seeing Woodlawn in nearby Pleasant Valley and meeting the large and lively family that Becky had spoken of so fondly.

Much to the girls' surprise and delight, Becky's father and older brother, Jed, arrived at the Academy in an open sleigh to collect them when classes were dismissed for the holidays.

Mr. Buchanan, a jolly man with a hearty laugh and a deceptive brusqueness, tucked them in with fur-lined blankets before he took up the bell-trimmed harness on the four horses and headed homeward. They skimmed effortlessly over the icy, rutted roads with the sound of sleigh bells ringing in their ears, while the cold wind reddened their noses and stung their eyes.

Arriving at Woodlawn, a sprawling fieldstone and frame farmhouse, Avril was hugged, kissed, and welcomed as warmly as Becky by her mother, grandmother, and two aunts who lived there. The house was fragrant with the smell of baking pies, the spicy scent of cedar boughs decorating the mantelpieces and windows, and the odor of bayberry candles lighting all the rooms.

Avril reveled in her first real taste of family life. From the day they arrived it seemed she was surrounded by loud, happy voices, laughter, and activity. The Buchanans had almost as many relatives as friends who thronged to this merry household about which life in the community seemed to revolve.

Strangely enough, there was no separation of age groups as Avril had known in Williamsburg and at Cameron Hall, but adults and young folk alike joined in all the noisy activities. Even very young children participated in the simple games, the square dancing, taffy pulls, and blindman's bluff.

There was outdoor fun to be enjoyed, too. Tobogganing on the snow-covered hill behind the house, snowball battles, and building snowmen added to the memories Avril was storing away.

She entered into all the gaiety with enthusiasm. It was impossible to be shy around the Buchanans. Becky's brothers were all tall, ruggedly handsome young men of high spirits, good humor, and a complete lack of self-consciousness, treating Avril with the same casual affection they bestowed on Becky. Only Jamison, the brother closest in age to Becky, who was promptly smitten with Avril, could barely find his tongue around her.

But one night, during a lively square dance, he surprised Avril by dancing her out of the parlor and into the hallway where a "kissing ball," an orange studded with cloves and beribboned with green and red streamers, swung from the chandelier. Positioning Avril directly under it, he kissed her soundly.

"I love you, Avril," he declared. "And I should very much like to marry you someday!"

Avril had no time to react, for just as quickly he danced her back into the front room that had been cleared of furniture, and she was soon skipping with another partner.

But she thought often of his romantic declaration and hugged to her the delicious idea that someone considered her a prospective bride! Perhaps Graham, too, would notice how mature she was becoming when next she went home to Montclair.

On the day Becky and Avril were to return to the Academy, Jamison thrust a box of sweetmeats into her hands. But, with the family encircling the girls, saying their good-byes, there had not been another kiss.

Avril experienced a decided sagging of spirits upon her return to school after the days of frivolity with the Buchanans. The stiff regulations and unrelenting regimen of the Academy seemed ever so much more oppressive.

A chill January merged into a sleety and windblown February, and just as the weather began to break, an epidemic of smallpox swept through the Academy. The younger girls became ill first, and the severity of the illness demanded more the nursing skills of the staff than the teaching ones. Classes for the older students were temporarily suspended, and those who had not come down with the "pox" had very little supervision.

For weeks the school was in quarantine. At first, neither Becky nor Avril contracted the disease. While the effervescent Becky found time dragging on her hands, Avril discovered an interest in painting with watercolors and whiled away many happy hours recreating scenes of Montclair—the gardens, the river, the woods.

Just when the seige seemed to be waning, both Avril and Becky felt the first feverish symptoms. A new wave of the illness hit the older girls with fierce tenacity, leaving them pale and shaky, though thankfully unscarred when they emerged from their beds several weeks later.

However, because of the extended quarantine and lost school days, the summer vacation period was canceled, and the Academy notified the families of the students that classes would continue during the summer months.

If it had not been for her close friendship with Becky and the fact that Woodlawn, less than a day's journey away, offered a welcome reprieve from classwork and drudgery, Avril did not know how she could have endured the long separation from Graham and Montclair.

At Woodlawn, where she was always received warmly, Avril was made to feel entirely at home. She quickly became a part of the group of young people whose plans for picnics, parties, and square dances went on all summer. Jamison, or Jamie as he was called by his family, was her constant and devoted escort, and although Avril did not take his promise seriously, she found his attention both flattering and fun.

For the second year in a row, ice-covered roads prevented a holiday trip to Montclair, and Avril again spent Christmas with the Buchanans. By the next, war was raging with the British and it was considered too dangerous for her to travel north to Virginia.

Feeling alienated and estranged from Graham and Montclair, Avril might have slipped into melancholia had it not been for an unexpected event at the Academy that third year.

It was, in fact, the announcement one morning at devotions that a noted evangelist was coming to New Hope Church and that any of the students wishing to attend his series of sermons might be excused from afternoon classes.

Three days later Avril made this entry in her journal:

> *So much has happened since I last wrote. Something strange, wonderful, and mysterious. I have confided in no one—not even Becky, so I alone know. For while I am unchanged in appearance, I know that on the inside I shall never be the same!*
>
> *For three days we have had opportunity to hear a series of special talks by a man named Henry Lowe. His calling is to travel about "bringing the good news," much like Jesus' early disciples.*
>
> *He told us that each of us is where we are in life because God has put us there. He has a plan and purpose for our lives, and every person who enters our lives does so, not by happenstance, but by divine appointment!*
>
> *For the first time I think I understand that even losing my parents was for a reason, and that Graham's coming into my life was in His plan, too. While I*

don't understand it all, I am certain it is God's doing. Now it is up to me to discover my part in His plan.

The last day of the talks, Mr. Lowe asked that whoever wanted to surrender their hearts and lives to the Lord should come up to the altar rail and he would pray for them. At first I was afraid to go. But feeling a sense of urgency, I obeyed the small voice within. Now I'm so glad I did.

When Mr. Lowe placed his hands on my head and prayed that the Lord would show me His "plan and purpose," I was overcome with happiness.

I will never find the words to describe all that has happened. I only know that now I am a child of God, and I don't feel like an orphan any more.

chapter
13

AVRIL WAS GOING HOME! The thought of spending Christmas at Montclair after such a long time brought a sparkle to her eyes, a glow to her cheeks, and the motivation to work very hard at her studies so that she could take home a splendid report.

Her efforts did not go unrewarded. As she got into the Montrose carriage Graham had sent for her, Avril carried with her a certificate from the headmistress that would be sure to make him proud.

Be it known that Miss Avril Dumont has completed this year well and this is a testimony of her general good conduct, following the rules of the school, pursuing her studies with all assiduity, gaining the goodwill and esteem of all the Tutoresses under whom she has been placed. She has shown a good understanding of History, Writing, Cyphering, Grammar, Geography, as well as a talent for Drawing and Painting. All of her instructors have been pleased with her progress and anticipate she will graduate this institution this next year with honor.

Signed at New Hope, North Carolina, Dec. 10, 1815

Avril could not sit still in the carriage, but moved from side to side, looking out the windows, still not quite believing she was really on her way home.

The fields and woods on either side of the road were silver-misted with a light snow that had fallen earlier, the dark green of the spruce trees dusted with glistening white powder.

She was thankful that the winter had been mild thus far, and if it should snow up a blizzard now, *why it might even mean being snowbound at Montclair!* Avril thought with a little surge of hope.

As they rounded the last bend of the driveway she saw the house clearly through the bare trees, and a lump rose in her throat. At last—at long last—home!

Inside, fires were burning in both the drawing room and library. As she entered she could smell lemon wax and the scent of applewood logs. She looked around at the familiar objects—the polished table in the hall with the blue and white Meissen bowl and matching candlesticks beneath the round, gold mirror topped with the crested eagle. She spun around in the middle of the floor, gazing at the paneled walls, the framed portraits marching along the staircase. Hector, who had opened the door for her, stood beaming.

"Shore is nice to hab yo' home, Miss Avril," he said.

"But where is Graham? Where is Mr. Montrose? I thought he would be here when I came?" she asked, a little pucker marring her smooth forehead.

"He had to go down to de storehouse at de las' minute jes' 'fo de carriage come up de drive. But he should be in sho'tly. I knowed he heered de horses."

"I'll wait for him in the library, Hector." She went through the double doors into her favorite room in the house. Her favorite, because it was filled with memories of so many happy hours spent here with Graham.

She moved over toward the fireplace, holding out her hands to the warmth of the crackling fire. Only a minute later she heard the sound of voices in the hallway and footsteps coming along the polished floor.

Slowly she turned to face the door just as Graham came through at a full stride. At the sight of him a wild kind of joy seized her.

Graham halted on the threshold. He drew in his breath sharply, and in spite of himself, his pulse thundered at the sight of the tall, willowy figure.

The firelight behind her shed a bronze sheen on her glorious auburn hair falling about her shoulders. At a glance he took in every detail of her appearance. She was wearing a traveling dress of gray kerseymere, a soft, finely woven wool, trimmed with russet velvet epaulets and cuffs. Its high-standing collar framed her slender neck, and the cut of the garment revealed the new feminine curves of her maturing body. Her bonnet, cape, and muff had been tossed on a nearby chair.

The last time he had seen Avril she had been a child. Here in her place was a graceful young woman.

As he stood there, at a loss for words, a mischievous glint brightened her eyes. A playful smile fetched a dimple winking at the side of her full, red mouth as if she were trying not to laugh.

It brought him around quickly. She had changed, yes, but there was still something of that impulsive, appealing child about her.

"Avril, my dear," he said, finding his voice. "Welcome home!"

Avril ran across the room ready to throw her arms around him, have him lift her and swing her around before setting her back on her feet as he had always done.

But this time she noticed a difference. Even as she hugged him she could feel him stiffen. Startled, she looked up at him, puzzled and hurt as he held her carefully from him.

"How was the journey, not too fatiguing, I hope?" Graham asked briskly. "And how was Aunt Laura when you stopped to see her in Williamsburg?"

He pushed her gently away, his expression composed enough. But there was something in his eyes Avril had never seen there before. Something indefinable that bewildered her. Was it her imagination? Or, in her long absence, had there been some subtle change in their relationship?

Perhaps he saw she had grown up, and that made him feel awkward. A perverse sense of pleasure in that thought gave Avril an unnatural boldness.

Stepping up to him, she took both his hands in hers, lifted her face, and asked pertly, "Have you missed me?"

"Of course," he replied with mock sternness. "The house has been quiet—and *peaceful* and *orderly,* I might add!"

"Well, I'm here to make it noisy again and disturb all your fine peace. So how do you like that?" She dropped his hands and pirouetted in front of him, setting her dark red curls bouncing and her skirt swirling to reveal her French-heeled boots.

Graham stepped behind his desk, unconsciously distancing himself from this enchanting creature. The skinny little girl he remembered had changed from a moth to a butterfly.

"Once the news is out that you've come home, we shall have the place full of young people in no time at all, I suspect. That is, if the young Camerons have anything to say about it. Both of them, Marshall and Logan, have ridden over at least twice already this week to see when you would be arriving. And they have a house full of guests themselves, so be prepared—" He gave a slight laugh. "I've given you fair warning."

His voice held a teasing note and yet he was conscious of a curious blend of emotions as he looked at Avril. With this girl he felt alive again, energized by her gaiety, her exuberance, her vitality. The sight of her gave him enormous joy. That was immediately followed by a feeling of regret that was entirely selfish. Graham knew he would have to share her with any young man who came within a mile of her.

Avril was looking at him now, her head tilted to one side in a questioning manner, as if awaiting his approval. He was at once aware of the ambivalence of his feelings toward her and felt his conflict anew.

There was something very different about her; more than the poise, the new attractiveness. It was a quality he could not quite define although he was very much aware of it. But with her new maturity she had not, thank God, lost that endearing, unaffected sweetness.

With her new womanly intuition Avril perceived the meaning of Graham's distress. Her transition from child to young woman had come as a shock to him. She cautioned herself to move slowly, not to upset the delicate balance of their relationship. She was sure that Graham still thought of her only as his ward, while she had come to believe they had a joint destiny, part of God's plan for both their lives. It was clear to her. But Graham had yet to be convinced.

So she seated herself on the sofa in a ladylike fashion and said demurely, "Thank you, Graham, for giving me permission to have Becky come for part of the holidays. Her family was so kind to me when I couldn't get to Montclair for the school holidays that I feel not only an obligation, but also a keen desire to show my appreciation."

"But, of course, your friends are more than welcome, Avril. Montclair is as much your home as mine."

Avril drew in her breath, feeling her pulses flutter. *Oh, I hope so, Graham. I do hope so,* she thought with yearning. But her voice was quite level as she continued. "I think you will like Rebecca. She is such good company. And isn't it fortunate that her older brother is visiting friends in Williamsburg for the holidays and can bring her to see us?"

For a moment nothing more was said and the only sound was the sputtering of the logs burning in the fireplace. Then the library doors opened and Hector came in, carrying a large, round tray with a silver tea service.

Seizing her chance, Avril spoke up with gentle dignity, "Thank you, Hector. If you'll put the tray right here, we'll serve ourselves." She indicated the low table in front of the sofa on which she had seated herself.

Hector followed her instructions and left the room, later reporting to Cookie, "Young Miss shore got her manners."

Watching Avril's graceful movements, Graham's eyes shone with indulgent tenderness as she poured the tea, adding cream to his and tucking the snowy linen napkin under the saucer of the cup as she handed it to him. Amused by her desire to impress him, he saw, nevertheless, her new command of the social graces. Indeed, she was a credit to her training, yet retained a quality that was uniquely hers, though he had yet to name it.

This new Avril presented a fascinating subject, Graham decided, observing her. The gold damask upholstery of the sofa set off her vivid coloring, her flaming hair through which the firelight sent golden lights. Perhaps she was not classically beautiful, but the combination of features was intriguing. All her freckles had faded and the stubby little nose had lengthened to an aristocratic shape, her large, luminous eyes the color of tide pools mysteriously changing from gray to green.

As if all at once aware of his gaze upon her, Avril gave a little bounce on the sofa pillows, breaking into his thoughts. "Isn't this cozy, just the two of us?"

"Indeed it is!" he exclaimed, surprised by her directness into telling her the truth.

She gave a delighted laugh and smiled at him over the rim of her teacup.

The spontaneous happiness he felt at her laughter was immediately discernible in his eyes and in the smile that softened the lines bracketing his mouth.

Avril felt a burst of assurance. Graham *was* happy to see her, glad she was home! She reached across the table and touched his hand.

At her touch the old familiar bond between them sprang to life, heightened by another element both felt but were not ready to express.

Patience, Avril counseled herself with a speeding heart. Time. That's all it will take. Time for Graham to get used to the fact that I'm no longer a child.

The firelight filled the room with a glowing warmth and the light patter of Avril's voice lulled Graham into a reflective mood. He remembered how many nights he had returned to this big house, feeling lonely and depressed. Now he understood why. Without Avril, this house—like his life—was empty.

chapter
14

AVRIL HAD FORGOTTEN with what enthusiasm Christmas was cele-
brated among the plantation dwellers along the James River and in
Williamsburg. She had become used to the quieter festivities at the
Academy, closely associated with the church and with the emphasis
on the spiritual observance of the season.

Invitations for all sorts of parties arrived at Montclair within days
of her return, and this year she was included in many of them.
Although she had not been formally introduced into society, Avril
was pleased to see both hers and Graham's names on quite a few of
the envelopes.

One morning shortly after her arrival, Avril came downstairs to
find a pile of varicolored envelopes on the silver tray on the hall
table. Flipping through them, Avril came upon one with a seal and
crest she recognized: *CF* in elegant initials. She picked it up and
held it for a long time. Instantly she felt all her old antagonistic
feelings for the fascinating Mrs. Fontayne sweep over her. She had
never forgotten Clarice's part in influencing Graham to send her
away to boarding school. Away from her beloved Montclair. Away
from Graham.

Avril tried to justify her dislike of Mrs. Fontayne, thinking that it
was more than irrational childish resentment. But she could not
deny that the seed planted by the Camerons—that Graham was the

target of the lovely widow's wiles—was the real reason for her antagonism.

Avril was still holding the square, rich vellum envelope with its intricate calligraphy when Graham came in from his plantation rounds.

"Another batch of requests for the honor of our presence at some soirée? It seems you have added immeasurably to my popularity, my dear. I can't recall ever having received so many invitations!"

There was nothing Avril could do but pick up the lot and carry them into the library for Graham's perusal.

Helping him remove his caped greatcoat, Avril talked gaily of all sorts of small, inconsequential things in an attempt to distract him from the task at hand. He would read all the invitations, then decide which to accept and which to decline regretfully. She tugged on the needlepoint bellpull, asking Hector when he appeared to bring a pot of tea and biscuits. Then she pulled up a stool and sat down beside Graham's easy chair in front of the fire.

The moment had come. She might as well be comfortable.

Sorting through the envelopes, Graham held up one, chuckling. "For the socially ambitious, here is the most sought-after invitation of the season—Clarice Fontayne's New Year Eve's party. There are some who would do anything to get in, I'm told, even going so far as to forge one of these."

Avril tensed as she saw Graham toss it onto one of the piles. Accepted or refused? Hope sprang up in her. Perhaps Graham had seen through the woman's artifice, after all, for she knew he detested sham in any form. But his next words dashed her hope.

"Wait until you see how she has redecorated the Handley house. Brought over all sorts of *objets d'art* from France and some grand furnishings from her English mansion. May raves about it. So shall we go see what all the fuss is about?"

"Becky will be visiting then," she reminded him. "Do you think, perhaps, that we could have a small party here instead?"

"Oh, I doubt that we could surpass the lavish affair that Clarice is sure to have. Don't you think your friend would enjoy a taste of elegance?"

Avril knew that Becky would be overjoyed to attend such a gala. She could just see those blue eyes widening at the gowns, the decorations, the food served at the Fontayne mansion.

Forced to tell the truth, Avril nodded. "Yes, I guess Becky wouldn't want to miss that."

Avril would have liked nothing better than to spend most of her holiday time alone with Graham, for they seemed to have found a new level of companionship, a new camaraderie. She felt that Graham respected her hard-won maturity, and she was looking forward to many happy hours of discussing the subjects into which she had gained clearer insight.

But that was not to be, for the next afternoon Logan and Marshall came calling. Their reunion, although marked with the natural enthusiasm of long friendship, had a new element as well, Avril was quick to see.

Marshall had simply grown taller, losing his adolescent awkwardness. But his face still held the boyish openness and ready smile. It was Logan who had changed most. Not only had he grown extraordinarily handsome, but his manner was decidedly different— especially in his attitude toward Avril.

She had felt his cool appraisal the minute they had arrived, and the interest kindled by her appearance gave her a distinct sense of satisfaction.

As they were leaving, Logan lingered a moment in the hall after Marshall had bounded down the porch steps where the grooms held their horses for mounting.

"You will be coming to our Open House on Christmas Day, won't you, Avril?" he asked. The holiday party at Cameron Hall was a countywide tradition.

"Of course," she smiled. "We wouldn't think of missing it."

"I'm glad," he replied, touching her arm. "Maybe we can find a way to slip away from little brother and catch up after all these years." There was a certain insinuation in his words that she found

116

vaguely exciting. "I never thought you'd grow up to be so beautiful, Avril." His smile broadened to his old teasing grin. "But you have!"

As it turned out their plans for horseback riding the next day were rendered impossible by an unexpected change in the weather. A light rain falling during the night turned to sleet and then to snow, making Montclair an impenetrable white fortress and preventing any visitors from negotiating the ice-encrusted roads and trails. Avril's concealed satisfaction at the pleasant isolation with Graham was short-lived, however. On the third day brilliant sunshine fast melted away any trace of snow, and the following day was Christmas and the occasion of the Camerons' open house.

After the Christmas morning gift-giving to the assembled house and field servants, a tradition at Montclair, Graham and Avril had their own private exchange.

Graham seemed pleased with the framed watercolor of Montclair that Avril had executed from memory during her time at the Academy, and he praised her talent extravagantly.

Among the several gifts Graham presented her was a velvet jewel box containing a tiny jeweled pin—a fleur-de-lis composed of aquamarines and pearls.

"Oh, Graham! It's lovely!" exclaimed Avril, clasping it to her.

"I'm glad you like it. I hoped it would be something you might enjoy wearing." He smiled tenderly, regarding the breathless young woman, whose cheeks bloomed with a color that rivaled her glorious hair.

"Oh, I shall!" she declared and immediately fastened it onto the collar of her spencer, the high-waisted jacket of her blueberry wool dress. "I shall love wearing it!" she said, thinking she would probably pin it to her nightie, so thrilled was she that Graham had chosen it for her.

Early Christmas afternoon they drove to Cameron Hall. Dressed in a short cape, the same bright blue as her dress and wearing the gray squirrel tippet and muff, another of Graham's Christmas presents to her, Avril felt she had never been so happy.

So far her holidays had been sublime. She and Graham had

enjoyed some unexpected moments alone together thanks to the unpredictable weather, and next week Becky was coming for a visit. Then in only a few months she would graduate from the Academy and come home to Montclair for good.

She looked over at Graham and smiled a secret little smile. Dreamily she imagined those long, leisurely days of summer when once again she and Graham would be together. This time, however, she would not be ticking away the days before her departure for the Academy. Her formal education would be complete and she could remain at Montclair forever!

Cameron Hall was beautifully decorated and filled with gaily attired guests. Auntie May, in a geranium-red taffeta gown, greeted them affectionately. It was the first time she had seen Avril since her return and she looked her over from head to toe.

"Oh, my! Now, I believe every word of Logan's description!" she exclaimed. "My funny little redhead has become a beautiful auburn-haired princess!" She beamed at Avril as though she herself were responsible for the transformation. Then she winked slyly at Graham. "Now, all we have to do is find her a proper *prince*."

"But how many frogs will she have to kiss first?" asked a deep, male voice from behind her, and Avril turned to see Logan smiling at her.

They all laughed at the jest except Graham, who looked a bit uncomfortable.

"Come along, there's food and punch and the famous Cameron eggnog," Auntie May urged, taking both of them by the arm and leading them toward the dining room.

Spread out on the festively decorated table, draped in lace and sparkling with crystal and silver and gleaming china, was a feast truly fit for royalty!

"Let me take your cloak, Avril," Logan offered, ready to hand it to one of the servants standing nearby.

"Just a minute," she said unpinning the fleur-de-lis from her collar and refastening it to her dress before surrendering her cape to him.

"A special Christmas gift?" he asked with lifted brow.

"Very special. Graham picked it out for me," she replied, unable to keep from blushing.

Logan was about to respond when Marshall appeared to join them.

It was a trio Logan seemed to find tiresome, for after they had filled their plates from the sumptuous buffet and the three of them were seated together, he kept sending Marshall off on errands.

"Get Avril some cranberry punch, why don't you, Marshall?" he would suggest.

"But she hasn't finished what she has," Marshall protested.

"A *good* host never allows a guest's glass to get less than half full," Logan said knowingly.

After Marshall's somewhat disgruntled departure, Logan would engage Avril in a spirited conversation, ignoring his brother's return with her refilled glass.

Avril was amused. It was rather fun to have her two former playmates vying for her favor. It was certainly a new experience to have Logan so attentive. She could not help feeling a sudden heady sensation of feminine power.

Then a gust of cold wind swept through the room and Avril experienced a sensation not unlike a woods creature's instinctive awareness of a predator. Without knowing exactly why, she shivered. Then turning, she witnessed Clarice Fontayne's arrival in a flurry of white fur and blue velvet.

The woman's heart-shaped face was framed by the fox-trimmed hood of her flowing cape. Gentlemen were flocking to her side to help her divest herself of it. But to Avril's dismay, it was to Graham that Clarice's attention was directed. As she watched with a sinking heart, Graham offered his arm and the two of them made a slow promenade of the room as Clarice was greeted as if she were a visiting empress.

Music floated in from the other parlor, which had been cleared for dancing, and Logan leaned down and whispered in Avril's ear, "Shall we venture in and see if our dancing skills are in practice?"

Anything seemed better than staying in the same room with Clarice and watching the men fluttering in her wake like moths drawn to an irresistible flame. How could Graham be taken in by her, let her use him so blatantly?

"You have a telltale face, Avril," Logan chided her as he led her into the parlor.

"What do you mean?" she asked indignantly, flushing.

"Ah, perhaps I know you too well, but those eyes of yours were flashing dangerously just now when the beauteous widow of Williamsburg arrived." His tone was bantering, but the eyes regarding her were grave.

Avril pressed her lips together, not knowing how to reply.

"Ladies must learn not to let their expressions betray their emotions. But I don't suppose they teach such frivolous things at that strict school you attend, do they?"

Avril shrugged. In spite of herself she glanced over at Clarice and Graham, who were now sharing a glass of punch.

"It's all part of growing up, you see, Avril," Logan went on. "It's even scriptural. Remember? 'When I was a child, I thought as a child . . . but when I became a man—or woman,'" he paraphrased, "'I put away childish things.' Grown-ups learn to dissemble."

"Then, maybe I don't want to be grown up!" she retorted. "Besides, you're misquoting Scripture, and you know what they say about that and who does it and for what purpose!"

"Far be it from me to argue the Scriptures with you!" Logan laughed.

They were at the edge of the polished floor now and Logan bowed and they moved into the graceful measured steps of the dance. "See, there are some pleasurable advantages to adulthood. At least now we are allowed downstairs."

Avril looked puzzled but before she could pursue his remark, she was swung into a twirl, her hand taken by another gentleman, before returning to Logan.

Logan was an excellent dancer. Probably he had had a great deal more practice than she, with the limited opportunities afforded by the Academy. But he led her through the steps with a gentle, sure touch, so that she found herself following with ease. He smiled his approval.

"So how does it feel to be all grown up, Avril?"

"Grown up?"

"Yes, have you forgotten the last time you and I danced together? It was on the balcony where we children were sent during the grown-up party."

"Ah, yes! I remember. Although it seems a long time ago." She smiled a trifle wistfully.

"You haven't answered my question."

She thought for a long moment. "It's a little frightening."

Logan gazed at her as they circled, took the measured steps, bowed, and he twirled her around. Then without her noticing, he danced her into the shadowed archway that led into the music room off the parlor.

"Don't be frightened, Avril," Logan said softly. "Being grown up can be quite delightful."

With that, he bent down and kissed her full on the lips. It was not at all like the awkward kiss Jamie Buchanan had bestowed that Christmas at Woodlawn.

"Logan!" she gasped when it ended.

But he already had his hand on her waist and was leading her back into the lighted parlor. He was smiling, a look of amused triumph on his handsome face.

When the music stopped Avril felt flushed and warm. She had been excited by Logan's kiss, but mostly confused by the feelings it had stirred in her. She excused herself to go into the downstairs bedroom that had been turned into a cloak and "retiring" room for the ladies. On the table under a wide mirror lighted by an elegant six-branched candelabra, she found bottles of cologne and dampened linen towels for the guests to use in refreshing themselves.

She was standing there lifting her heavy hair to cool her neck when Clarice's reflection appeared beside hers in the mirror. Even while acknowledging the woman's ravishing beauty, she could not stem the helpless tide of animosity that flooded her.

"Why, Avril!" Even Clarice's exclamations were delivered in smooth honeyed tones. "I hardly knew you!"

Slowly Avril turned to face her, knowing in her heart that she could never compete with this polished charm, this sophisticated confidence.

To her surprise Clarice seemed to be appraising her with a different kind of interest. Eyes narrowed speculatively, her glance swept over Avril, not missing an inch of the girl's slender height, the soft new roundness of her bosom, her creamy skin, and auburn hair. It was as if she realized she was confronting a young woman instead of a child, one whose emerging beauty rivaled her own.

In a matter of seconds, a swift exchange of looks passed between them, then a shrewd half-smile touched Clarice's lips.

"So, how is it to be home after all this time?" she asked indifferently, moving on to observe herself in the mirror with evident satisfaction.

"Oh, it's quite wonderful, Mrs. Fontayne," Avril replied, feeling an urge to somehow squelch that studied ennui Clarice always affected. "Graham and I have been having some lovely times together." This seemed to elicit a little response from Clarice, who glanced her way again. Avril, sensing this, felt her courage soar. "We ride together almost every day and read or play chess or just discuss books we've read or music we like—" She gained momentum as she thought of Graham's obvious pleasure in having her back at Montclair, his delight in their shared interests. For a moment she enjoyed a feeling of superiority. Clarice did not ride nor did she read. In fact, according to Auntie May, the lovely widow's days were filled with shopping and visiting, her conversation limited to fashions, fads, and trivial gossip.

But that brief feeling of confidence was snatched from her. Clarice, finished admiring herself, turned slowly toward Avril and, seeing the fleur-de-lis pin, reached out and touched it lightly.

"Oh, I see you are wearing the pretty pin. Do you like it? I so

hoped you would. I was with Graham when he bought it for you."
Beneath the smooth sweetness of her softly modulated voice was an
underlying mockery.

Clarice might as well have slapped her. The casual remark,
implying that *she,* not Graham, had selected the jewel for her,
wounded Avril to the quick. More than the lovely pin itself, the fact
that Graham had chosen it for her himself meant most to Avril.

Avril felt the stinging rush of tears, but she willed them away.
She whirled around, her back to Clarice, and picked up one of the
silver-handled brushes provided for guests and began to brush her
hair vigorously.

Clarice was patting her creamy neck and shoulders with a
maribou powder puff, apparently indifferent that her careless
comment had broken Avril's vulnerable heart and ruined Christmas
Day for her.

chapter
15

"WELL, *THAT'S* OVER!" declared Avril, sighing, as she dropped into a chair, slipped her feet out of her yellow satin slippers, and began unbuttoning her long kid gloves.

"*Over!*" exclaimed Becky, with a shocked expression. "You make it sound as though we've just come from a funeral, not a ball!"

Avril pressed her lips together as she cast a look at her friend's shining face. No use to spoil her guest's afterglow of happiness with her own dismal mood. She herself could not wait to leave Clarice's party and come back to the Barnwells' home where they were sharing the guest room at Aunt Laura's. The ball had not been over until much too late to return to Montclair that evening.

Avril would have preferred her original plan to hold a small New Year's Eve party at Montclair instead, but once Becky had heard about the extravagant gala from Logan and Marshall, she had been eager to go. So in spite of Avril's premonition of disaster, she had been forced to consider her guest's wishes instead of her own.

"Why do you say that, Avril? You looked perfectly beautiful in that stunning dress! And every time I saw you—why you danced every dance!"

Not waiting for an answer, Becky held out her own pink sarcenet skirt and spun around happily. "It was the most marvelous party I've ever been to and I had a splendid time!"

"I'm glad, Becky. Maybe I'm just tired. I've the beginning of a headache, that's all." And worse still, *a heartache,* Avril admitted silently.

She stood to unfasten the row of tiny looped buttons on the bodice of her dress of jonquil silk barege. Becky was right. It was a lovely gown, the neckline corded in deeper yellow satin, the skirt and tiny puffed sleeves ornamented with satin bows, the color enormously becoming.

There was no use explaining to Becky that it was not the party itself but the hostess she wished to avoid—especially after that shattering encounter with Mrs. Fontayne at the Camerons' on Christmas Day. But of course she had to go. There had been no possibility of escape after Becky's arrival. As soon as she learned about the glittering social event, her friend had talked of little else. Clarice's parties had become widely known in Williamsburg and beyond, providing weeks of anticipation and months of gossip afterwards.

But Becky's spirits were not easily dampened. As they got ready for bed, she chattered endlessly about the party.

"I think Logan Cameron is very handsome and gallant, but Marshall is so much nicer, really. Maybe he's more like my brothers, not so formal, so I feel more comfortable with him. They were both extremely flattering, though, and filled my dance card with the names of many other young gentlemen. Marshall made sure he had the dance before supper and the last dance of the evening and—well, I do believe I liked him best."

Avril's mind was wandering and it was only Becky's next remark that brought her sharply back to the present.

"Don't you agree? I'm hardly ever mistaken about such things."

"What on earth are you saying?" demanded Avril.

"It's as plain as the nose on your face!" retorted Becky. "There is something going on between Mrs. Fontayne and your guardian."

"What do you mean? What did you notice?"

"Oh, it's very obvious. At least to me. Didn't you see how she singled him out all evening, how she looks at him, flirting and yet very possessive as if there is no need to flirt. The kind of intimate teasing that only exists between people who are very close? And your guardian, too. Didn't you notice how solicitous he was of her? He went to fetch her shawl, brought her supper, kept her punch cup filled all evening—all the little things that people do who care deeply for each other."

"But that's the way Graham is!" protested Avril. "He has impeccable manners. He treats all ladies graciously."

"Perhaps. But there was a difference in the way he was acting with Mrs. Fontayne," said Becky with a wise air. "Just watch them the next time they're together. You'll see. I know *she* is interested in him. But, if as you say, he conducts himself in the same way toward every lady"— There was a definite touch of doubt in Becky's tone— "then I'm not sure about him."

"You're imagining things," sniffed Avril. "I don't believe a word of it."

"It's because you don't want to." Becky gave an indifferent little shrug. "But, mark my words, Mrs. Fontayne strikes me as being a very clever lady. If she wants something, I'm sure she would do anything to get it."

Avril felt a growing sense of uneasiness. Becky was often remarkably perceptive. And it was true that her observation was something Avril would rather not believe. Now she felt cold and numb at her friend's words.

Gradually her dismay took the form of anger. For a few minutes she even wished she had never invited Becky to Montclair for the holidays. Then she would not have attended the ball tonight and noticed whatever it was Becky saw between Clarice and Graham. She certainly could not have repeated it!

Resentment flared within her and she said crossly, "Let's not talk any more tonight. I'm tired and want to go to sleep." And with that, Avril snuffed out the candle on her side of the bed and burrowed under the covers, turning her back on Becky.

She heard Becky moving about the room, finishing undressing, making deliberate little noises—the bang of a hairbrush, the scrape of the armoire door as she hung her ball gown—taking longer to settle as if in silent protest to Avril's behavior.

Finally the bed creaked, the mattress jiggling as Becky climbed in beside her in the big, four-poster canopy bed. But tonight they didn't warm each other with conversation, nor did they sleep curled up like spoons.

Soon Avril heard Becky sigh and in awhile she could tell by her friend's breathing that she had fallen asleep. But there was no rest for Avril. The headache she had pretended was now a throbbing reality. All the impressions of the evening came flashing back into her mind punishingly. For in spite of the disbelief she had professed to Becky, she, too, had been aware of the disturbing appearance of Graham's attentiveness to Clarice.

She recalled coming downstairs and seeing Graham in the hall waiting to escort them to the carriage for the ride to Mrs. Fontayne's townhouse. How splendid he looked in a dark sateen waistcoat, cream silk cravat, high stiff collar. But there was no joy in her heart, only dread premonition of the evening ahead.

He had complimented both of them, but the words seem to drift by Avril as if she had not heard them. She remembered little of the ride—only that Graham and Becky kept up a lighthearted patter into which she rarely entered though they prodded her with an occasional question.

But arriving at Clarice Fontayne's home was a distinct image. She would never forget her first impression of the grandeur. A liveried butler opened the door for them and Avril had the sensation of dazzling light, the sound of music, the murmur of voices. She heard Becky's own awed little intake of breath.

The house was even more lavishly decorated than Cameron Hall, which Avril had always considered the most luxurious of homes. Here were rose brocade draperies, elaborate crystal chandeliers with tinkling pendants dangling like fine jewels from a lady's ears—no doubt an import from one of the foreign countries in which Clarice had lived. There were parquet floors, graceful French furniture, exquisite Persian rugs. No expense had been spared. Indeed, when

Avril glanced into the drawing room, she had the impression that all of this elegance was only a setting to complement the rare jewel who occupied these quarters.

There, Clarice was seated in a high-backed, throne-like chair, as if posed for a portrait. She was gorgeously gowned, something gold and blue, with a filmy tulle stole about her sloping ivory shoulders. In her stylishly coiffed hair was a sparkling jeweled star.

In an adjoining room guests were playing cards, seated at small card tables of polished wood, with brackets at each corner for lighted candles. Crimson-liveried servants were moving about with serving trays of delicacies and wine carafes. Stationed in one corner was a quartet of musicians, playing soft music.

Avril was grateful when she saw Logan and Marshall heading toward them from across the room. Marshall immediately claimed Becky for the first dance, and just as Logan bowed and was about to ask Avril, Avril spied Jamison Buchanan over his shoulder. She knew, of course, that he had escorted his sister as far as Williamsburg on her way to Montclair, but she had not expected to see him at the party.

That was soon explained. As the houseguest of the Langleys, he had been included in their invitation.

In his well-tailored evening clothes, Jamison made a strikingly handsome figure. He was taller now, but the merry blue eyes, so like his sister's, had not changed, nor had the engaging smile and easygoing, natural manner.

His eyes sparkled with excitement as he told Avril, "I'm enrolling at the College of William & Mary for my next year. Then I plan to read law with a friend of my father's here. So I shall be around when you graduate from the Academy and come back to Virginia."

He stepped beside her as a line formed to greet their hostess. After that, Jamison rarely left Avril's side all evening. To distract herself from the ever-present irritation of Clarice, Avril flirted outrageously with Jamison as well as the many other young gentlemen who requested her as a partner.

Every once in awhile her eyes sought Graham, but he seemed

always to be either occupied in conversation or dancing. She saw him only once with Clarice, but even then she felt a cold fury. It sickened her that she should feel so hideous an emotion.

She had spent the rest of the evening dancing alternately with Jamison, Marshall, Logan, and Jamison's host, Peyton Langley, who seemed quite intrigued with her. She had flirted and laughed at the silly jokes, the compliments, and banter. She had played the games and, as Becky pointed out, had not missed a single dance.

The flame of the night lamp on the mantelpiece flickered, making strange shadows on the wall. A log in the fireplace cracked and fell, sputtering in a burst of sparks. Eventually both lamp and fire went out, leaving the room in a darkness as deep as that she felt in her heart. Sleep still did not come, and Avril lay staring into the blackness until finally she slipped into troubled dreams.

New Year's Day dawned gray and rainy. After breakfasting with Aunt Laura, during which Avril had to listen again to Becky waxing lyrical over the decorations, the food, the gay company at the party, they said their good-byes and set out for the long ride back to Montclair.

Riding along the cobbled streets of Williamsburg, then onto the winter-rutted country roads, Avril was noticeably silent. Graham cast several puzzled glances in her direction and valiantly carried the conversation with Becky as best he could. Avril's friend, still miffed by her hostess's attitude the night before, ignored her. Avril, feeling guilty, pleaded a possible cold coming on and huddled in her corner of the carriage all the way home.

The rain that had begun as a light drizzle in Williamsburg persisted throughout the ride, and when they reached Montclair at last, Avril was glad for the privacy of her own room, where she need not pretend a spriteliness she did not feel.

Cheered by the promise of another party at Cameron Hall the next afternoon, Becky went to put her hair up in rags, so as to look her prettiest for Marshall when she saw him again.

The next morning continued bleak and rainy when they breakfasted and prepared for the ride to Cameron Hall. It was a bone-chilling rain, and even with warm lap robes over their knees in the carriage, the girls were shivering from the cold. Almost as cold was the strained politeness between them.

But when they reached the Cameron plantation home, the atmosphere was so jolly and festive that they were soon caught up in the fun, forgetting their earlier estrangement. And by the time they were on their way back to Montclair, the coolness between them had been resolved, and though neither of them ever mentioned the incident that had precipitated their tiff, the two were soon back on their old amiable footing.

Friends should be friends forever, thought Avril with remorse, regretting her childish petulance, *like my father and Graham.* And she wondered what her fate might have been had they not signed that boyhood pact so long ago.

chapter
16

AVRIL STARED at the questions on her examination paper, then raised her head and looked out the window where the early spring day beckoned invitingly.

It was hard to concentrate when so many exciting things were happening. The most thrilling for Avril was the fact that Graham was coming to New Hope for her graduation. It would be his first visit here, and Avril was looking forward to his coming for more than one reason. She did want to show him around the campus, but more importantly, she wanted her friends to meet her handsome guardian!

Avril forced her attention from her daydreams. In order to graduate with honors, as Graham would expect, it was imperative that she do well on her final examinations.

She glanced over the questions. Graduates were examined on all the subjects they had studied. Under the heading of History, Avril read the first one: "How long has the United States been independent of Great Britain?" then wrote, "On the fourth of July, it will be thirty-seven years." History, both world history and American history, was one of Graham's avid interests, so Avril had taken pains to learn as much as possible in order to converse intelligently about great events of the past, especially those taking place in Virginia where his ancestors had been among the early settlers.

Avril completed this portion of the test with ease and went on to geography, which she found a little more difficult. She pondered the correct definition of "isthmus," frowned and chewed on her pen over the instruction to "name the boundary between New Hampshire and Vermont," then quickly scribbled in the name of "the most important city on the banks of the Danube."

Arithmetic had never been a strong point and Avril squirmed, using her fingers and puckering her brow as she tried to "calculate the interest for 6 months on 475 dollars at 6 pr. ct."

Avril paused, remembering how Graham had called her into his plantation office one day when he was going over the ledgers. He had pointed out the column indicating the income from the crops and the sale of some of the calves and tobacco, then the column itemizing expenditures, and had explained how one must wisely balance both so as not to operate at a loss. He had been very patient, very precise, but Avril had fidgeted, gazing longingly out the window toward the stable, where she knew Fancy would be waiting for a ride.

Then Graham had taken her by the chin and lifted it so his eyes, very clear and dark, were on a level with hers. "Listen to me, Avril. Someday you will be a very wealthy woman, so you must begin now to understand the importance of handling money wisely. There are unscrupulous people about, who, unless you are alert and knowledgeable, might manipulate, defraud, or otherwise cheat you. A great fortune is a great responsibility. It is your duty to guard it well."

That was perhaps the first time Avril had been made truly aware of what she had known for some time—that when she became twenty-one she would be very rich. She had simply never considered the notion that she herself would be responsible for managing her inheritance.

Even that day, when Graham had tried to impress upon her the future task that would be hers, it did not seem real. Twenty-one seemed such a distant age and so remote from this moment. But this summer she would be a graduate of this institution—if she kept her mind on her studies a bit longer! After that, what then? She continued to muse, twiddling a russet strand of hair between two fingers.

"Is something wrong, Avril?" The voice of Dame Whitley, who was monitoring the examination, caused Avril to start and look up. She shook her head.

"Then you best get on with your work," the teacher cautioned, pointing to the wall clock. "I will soon be collecting the papers."

Avril ducked her head and set to work again. There was plenty of time to think about her fortune, to plan for the future. There wasn't much time to finish her examination!

The last section was comprised of questions on religion. "How is faith accomplished?" Immediately Avril wrote down the words to a verse of Scripture from the book of Romans: "So then faith cometh by hearing, and hearing by the word of God" and added the reference "(tenth chapter, seventeenth verse)." She thought a moment longer. Though the answer seemed simple, Avril had not found the living of the Christian life to be an easy matter. Acquiring a strong, sustaining faith involved struggle, she had learned. Even after that ecstatic first coming to the Lord, believing the gospel to be the truth, the reality she had been searching for, Avril knew she had not yet overcome certain unbecoming characteristics of her nature—and she thought of her resentment of Clarice Fontayne with a sinking heart.

She had often wished Mr. Lowe, the evangelist, would come to the Academy to preach again. Now that she had studied the Bible and memorized many of the Psalms, there were questions she wished to ask him. Do God's promises stand the test? Are prayers really answered?

The headmistress told her once when she had asked about him that Mr. Lowe went "wherever the Lord leads," and she could not tell Avril when that path would bring him next to New Hope.

Avril wished she could feel again that joy, that exhilaration she had experienced the day she had responded to the altar call. She wondered what she would do about church attendance this summer at Montclair. It was too far to go in to Williamsburg every Sunday, though she always attended with Aunt Laura when she was there for a visit or shopping, sitting in the pew with an engraved brass plaque bearing the name "Barnwell" and opposite the one marked "Montrose."

Perhaps if she asked him, Graham would go with her. He also attended services when they were in Williamsburg, but never mentioned it otherwise. He seemed thoughtful during the sermons, but Avril did not know whether he was moved by them or ever gave them a second thought.

There the services were nothing like the fiery exhortations given by Mr. Lowe, urging the hearers to repentance, often accompanied by tears of remorse. Instead, the sermons were short, usually cheerful, the singing pleasant but certainly not spirited.

Avril sighed and turned to the last few questions. She had just completed the last of them when Dame Whitley tapped the warning bell and began gathering the examination papers.

Within a few days the results of all tests were posted and Avril and Becky found their names on the list of students to be graduated.

The following week was a whirl of preparations for the big day. Becky's family was coming en masse, and as the girls got ready for the occasion there was much excitement.

"You know, Avril, Jamie arranged to take his examinations early in order to be here. Mostly to see you, I expect!" she teased.

Since Christmas Avril had regularly received letters from Jamison Buchanan, Esq., postmarked Williamsburg, where he was in his third year at William & Mary.

Avril pretended shock. "Not at all! He told me he had to see with his own eyes the miracle of your passing your examinations and actually being graduated from this institution of higher learning!"

"Oh, *you!*" exclaimed Becky, aiming a patchwork pillow unerringly at her roommate. This initiated a furious exchange of pillows, petticoats, and stocking balls and ended in leaving both girls breathless, laughing, and collapsing on their beds.

When she could speak again, Becky sat up, her round, flushed face serious, and said plaintively, "Oh, Avril! I shall miss you so! What in the world will I ever do without you? You've been like the sister I never had and always longed for! I shall be desolate!"

Then her eyes widened as if with sudden inspiration. "Oh, Avril, why don't you marry Jamie? I know he adores you! Then you could come and live at Woodlawn and we'd truly be sisters!"

Avril regarded Becky's eager face, tempted to tell this dear friend the truth about the legal union between herself and Graham that precluded the thought of a marriage for several years. But only the two lawyers, Judge and Mrs. Cameron, and Avril and Graham knew of that secret ceremony that had taken place in the drawing room at Montclair. Six witnesses to a well-kept secret that had given Graham trusteeship of her inheritance as his wife. A vast inheritance she had come to understand.

She knew Graham had made several trips to Natchez over the years, telling her only that he must see to her property. Often he had seemed worried before he left, but upon his return he would tell Avril that matters had improved or had been corrected. Sometimes she had the feeling that some danger threatened. But most of the time she soon forgot about any problems. Graham was in charge, after all, and he would manage. He always had, hadn't he?

If Avril were about to waver and confide in Becky, she was interrupted by a knock at the door, and one of the younger girls entered to deliver a package for her.

It was the first of many graduation gifts, and Becky was as excited as Avril when she opened it. It was a sterling silver toilette set— mirror, brush, and comb, with sculptured intertwined roses on the backs and the initials A.D.

Inside was a card from Graham, giving the date of his arrival in New Hope. But Avril did not know how to interpret the last bit of news: "I'll be bringing along a surprise."

chapter
17

"I WONDER what Graham's surprise can be?" Avril was to ask Becky many times in the days that followed.

Of course she did not really expect an answer, but her anticipation mounted as the date of his coming neared. Once they had received the results of their final examinations and knew they would graduate, the girls were free to spend their time in preparation for the many events of graduation week.

For the graduating students many of the Academy's rules were bent and they were given permission to shop in New Hope in the afternoons while the younger girls were still in class.

Graham's letter had suggested that, on the evening of his arrival, she should join him for dinner at the Inn, where he would be staying. All the graduates had similar plans to meet with family and friends, as long as they were back at the Academy by nine. The Buchanans would be arriving, too, and both girls talked endlessly of what they would wear for that momentous event.

After months of wearing the required uniforms, the idea of dressing in a pretty frock was appealing. Avril especially wanted to look stylish and mature when Graham saw her, for more depended on this reunion than she cared to admit, even to herself.

She had tried on her chosen outfit for Becky in a kind of dress rehearsal and had been pronounced "perfect." But as she dressed that evening, she examined her reflection in the mirror critically, trying to see herself as Graham would see her.

Her dress was of pale yellow, ribbed fabric, fashioned with a pelerine-effect bodice, and long, puffed sleeves, tied at the wrists with lilac satin bows.

On impulse she had purchased a wide-brimmed leghorn hat of canary-colored straw, trimmed with silk pansies and lilac streamers. Finally she confessed to Becky that she had "gone completely mad" with the addition of lilac kid gloves and soft yellow moroccan leather shoes.

Her heart was thumping wildly as she entered the front parlor of New Hope Inn. Halting on the threshold, Avril looked for Graham. Then she saw him coming toward her, and she felt faint.

How elegant he is, she thought breathlessly. *How distinguished!* The well-fitting dark broadcloth jacket, blue cravat, striped waist-coat, buff trrousers were enhanced by his erect carriage. There were a few silver strands threaded through the dark, wavy hair, some new lines around the deep-set eyes. But the classic, aristocratic features in the lean face, tanned from his days outdoors, were the same. Graham was still the most intriguingly handsome man she had ever known.

As he came toward her, his expression aglow with pleasure, Avril's throat went suddenly dry. She felt warmth rise into her cheeks and she stood quite still, unable to move. Graham held out both his hands and numbly she placed her small, gloved ones into them.

His eyes swept over her, taking in every detail, and she held her breath unconsciously waiting for his comment.

"If you aren't a picture!" he said, gazing at her.

So aware of his nearness and her own reawakened feelings for him, Avril felt her composure slipping away, and to her horror, instead of accepting his compliment with gracious coolness, she stammered childishly, "Do you really like it? It isn't too much—too gaudy, perhaps?"

She could have bitten her tongue the minute the words were out of her mouth. He must think her inane!

But Graham merely chuckled and slipped her arm through his, patting her hand reassuringly. "Not at all! You look utterly charming. Now, come, as a special treat I've arranged for us to take our supper in a private dining room."

A *private* dining room! Avril's feet barely touched the floor as they walked arm in arm through the lobby and up the stairs.

A waiter, standing at a closed door at the top of the stairway, smiled and bowed as they reached the landing, then opened the door with a flourish.

Graham stepped back to allow Avril to precede him. Just as she started through, she heard a chorus of voices. "Surprise! Surprise!"

Three familiar laughing faces came into view—Auntie May, Logan, and Marshall Cameron! Her initial confusion was quickly followed by dismay. It took all her power to disguise her disappointment and feign an enthusiastic happy response when her heart was breaking inside.

"You didn't think we would let you graduate with only one person to applaud and cheer as you received your honors, did you?" asked Auntie May. "So when I suggested we come along, Graham thought it a grand idea."

For weeks Avril had dreamed of her reunion with Graham, looked forward to spending precious time alone with him. Now it was slipping out of her grasp. Her surprise was so genuine that the other emotions she was struggling to hide went unnoticed in the laughter and animated conversation going on around her.

They all seemed so pleased with themselves for bringing off such a feat that Avril had trouble holding back tears of frustration. Logan and Marshall were in high form and the table talk was spritely, full of teasing jokes and lively witticisms. In a way, Avril was relieved that she did not have to force any of her own, since all that was required of her was to smile and nod in response.

Even when dinner was over, there was no chance to see Graham alone on the short walk back to the Academy, as Logan and

Marshall Cameron, hoping for a glimpse of Rebecca Buchanan, had asked to accompany them.

Upon entering the visitors' parlor, they found Becky returning with her family from their evening together. At once Jamison was at Avril's side, open adoration on his face.

Graham was introduced to the Buchanans, while Marshall and Logan lost no time in renewing their acquaintance with Becky. With still a half-hour remaining until curfew, the Buchanans immediately engaged Graham in a discussion of education for young ladies, to Avril's added irritation. Becky, looking particularly fetching in her new blue dress and bonnet, at once caught the combined attentions of the Cameron brothers, thus leaving Jamison without competition for Avril.

"I received special permission from my instructors to take some of my examinations early so I could attend my sister's graduation," Jamison told Avril, then lowered his voice significantly, "but my *real* reason was that I had to see you again."

Avril, whose attention was distracted by Graham's presence across the room, was only half listening. What annoyed her most about the present situation was that almost immediately the company had been divided into two groups—on one side, Graham with the parents; on the other, the young people!

"Did you hear me, Avril?" Jamison was saying. "I will be in Williamsburg at the end of the summer so I can finish up my work before the fall term begins."

Avril turned to regard him blankly. His eyes were holding hers in an adoring gaze.

"I hope to see a great deal of you then," he said.

"Oh . . . well . . . yes, of course, Jamison," she replied without enthusiasm. Something that was being said on the other side of the room reached her ears and filled her with apprehension.

In response to some question from Mrs. Buchanan, she heard Graham reply, "I shall be leaving directly from here, right after the graduation ceremonies."

Every nerve tensed as Avril strained to hear more.

"To Scotland, you say? How interesting."

"I have always wanted to visit the land of my ancestors, especially the area on the coast called Montrose, from which our family's surname is derived. And the home of the clan, the 'gallant Grahams,' for which I personally was named. History is one of my passions, and to trace our family history should prove very fascinating."

Avril gasped, feeling almost as if Graham had struck her. Graham—going to Scotland right after graduation? Why hadn't he told her? Or why could he not take her along with him? Was that the "surprise" rather than a stupid dinner party? Hope sprang into her heart, setting it pounding. But Graham's next words banished even that frail expectation.

"Oh, Avril will be returning to Williamsburg with my friends, the Camerons. She will stay with my Great-Aunt Laura there, who is quite elderly and will be glad of young company this summer."

"Perhaps Avril could spend part of the summer with us at Woodlawn, Mr. Montrose. We would love to have her and I know Rebecca will find it easier to part with her if she knows Avril will be coming for a visit."

"I think that could be arranged."

There was further murmured conversation between them, but Avril heard no more. The long-anticipated summer at Montclair with Graham, his getting to know her again on a new and more equal basis, faded like a misty dream.

The bell, announcing the end of visitation, echoed through the hall and everyone rose.

Avril followed Graham out to the entryway. "Why didn't you tell me you were planning a trip to Scotland?" she asked, managing to keep her voice steady.

"I was planning to tell you, my dear. I was just waiting for the most opportune time."

Making an effort to keep her lower lip from trembling, she said, "You might have told me sooner." She hadn't meant for it to come out like that—like the complaint of a fretful child.

Graham touched her arm, "I'm sorry. Perhaps I was wrong, but I didn't want to spoil this special time for you in any way."

"Well, you have!" Again the note of childish petulance. Fighting foolish tears she was thankful the shadowy hallway prevented Graham from seeing them.

"Avril—" Graham began, but just then Logan and Marshall joined them and their laughing farewells and parting remarks to Becky prohibited anything more being said on the matter. The headmistress had come into the entryway to bid the Buchanans farewell, and Avril's distress was covered. She moved away from Graham and then he was gone.

It was only when they were in the privacy of their shared room that she vented her feelings to Becky.

"It's not fair how my life is always being planned for me!" she said indignantly as she paced up and down their small room. "I'm almost nineteen and I'm still treated as a child."

"But at least you're coming for a long visit with us at Woodlawn, Avril! Mama told me your guardian gave permission. We'll have such fun! I'm so glad when we say good-bye that it will just be until the end of the summer!"

The end of the summer! Avril moaned to herself as she lay sleepless in her bed long after Becky had fallen asleep. The end of the summer, when Graham would return, seemed a lifetime away! Somehow she would have to find some way to survive until then.

Avril felt angry, betrayed! It wasn't fair. Why weren't her prayers answered? She had tried to be good, to be patient, "to delight in the Lord," "to wait upon him." According to the Scriptures she was, in turn, promised "the desires of her heart." Why had He not brought it to pass?

Her heart felt heavy and rebellious. How long must she wait?

She thought of the summer ahead in Williamsburg. She had come to love Graham's Great-Aunt Laura, but to spend the entire summer in town and not at Montclair seemed a terrible lesson in patience.

As she lay there, Brother Lowe's words echoed in her mind:

"Trust in the Lord and lean not on your own understanding." Avril gave her pillow a little thump and turned it over. Well, that's what she would have to do because she couldn't understand. Not a bit of it! But she would try.

The next day as the two girls donned their graduation dresses of white lawn with lace collars, and pinned on the filmy white caps adorned with white ribbons to signify their status as graduates, they were unusually quiet.

It was as if they were realizing that this day was both an end and a beginning. Even though they had often bemoaned the strict rules of the Academy, they knew these years had been important and their impression would mark them forever.

This time of introspection was soon broken with the delivery of several bouquets.

It was a tradition at the Academy for friends and family to send bouquets of flowers that would later be displayed with the sender's cards around the dining hall where a reception was held after the ceremonies.

With each new delivery, the girls ooh-ed and ah-ed, finding and opening the congratulatory cards revealing the identity of the sender.

Becky was still starry-eyed over a card from Marshall that had accompanied his bouquet, when Avril discovered a note in an unfamiliar handwriting resting in a bouquet of Michaelmas daisies and jonquils.

> *Another step along the way, dear Cousin. I look foward to the time when I may present my felicitations openly without fear of rebuke from those who "protect" you. Until your twenty-first birthday.*
>
> > *Always your affectionate cousin,*
> > *Claude Duchampes*

The memory of his unexpected visit to the Academy years before returned vividly to Avril's mind, and with it the same vaguely uneasy feeling she had experienced then. There had been—for all his good looks and debonair manner—something sinister about Claude Duchampes. The fact that he had pledged her to silence, not wanting Graham to know of his contact with her, seemed unprincipled. And why had he insinuated that Graham's guardianship was unwarranted?

Hurriedly Avril tucked the card into her pocket and later tore it into tiny bits. When they took their bouquets downstairs to be placed on display, Avril left that one behind, grateful that Becky was too absorbed in her own happiness to notice.

Then before they left for the church, where the graduation ceremonies were to take place, Avril removed a single rose from the bouquet Graham had sent and pinned it to her sash.

As the graduates filed into the church and took their places, at least two people in the audience focused their gaze on the tall, graceful, young woman whose flaming hair contrasted strikingly with her white attire.

May Cameron leaned over to Graham and whispered, "How pretty and poised Avril looks. Sending her to this school was a brilliant idea, if I may say so. She has turned out beautifully."

Graham nodded, not moving the direction of his eyes.

Although he was seated in the section reserved for parents, he felt anything but parental. He had slept poorly the night before, troubled by the expression on Avril's face when she had confronted him about his trip to Scotland—one of the few impulsive decisions he had ever made. Yet how could he have explained to her that *she* was the reason he must leave—and soon? For it had occurred to him that, after graduation, she would be returning to Montclair to stay and—what then? In the face of that disturbing question, he had been compelled to face the fact of his changed feelings for her.

Since Christmas Graham had been uncomfortably aware that, since he had brought Avril as a child into his home, the sympathetic affection he had felt for her then had changed into a man's intense longing for the woman she had become. Not until that day in December, when he had first seen her after their long separation, had he recognized the powerful emotion as love. In that moment of recognition, however, everything had changed—and therein lay the danger.

Never, Graham determined, by any careless word or deed, must anyone learn of his secret love—least of all, Avril herself. To reveal his heart would be to destroy the trust between guardian and ward. That trust must be kept inviolate at all costs. And the cost would be great—to put as much distance between them as possible, for the duration of his guardianship. After that? Only God knew. Graham was certain only that her future was his responsibility, a sacred duty he would never betray.

Avril, from her place among the graduates, searched the audience for the one face most dear to her. Finding it, she smiled tremulously.

Oh, Graham, if you only knew how much I love you! her heart cried, wishing he could hear its secret message of longing. *But one day you will know, I promise. I will tell you and you will have to listen. You will have to know that I love you—no longer as a child loves but as a woman loves!*

Unconsciously Avril's fingers touched the delicate petals of the rose from Graham's bouquet. Again her eyes sought his and in that one unguarded moment the answer was clear. Convinced as she was that their love was in God's plan, Avril felt a certain peace in her pain. *If it takes forever, I'll wait, for one day you will love me, Graham, as I love you.*

At last the ceremony was over and the graduates mingled with the proud parents, relatives, and well-wishers. Auntie May told Avril they would be leaving in the Cameron carriage the next day for Williamsburg, while Graham would take the stage to Wilmington, then on to Charleston, where he would embark on the ship for Scotland.

Then came the time for good-byes.

With gentle fingers Graham lifted Avril's chin and wished her a happy summer, promising to see her at summer's end.

"Will you be back for my birthday?" she asked him, holding back the tears that threatened to spill.

"Of course," he smiled. She lowered her eyes, her lashes veiling what he might easily have read there.

Then he was gone. As she watched him walk away, Avril felt the pangs of remembered loneliness she had felt so often before on parting. She knew Graham was all she wanted, yet he seemed further beyond her reach than ever.

Part IV

Exile

1815–1816

The Lord watch between me and thee, when we are absent one from another.

Genesis 31:49

chapter
18

DURING THE TIME Avril spent in Williamsburg with Aunt Laura, she was continually amazed by the woman's energy. Despite her age and deceptive fragility, Laura Barnwell was a tiny dynamo of activity.

She gave herself unceasingly to family and friends. Rising early to work in her gardens, she gathered fruit and flowers, preparing bouquets and baskets to be dispatched to friends who were ill, as well as providing artistic arrangements for the altar at the church each week. In addition, her house always smelled of lilacs or roses for she placed fresh-cut flowers in each room daily, and there was always a new centerpiece for the dining room table.

After "doing" the flowers, which occupied a good part of the morning, Laura then paid a visit to the kitchen, where she often prepared special dishes with her own hands. These might be delivered by one of the maids to tempt an invalid's appetite or appear as a delicate dessert at one of her frequent dinner parties.

Upon observing the old lady, always impeccably attired in colors suited to her silvery hair and manifesting grace and charm in all circumstances, Avril was forced to reconsider her earlier hesitance in spending the summer here. The time, instead of being tedious and dreary, had been infinitely rewarding, for she had learned much of gracious hospitality and genuine compassion. Then, too, living with an elderly person who was both hard of hearing and somewhat frail had taught her patience on a very personal level.

Avril's greatest lessons, however, came from the discovery that Laura Barnwell's enduring strength was drawn from the Lord. Since her eyesight was failing, Avril was called upon to read a chapter of the Bible to her in the evenings before bedtime. Thus, the old lady and the vibrant young one became abiding friends.

Avril had promised Becky that she would visit Woodlawn before Graham returned, so at the beginning of August she left for Pleasant Valley. She planned it when she knew Jamison would be away during her stay. As much as she liked him, she could not face the thought of his coercing her into making any sort of promise she might not be able to keep.

Upon Avril's return to Williamsburg she learned that Graham was back at Montclair, and lost no time in sending for a carriage.

The August day was humid and the trip along the dusty country roads seemed longer than usual, but it did provide her with time to remind herself that this homecoming would be different. With a whole summer to think about her relationship with Graham, she had decided that she must not be imprudent nor act impulsively. Gradually, she would simply demonstrate to him that she was now a woman, ready to love and be loved.

As she neared the turn-off to Montclair, Avril could hardly contain her excitement. It seemed an eternity since she had said good-bye to Graham at the Academy. She remembered contritely how childishly she had acted before he left for Scotland and was determined to behave quite differently when she saw him again.

When they rolled up the driveway and she saw the Camerons' carriage drawn up before the veranda, Avril gave an impatient sigh. "Oh, no! And I had so hoped to have this first meeting with Graham by myself!"

Again she felt the rebuke of her conscience. "Patience," she told herself, and with only a slight tightening of her mouth, she composed herself and alighted from the carriage to greet her guests.

Afterward, Avril was grateful for May's presence, for Graham's greeting was so reserved as to be construed as indifference. May, on the other hand, had been so delighted to see Avril that her spirits lifted for the moment. In fact, Avril had no time to ponder Graham's constrained manner, for Auntie May launched immediately into a subject about which she was utterly enthusiastic.

"We were just talking about you, darling!" she told Avril, giving her another hug, "and we have so many lovely plans." Taking Avril's arm, she led her into the parlor.

Here it was refreshingly cool. The louvered interior shutters closed out the heat of the early afternoon and the French doors were open to the side of the house that faced the river, admitting a gentle breeze into the room.

Auntie May poured Avril a glass of lemonade from a tall cut-glass pitcher, then patted the cushion beside her. "Sit beside me, my dear. It is time, I was telling Graham, for you to make your formal entry into Mayfield society and of course the most acceptable way is a ball. I suggested we hold it at Cameron Hall, for Hugh and I would love to host your debut. But Graham insists it be held here at Montclair. So, I agreed. However, he has graciously consented to allow me to arrange the entire affair, since I will never have a daughter of my own." She gave a happy laugh and glanced gratefully at Graham.

Avril looked from one to the other. Attempting to disguise her horrified reaction to Auntie May's plans, she gasped. "But that's so much trouble, Auntie May!"

"Trouble?" echoed May. "My dear, I'll adore every minute."

Avril tried to quell her aversion for the idea. The last thing in the world she wanted was to make her bow to society. She cast one desperate look at Graham, but if he saw her silent plea for help, he did not acknowledge it. He remained aloof, smiling indulgently at May, who prattled on and on about guests, flowers, music, and refreshments.

Avril tuned out May's voice, wondering how she might escape the web that seemed to be weaving itself ever more tightly about her. She concentrated on Graham, hoping against hope to catch his eye and signal her distress, praying that he intervene in this frivolous event Auntie May seemed determined to orchestrate for her.

A sense of futility eclipsed her, and Avril experienced the

complete collapse of her hopes for the last weeks of summer, when she had dreamed that she and Graham, alone in the seclusion of Montclair, could come to know each other again. Know each other as equals—not as child and guardian—but as two people drawn together and destined by God for a future together.

Now that was not to be, Avril realized hours later as she unpacked in her bedroom.

Auntie May had left in a flurry of last-minute promises to be back the next day with a guest list for their approval and appointments with dressmakers in Williamsburg for Avril's new debutante wardrobe.

Avril's emotional reaction to the whole idea of a debut vacillated between hopeless acceptance and furious resentment.

She had come home an honor graduate, expected to be treated accordingly, and within minutes of stepping in the door, had been relegated once again to the status of a dependent child for whom a party was being planned—a party she neither needed nor wanted.

Suddenly she heard horses' hooves on the drive below. Flinging down her pile of petticoats, she rushed over to the window just in time to see Graham mount his horse and canter down the driveway.

Her fists clenched convulsively and she slumped down in a disconsolate heap on the floor. He hadn't even asked her to go with him! In the old days he would have whistled up the stairs for her.

"Come, Avril," he would have called. "Leave whatever you're doing. It's a fine evening. Let's go riding!"

She had yearned to grow up, could not wait for the day when she would be eligible for Graham's adult companionship, his love. Yet as Dilly had often warned, "You cain't hab yo' cake and eat it, too!" It seemed that in coming of age, Avril was losing much more than she had gained. In retrospect, those innocent days of childhood, when Graham had been hers, if only in the role of mentor, confidant, and guide—were to be preferred to this complete exile from his company.

That a subtle estrangement existed between them was all too

clear. Where was the wonderful bond that had never needed words of reassurance, open declarations of affection? Gone. All gone?

She thought of those lovely sunlit days before she had ever gone away to boarding school, and they brought scalding tears coursing down her cheeks. She wrapped her arms around her shoulders, rocking back and forth, remembering how much they had enjoyed each other's company. Surely those happy times were not all in the past!

Yet perhaps all she would have of Graham resided now in her memory. This summer with Great-Aunt Laura had taught her the value of memory. The dear old lady, who was well into her eighties, might easily forget a neighbor who called every day or where she had put her thimble or even Avril's name, but the summery days of her youth were crystal clear. Laura recalled vividly episodes from her own past when she and her sister were little girls and when Noramary Marsh, Graham's grandmother, had come from England to live with them. Would it be that way for Avril too when she was old? Would she live in the dead past of her love for Graham?

She was not sure when her love for him had grown from the adoring worship of a child into the full-blown love of a woman— only that it had happened. That it might never be recognized nor fulfilled now became the reality replacing the dream.

The next day Logan and Marshall arrived on horseback to welcome Avril home. Marshall was full of questions about Becky, and Avril's stay at Woodlawn.

Later Logan told Avril, "He's quite smitten with your friend, you know. He keeps telling Mama to be sure to put the Buchanans on the guest list for your party!"

"The party!" Avril groaned.

Logan's eyebrows lifted quizzically. "You're not looking forward to making your bow to local society?" he asked, amused at her reaction.

"It's mostly your mother's idea, bless her heart! I know she thinks I should be thrilled. But I'm not. Quite frankly, I was looking forward to a quiet summer here with—" She stopped and felt herself blush.

Logan gave her a knowing look. "Don't tell me that school turned you into a 'blue stocking'—all books and Scripture verses and poetic walks in the woods!" he exclaimed in mock horror.

Avril laughed a little. "Not really. But it has been a long time since I had time of my own to do just as I wish. To ride, to read, and yes, even *to take walks in the woods!*" She mimicked his scoffing tone.

"Poor Avril," he said softly. "They're bound and determined to make a lady of quality of you. You know the whole show is to announce to all eligible bachelors and their matchmaking mamas that you have been refined, molded, polished, and turned out fashionably and are now a marriageable item on the market."

"Logan!" Avril remonstrated, shocked. "How dreadful!"

"I agree." He shrugged and smiled. "But it's the truth. Of course, no one will admit it, least of all my mother. She is having the time of her life planning this affair for you."

"I know." Avril shook her head sadly. "And it's such a waste. I don't want to be married—" She pressed her hand to her mouth, realizing what she had said.

Logan looked at her curiously. "You mean—not ever?"

Avril knew they were treading on dangerous ground and quickly changed the subject. "Oh, not for years and years," she said blithely.

Fortunately for her, further discussion was interrupted by Marshall's return from the stables, where he had gone to get their horses.

After the Camerons had ridden away, Avril realized how close she had come to blurting out her feelings about Graham to Logan. The fact that her love must remain hidden indefinitely depressed her. All Auntie May's plans to present her seemed so pointless when Avril knew that it was only Graham she loved. And if she could not have Graham, she would have no one.

As they dined alone that night, Avril's secret weighed heavily. Being with him only confirmed what she felt. Glancing down the length of the table at his lean, handsome face, its interesting planes lighted by the flickering glow of the the candles, her heart contracted.

It was only his question when Hector had removed their dessert plates that jolted her out of her dreamy fantasy. "Would you come into the library with me, Avril? There are some important papers I need you to sign, some matters that have recently come up that must be discussed."

She followed him wonderingly.

He went behind his desk and brought out a portfolio, then looked at her with something of the old mischief in his manner. "I'm sure what I have to say will be far less compelling than all the discussions you and May Cameron have been having lately. But life sometimes interrupts even the most pleasant of pastimes."

She was about to deny his statement, declare that being with him mattered more than anything else in the world, but Graham was serious now, leafing through what appeared to be a sheaf of legal documents as he waved her to a chair.

"Sit down, my dear. I shall try to make this as brief as possible, but it is important that you understand. First, I must tell you that I came home from Europe by the southern route, landing in New Orleans, then traveling by stage to Natchez."

"Natchez?" The familiar name sprang to Avril's lips in a question.

"Yes. It was not until I returned from the Continent to England that my mail caught up with me. Unfortunately I received some disturbing news. It seems a relative of your mother, a distant cousin, is contesting the disposition of your property that will come to you from your mother's inheritance, actually. In Mississippi, a woman's property goes to her husband at marriage. In Eva's case, however, her land was never legally transferred to Paul, and, therefore, the claimant is going to court to obtain it. Since your parents did not leave a will, all this must be validated after their deaths. The cousin is suing to have the Duchampes property returned to him."

Avril frowned. It sounded hopelessly complicated.

"While I was in Natchez," Graham continued, "I consulted with

155

a lawyer, a friend of your parents. Together we drew up what we believe to be unassailable protection and a countersuit to this man's claim. Since you have been under my guardianship as well as legally a Montrose with our—" He cleared his throat— "marriage . . . he feels this document should stand up in court."

Avril's pulses were pounding. This was the first time in all these years that Graham had mentioned the secret marriage.

"We also arranged for the lease of the house in Natchez to a young couple who are building their own house upriver. In five years, when the lease is up, you will have reached your majority and we can reassess what needs to be done at that time."

Graham slid some papers across the desk top and handed her a pen. "Now, if you will just sign where indicated on that line. Your full legal name, please."

Carefully she wrote, using her best penmanship: AVRIL DU-MONT MONTROSE. *How beautiful it looked—written out like that*, she thought. Avril started to say something but Graham reached for the document, saying, "Thank you, my dear. That should take care of it."

She stood up, hoping Graham would see the longing in her eyes. But he was preoccupied with the papers.

At length he looked up absently as if surprised to find her still standing there. Smiling, he said with a tone of dismissal, "That will be all, Avril. You may go now."

With a feeling of incompleteness, she left. It seemed there should have been more for them to say to each other. Avril stood outside the closed library door for a moment longer. Then, with a heavy heart, she climbed the stairs and went into her bedroom.

After undressing slowly, she lay on her bed and watched the shadows turn the summer twilight to dusk, the dusk to blackest night. The wind rose, lifting the filmy curtains at the windows into billowing sails.

Avril lay there, for how long she did not know. Downstairs, she heard the clock strike, then the sound of Graham's footsteps on the veranda beneath her window. She got up and crept over to the window and looked out to see him, hands clasped behind his back, walking along the paths of the rose garden.

What was he thinking? What was he feeling? Avril ached to know. He looked so lonely. She wanted to run to him, fling her arms around him, comfort him, saying *"I'm* here, Graham! You have *me!"*

Shortly she heard him come inside, close and lock the front door, and walk down the front hall to the master suite.

Sleepless, she tossed restlessly on her bed. The wind outside blew through the trees with the sound of sobbing, and some deep, unfathomable longing rose within her. Was it a longing destined to go unsatisfied?

chapter
19

ALMOST AS SOON as she awoke, Avril got out of bed. Within days of her return to Montclair, she had learned that lying abed for any length of time only increased her sense of depression. Staying active helped to dispel the dreary fact that even though she was in the same house with Graham, he might just as well still be in Europe for all she saw of him.

Of course Auntie May was partly responsible for taking up so much of Avril's own time. There seemed to be an almost endless list of things that must be done for the party. Almost every day she dropped in to check with Avril on one thing or another.

If Avril did not get an early morning ride, chances were that Auntie May would have so many other plans for her that she would never get out to exercise the gentle mare that Graham had given her to replace Fancy, who had been put out to pasture.

She went over to the windows and opened the shutters. Early morning haze shimmered like gossamer over the river where little clouds of mist were rising.

She took her dark blue riding habit from the armoire but left off the jacket, knowing that the hot August sun would be bearing down even this early in the day. She braided her hair in the old way, tucking it under and securing it with a ribbon. Picking up her boots, she slipped down the stairway in her stocking feet so as not to disturb anyone.

At the stables Avril roused a sleepy stable boy to saddle Ginger and bring her out to mount.

Avril trotted down the driveway, then took the fence at the end of the meadow. Once clear, Avril gave Ginger her head and the mare hit her stride at the entrance to the sunlit woods. The air was fresh and cool, the horse under her moving in gentle rhythm, and Avril relaxed, feeling a revival of the old joy.

The morning sun slanting through the trees touched Ginger's mane with fiery fingers and set it aglow, echoing Avril's own coppery hair.

No sound disturbed the tranquil moment except the muted clop of Ginger's hooves on the pine-needled trail. Approaching a clearing, they jumped a fallen log, then cantered to the crest of the hill overlooking the river. Reining in, Avril slowed the mare to a walk and guided her to a place where, by rising in her saddle, she had a clear view of the water below—dappled with sunlight and rushing over the rocks.

Just then Ginger's ears twitched. Thus alerted, Avril tilted her head, listening. Even before he rode into sight, some instinct told her who was coming.

High in the treetops she heard the burst of a bird's morning song. She turned in her saddle to see Graham riding toward her and gave him a radiant smile as he drew up alongside her, her heart singing, too.

"You're out early," he said, returning the smile.

"Want to race?" she challenged him.

"Why not?" His smile broadened and before she knew it, he had given Chief a kick and passed her in a gallop, throwing her a laughing glance as he did.

Avril clicked her reins and went pounding after, straining to catch up. But Graham had already dismounted and tethered Chief lightly to a tree to graze when she approached the hillock where he waited. It was a place they had often paused to rest after a hard ride. From here they could see the river, winding through the verdant land like a sparkling ribbon.

Silently she looped her reins to a slender tree to let Ginger munch on the lush woodsy brush, then joined Graham where he stood looking down on the peaceful scene.

Suddenly filled with an indescribable joy in this intimate reunion after such a long separation, Avril put her hand on his arm in a spontaneous gesture.

"It's so wonderful being here with you, Graham! I've missed you so!"

Almost at once he moved away, and she saw a flicker in his face she had never seen there before. She had always been sensitive to Graham's every expression that indicated what he was thinking or feeling. But now she was bewildered. Was he angry?

"What's the matter, Graham? Did I say something wrong?"

He frowned and shook his head, answering brusquely, "No, of course not. I'm glad you're happy to be home. It's just that—" He stopped, flung out his hands in a kind of helpless gesture— "things are different now. I mean, when you were a child—" He groped for words. "But now you are a young woman and perhaps—"

"I should be less honest and open?" she said in a slightly sarcastic tone.

Graham's mouth tightened. He ran one hand through his thick, dark hair but made no reply.

Avril gave a short laugh. "Oh, of course. It is expected of children to blurt out their feelings, but adults are expected to dissemble. I find it contradictory. Why are children punished for lying, but grown-ups encouraged not to tell the truth? That seems a very strange sort of behavior. It is certainly not what I was taught at that fine Christian school you sent me to, nor what I now believe!"

Graham looked distressed. "I'm sorry, Avril, I only meant—"

"I think I know what you meant, Graham." With that she whirled around, walked over and untied Ginger, and pulled the reluctant horse from her feast.

"Wait," Graham called, coming over, placing one hand on Ginger's bridle, the other on the velvety nose. "I didn't mean to hurt you, Avril. You may have misunderstood—"

"You made yourself very clear, Graham. I don't think I misunderstood," she said tightly, trying not to cry.

"Come, we'll ride back to the house together, have breakfast, talk—"

"No, thank you, Graham. I think I'll ride a little longer." She tugged at the reins, turning Ginger's head. Then, flicking the mare's neck with the reins, she cantered off in the opposite direction, nearly blinded by streaming tears.

Given her head, Ginger thundered freely along the winding woodland path before Avril checked her back into a rolling canter. As she slowed the mare, Avril realized they had ranged quite far in a broad circle and were headed back toward Montclair by a path she seldom took.

Looking around, she spied a vaguely familiar structure, outlined through the dense foliage. Once before, a long time ago, she and Graham had come upon this same spot. It was the little house, Eden Cottage, the traditional first home to which Montrose men brought their brides.

Avril raised herself in the saddle for a better look. Then she walked Ginger closer, guiding her through the tangled underbrush until she had an unobscured view.

What must have once been a small replica of the lovely gardens of Montclair was now wildly overgrown, with thistles thrusting up among the gnarled rosebushes.

Avril felt a deep sadness as she gazed thoughtfully at the small abandoned building. Would it ever be a "honeymoon house" again?

Pausing there in the quiet glade Avril had a strong sense of some other Presence. Unbidden, the words of the Psalmist came to mind: "Be still and know that I am God."

For a moment Avril's very soul was touched with awe. God seemed to be speaking directly to her! In this beautiful place He was reminding her that He was present in her life and His perfect plan for her would unfold. She needed only to be patient, to wait upon Him and He would give her the desires of her heart.

Remorse filled her. All her frustration and fury at Graham's earlier rejection evaporated. Her love for Graham would wait until he was ready to accept it. In spite of anything he said, any denial he made, Avril was sure she had seen something in his eyes this morning, something more than words could have expressed.

Slowly she turned Ginger around and started back to the house. She must find Graham and apologize. He did not deserve her anger. He needed her understanding. And she needed God to show her the way.

Leaving Ginger at the stables, Avril intended to slip into the house, go up by the back stairs, change, then go in search of Graham.

But when she walked into her bedroom, she found Auntie May in a state of excited animation.

"Come see, dear child. These just arrived yesterday and I brought them over as soon as possible!"

Avril looked past Auntie May to the two gowns spread out upon the bed. Wide-eyed, she sought an explanation from May.

"Yes, you lucky girl, they are for you!" May clasped her hands together happily. "From Paris!"

"Paris? But how?"

"Graham had them made for you when he was there this summer," beamed May. "Wait until you see the workmanship, the exquisite seams and embroidery."

Slowly Avril moved over to the bed and lifted the flounce of one of the gowns, then turned bewildered eyes again to May.

"But I thought Graham went to Scotland—"

"He did, of course. First. Later he traveled to France."

"I didn't know he went to Paris . . . ," continued Avril, still puzzled. "He didn't say—"

"Aren't they lovely? Which one will you choose for your debut party?"

"I'm not sure." Avril was still overwhelmed that Graham would select such extravagant gowns for her. "But, Auntie May, I don't understand. How would Graham know my measurements or how to go to a dress salon or—"

May seemed a bit disconcerted, then giving a small shrug, said, "Well, actually, on the ship going over last spring, Clarice gave him the names of some of the shops she prefers when she is in Paris—"

"Clarice Fontayne?" Avril felt some of her elation drain away at the mention of the name.

"Yes, she had been visiting relatives in Charleston and had booked passage on the same ship as Graham. She owns a small house in the south of France and I think was returning to place it for sale. Anyway, I suppose Graham discussed what he wanted to do and asked for some suggestions—"

"You mean Clarice picked out these gowns?" Avril wrinkled her nose slightly.

"Oh, no! Graham chose the materials, the colors—everything! He has marvelous taste, don't you think?"

"But how did he know they would fit?" Avril persisted.

Auntie May looked smug. "To be truthful, I thought there might be a chance, and I gave him your measurements before he left, just in case—"

All her pleasure in the wonderful surprise returned. How thoughtful, how dear of Graham. Spontaneously, Avril hugged May.

"Thank you, Auntie May, thank you!" she said rapturously. Then she picked up one of the dresses, held it up to her, and spun around. "I feel like Cinderella," she laughed, "with a real fairy godmother!"

"A kind and loving guardian, I would say," corrected May.

And perhaps one day he would be something more! Avril smiled a secret smile.

chapter 20

DRAWING ON her long white kid gloves and buttoning them at her wrists, Avril could think only of Graham. Would he think her beautiful tonight? What mattered was his opinion and his alone.

She confronted herself severely in the bedroom mirror. Her dress, of course, was perfection. One of the Paris creations, it complemented her coloring and made the most of her slender figure. Of pale blue crepe-lisse, ornamented with Persian roses and satin ribbons, it was fashioned on Grecian lines, the delicate fluted tiers of the gauzy fabric fluttering with every step.

Copying a picture, Avril had plaited her hair and drawn the braids up in loops, entwined with satin ribbons pierced with seed pearls. As a final touch she had pinned the fleur-de-lis pin on the tucked bodice. Tonight she would not allow the memory of Clarice Fontayne to spoil anything for her. To her vast relief the widow was out of town and would not be present at her party.

In the last few days Avril had been filled with a new determination. With her debut she entered into a new phase of her life. Inadvertently Auntie May had given her the clue by saying that many girls married within the year of their bow to society. This being proper, then publicly acknowledging her secret marriage to Graham should not be at all complicated.

Ever since that day in the woods, Avril had become more and more convinced that Graham was fighting some deep feeling for her that he did not wish to acknowledge, even to himself. Possibly he felt that such feelings for his ward were unseemly and would create gossip damaging to both of them, or that he was too old for her. Whatever his reason, Avril felt sure he needed only her declaration to believe that it was not only possible, but inevitable that they should spend the rest of their lives together.

With new confidence Avril floated out of her room and down the stairway on a cloud of anticipated happiness, never imagining it was as precarious as it was precious.

She wanted a few minutes alone with Graham before the guests arrived. Already she could hear the musicians tuning their instruments, could see the servants scurrying about, carrying cut-glass punch bowls and silver trays of sparkling crystal glasses. Her excitement mounted. This promised to be the most wonderful evening of her entire life!

She halted midway down the stairs to glance, as she always did, at the portraits of the brides of Montclair. With a new sense of the rightness of her "heart's desire," Avril knew that one day her picture would hang beside them.

She found Graham in the pantry, consulting with Hector about the beverages to be served during the evening. She stood watching him, thinking how magnificent he looked in his elegant evening attire. Graham seemed to grow more handsome, more distinguished-looking with each passing year. The brush of silver at his temples enhanced the tan, healthy look of his smooth skin. His carriage was as erect, his body as muscularly slim as when she had first met him. The clothes he had had tailored in London fit superbly. Avril had not the slightest doubt that Graham would be the finest-looking gentleman at the ball tonight.

When she called his name softly, he turned, seeing her for the first time. A look of affection and admiration passed across his face as he took in everything, from her charming hairstyle to the tips of her blue satin slippers.

Avril pirouetted in a slow circle, fluttering her fan, holding out her train, a slender, graceful figure.

"Do you like it?" she asked eagerly.

"No Parisian lady-at-court could look more beautiful!" he declared.

She laughed delightedly, her eyes sparkling. She had never felt so happy, for in that brief unguarded moment she had seen in Graham's face all that she needed to confirm her own inner belief.

"He must *love me! He* will *love me as I love him!"* she whispered in her secret heart, ignoring the thought that followed, *"And what if he* doesn't?"

But she would have tonight. Tomorrow was only a dim promise. The future, after all, was in God's hands.

"Come into the library with me for a minute," he said, offering her his arm. "I have a little birthday gift for you."

She slipped her hand through it and together they walked across the hall and into the library. Graham went over to the desk, opened a drawer, and brought out a small box. He seemed hesitant.

"I hope you like this."

"Why shouldn't I?" she asked, puzzled.

"Well, open it and see. Then I'll tell you why I had my doubts."

She took the box, touched the spring that opened the lid, and saw inside a pair of aquamarine and pearl earrings in the shape of tiny fleur-de-lis.

"Oh, they're lovely!" she breathed. "Why would you ever think I might not like them?"

"Because I have never seen you wear the pin of the same design since last Christmas—"

Avril felt a small clutch of regret. How could she tell him that knowing Clarice had picked it out had spoiled the gift for her?

"I ordered them made up at the same time as the pin, but they were not ready in time for Christmas, so I planned to give them to you for your graduation. But when I never saw you wear the pin—I assumed you didn't care for it—although Clarice Fontayne, who happened in to the jewelry store in Williamsburg, thought it was lovely when I showed it to her."

Avril realized with a shock that Clarice had deliberately let her believe the lie that it was *she,* not Graham, who had selected the pin. What a cruel, spiteful person she was!

"Oh, Graham, I'm so sorry about the misunderstanding, but I do love the pin and am wearing it tonight as you can see. And the earrings are exquisite. That you had them designed and made up especially for me means so very much."

Impulsively she reached up, bent his head toward hers, and would have kissed his lips, but at the last minute he turned his head and her kiss landed on his cheek. *No matter,* Avril thought happily. *At least that mystery has been explained.*

Oh, what glorious news! she thought. *He loves me! I knew it all the time. What does it matter that Clarice tried to trick me. Tonight, after everyone is gone and we are alone, I shall tell him how long I have loved him and he can tell me!*

So sure was Avril of the evening's happy outcome that her countenance glowed and her eyes sparkled so that everyone declared she had never looked so beautiful.

Carriage after carriage drew to a stop before the portico, and one after the other deposited its passengers, the ladies in billowing silks and laces, the gentlemen in fine broadcloth and ruffled linen. The drawing room, center hall, and dining room soon resembled a swirling garden of bright flowers as guests milled about through the rooms.

When the music for dancing began, pairs of couples took their places, moving, swaying, bowing in rhythm to the spritely tunes. Avril was immediately surrounded by young men clamoring for a dance, and as she passed her card among them, each in turn scribbled in his name.

Standing in the hall, waiting to receive any late-arriving guests, Graham observed her. In the glittering glow of the dozens of candles in the crystal chandeliers overhead, Avril's hair shone with amber lights. Her blue gown set off the creamy shoulders, the slender neck, the interesting profile of her head lifted to her dance partner.

How lovely and graceful Avril was tonight—how different from that scrawny little waif he had brought here seven years ago. He felt his chest constrict as she drifted from partner to partner. The yawning difference in their ages, their positions, struck him with new awareness. Just then Avril caught his eye and, over the shoulder of her dancing partner, smiled and gave him a little wave. She looked so joyful, so full of youthful exuberance that his own heart ached to share it—every thought and feeling, to share her life!

"Graham, my dear!" he heard May's voice calling behind him and turned to see her entering from the open front door. "Look who came back in time to attend Avril's party!"

Both Graham and Avril looked and, at the same moment, saw the one who had accompanied the Camerons to Montclair on the night that was to have been Avril's happiest.

"Clarice," murmured Graham, bowing low over the lady's proffered hand. "What an unexpected pleasure."

Avril's heart was clutched by icy dread. Why, tonight of all nights? All her happiness drained away, and, as it did, her eyes met those of Logan Cameron. He was looking at her with something very like sympathy, but she felt as if he were reading her mind. With a purposeful stride, he crossed the room and, taking her dance card, scratched out the next name and wrote in his own.

"The privilege of an old and trusted friend," he explained to the disappointed young man who had just stepped up to claim Avril.

Even with Logan, Avril did not feel she could give full vent to her emotions, so she attempted a charade of frivolous conversation. She was grateful and relieved, however, when he tactfully took charge, dancing her skillfully out of the room, through the French doors, and onto the veranda.

"What a lovely idea," she thanked him. "It was getting much too warm in there."

Taking his cue from her, Logan also struck a light touch. "Especially for the belle of the ball who has not missed a single dance, I'll wager." In his voice was the teasing affection of long friendship. "So now it's official. Miss Avril Dumont, turned out like a Parisian mannequin, gilded and coiffed to a fare-thee-well, on display for all Mayfield gentry to see, inspect, and put up their bid. Now the question remains: Who shall win this prize?"

"Logan! You are awful! Incorrigible!" scolded Avril, but she could not help laughing.

"Besides the poor, besotted Jamison Buchanan, whom else have you considered giving your hand in marriage?"

"I thought I told you, Logan—" Avril began.

"I know what you told me, Avril. But I also have ears. I am privy to much discussion, much speculation, much conspiring among the elders, and somehow your name is constantly cropping up. Why is that, do you suppose?" Logan asked, all innocence.

"I don't know what you're talking about!"

"Why not? Unless, like an ostrich, you're sticking your head in the sand?"

"Marriage is the farthest thing from my mind," Avril retorted archly.

"Well, that isn't the case with everyone else."

"Why are we talking such silliness on this beautiful evening?" She was growing annoyed now.

They were quiet for a few minutes, leaning on the porch balustrade, looking out at the garden, barely silvered by a rising moon.

Then Logan broke the silence. "You know, Avril, my mother would be very happy if you married one of us. So why not consider it." His tone was half-joking, half-serious.

She turned to look at him in amazement. Auntie May herself had witnessed the signing of the document of marriage between Avril and Graham. Evidently she had kept the secret well. So why this hint of a possible marriage to one of her sons?

Avril smiled up at Logan and said in soft reproach. "You aren't in love with me, Logan. That's reason enough."

Logan placed his hand over hers where it lay on the balustrade.

"That wouldn't be difficult. Not difficult at all," he said seriously, then shifting to a lighter tone went on, "Anyway, from what I've observed of marriages, the most successful ones are not made in heaven, but are very down-to-earth affairs. Common backgrounds, interests, family. We certainly have that!"

"The same is true of Marshall and me!" she laughed.

"Oh, Marshall!" scoffed Logan. "He's so far gone on Becky he can't see anyone else!"

"I'm glad," declared Avril. "Becky is a darling. I'm sure they would be ideally suited, very happy together."

"Not to change the subject, but just what plans do you have for your future?" Logan asked.

"Nothing very different from now. To stay on here at Montclair, ride in the woods, spar with you in these—interesting—verbal battles!" she teased.

"You mean stay on here at Montclair—with Graham?"

"And what would be wrong with that?"

"Well, there is the possibility that he will marry one day, when his guardianship is over. Or even before, if Clarice Fontayne has anything to say about it. Then what would you do? There can't be *two* mistresses of Montclair."

Logan's words pierced Avril's complacent happiness like a stiletto. The night that had shone for her like a thousand stars splintered and crashed around her like a house of cards swept away by a careless wind. She straightened and stared at him.

"What are you talking about?"

"The fascinating widow of Williamsburg!" Logan replied satirically. "Haven't you heard the rumors? You must be deaf and blind, Avril, not to see what is going on right under your pretty little nose."

Avril felt a vice of pain grip her throat. "It can't be true," she managed to say over the swelling lump that thickened her voice. "Graham is much too—too—intelligent to—"

Logan's sarcastic laugh stopped her. "Too intelligent not to be intrigued by a sophisticated beauty like Clarice? When did intelligence have anything to do with being enamored?" Logan put his hand to Avril's hair, twisting one of the straying tendrils around his fingers. "You'll have to wake up, Avril, grow up. Life is not a fairy tale that always has a happy ending. I say this not to hurt you, but to save you from greater hurt. It would be foolish to ignore the obvious."

An indignant denial sprang to Avril's lips but was instantly halted by the sound of an affected little laugh nearby. Turning in the direction from which it came, they saw two figures emerging from the shadows of the garden. Graham and Clarice! As they approached the steps of the veranda and saw Avril and Logan, they stopped.

Avril's heart felt leaden within her at the sight of Clarice. The older woman was a vision in blond lace over satin. A tulle scarf, embroidered with glittering beads, swathed her bare shoulders and décolletage. Her pendant earrings were diamond and gold as were the bracelets she wore over her gloves.

"Good evening, *sir.*" Logan spoke first and Avril could have kicked him. With that deferential address he had immediately set Graham apart from them, and she suspected that it had been intentional. She threw him a scathing look, and to her horror, realized that Clarice had seen it!

Clarice looked amused. "Are you enjoying your debut, Avril?"

Avril, disguising her resentment, gripped her fan so tightly that she heard one of its fragile spokes snap in two. "Oh, yes! It's quite the most delightful evening I've ever spent."

"Did you put me down for a dance?" Graham asked.

Wounded as she was, Avril's only thought was to strike back, not caring that the target was the one she loved most in the world.

"Oh, Graham, I'm so sorry. I forgot and I'm completely filled up!" She held up her tasseled dance card.

A curious look crossed Graham's face, and for one startled moment, he appeared hurt. Then he said gently, "Of course, my dear. I should have known."

Avril felt Logan's eyes burning into her, but she kept a smile fixed on her face.

Graham said to Clarice, "Shall we go in and join the dancing?"

Clarice gave Avril a long speculative look, and as she and Graham started toward the house she paused. Cupping Avril's cheeks with her smooth gloved hands, she murmured, "What a child you are!" Then she passed on.

Avril let out her breath after they had disappeared inside and rapped her closed fan sharply on the balustrade. Logan, standing behind her, said nothing.

Then Avril spun around and, taking his arm, lifted her chin bravely. "Take me in now, Logan. Jamison is waiting."

chapter
21

LONG AFTERWARD Avril would ask herself how something that had begun in such hope and happiness could end in disaster and despair. That it was her own fault made it no easier to bear.

For weeks after her debut party, Avril went over and over the events of the evening—what she might have said differently, how she could have avoided the confrontation with Clarice altogether. Agonizingly she relived every detail, each time punishing herself the more.

With the chance meeting of Clarice and Graham on the veranda, she realized that she had completely lost her composure. From that point on the evening ceased to be a joyous occasion and, as it proceeded, grew worse.

When she had reentered the house, Jamison was impatiently waiting for his set of dances with her. And here is where Avril reproached herself most. She had deliberately used Jamison to vent her own frustration, had used his obvious devotion to soothe her wounded vanity. Applying every scrap of charm she possessed to captivate and enthrall him, she acted as if there were nothing she wanted more than to dance the rest of the night away with him as her partner.

When the buffet supper was served, Avril suggested to Jamison that they take their plates to one of the secluded alcoves at the far end of the dining room where there would be more privacy.

They had just started eating when Graham walked over and, looking down at her, asked sternly, "Don't you think it's rather rude to be so exclusive? Shouldn't you be mingling with your other guests, Avril?"

She tilted her head up and let her eyes drift over him before she answered coolly, "Oh, I don't know why, Graham. Everyone seems to be having a perfectly good time without me."

Then she deliberately turned away and smiled demurely at Jamison. He was so dazzled he did not see the flash of fire in Graham's eyes, nor the flex of the muscle in his jaw as he glared at them both.

Avril knew Graham was angry and for the first time in her life she did not care. Although she willed herself to keep up a flattering attentiveness focused on Jamison, Avril was churning with inner turmoil. She had never behaved with such calculated defiance toward her guardian. Her cheeks burned. Her nervousness made her more talkative. The laughter from their alcove brought many curious glances. The casual observer would get the impression that the two of them were totally absorbed in each other.

"Would you like me to get some dessert or perhaps some more punch?" Jamison inquired.

Avril handed hand him her plate, ignoring Graham's presence. "Why don't we take a walk in the garden instead?"

There was a certain playful insinuation in her suggestion, and Jamie's eyes lighted up. He needed no persuasion. They stood quickly and started toward the open French door.

Over her shoulder Avril glimpsed Graham's quickened pace. There was something in that forceful stride that both excited and frightened her. Tugging at his hand she hurried Jamison out onto the veranda and ran down the steps.

Pulling him along the garden path, Avril glanced back and saw Graham's tall figure in the doorway, silhouetted against the light from the drawing room.

Knowing he could see them, a perverse streak of rebellion coursed through Avril. Without being quite sure why, she impulsively took both Jamie's hands and placed them on her waist, then putting her arms around his neck, drew his head down to hers and kissed him on the mouth. For one stunned moment Jamison hesitated, then eagerly pulled her closer and kissed her again. His ardor startled them both and Avril drew back, but he held her fast.

"Oh, Avril, I do love you with all my heart," he whispered fervently.

Before she could gather her wits, Graham's voice cut through the soft evening. "Avril, will you please come inside. Your guests are waiting."

There was no mistaking the note of authority in Graham's voice. There was something else as well—a steely hint of anger that Avril had heard only twice before. She shivered involuntarily.

Immediately Jamison's arm went around her in a protective gesture as Graham's voice sounded for a second time, slashing like a whip. *"Now,* Avril."

"He has no right to speak to you like that!" Jamison muttered under his breath.

"Yes. He has every right," Avril corrected him. Already she was overwhelmed by self-reproach at her recklessness.

Her heart hammered. Suddenly she realized how foolish she had been to deliberately provoke Graham. And to what end? To feed some selfish need? Instantly she was contrite.

Graham remained on the veranda like a sentinel, waiting for them. When they reached the bottom step, he gave Avril one scathing look, then turned, marched to the door, and stood aside for them to pass through ahead of him.

For Avril, the rest of the evening passed in a kind of miserable blur. When at last everyone had gone, she and Becky, who was staying over for a week's visit, went upstairs to her bedroom. She was just grateful that Becky was too much in a romantic trance over Marshall Cameron to notice Avril's depression.

Long after Becky slept the slumber of the newly-in-love, Avril kept mentally flogging herself for her heedless actions. Why, oh why had she felt it necessary to flaunt herself so brazenly? She had given

Jamison false encouragement. Worse, she had hurt and angered Graham.

Avril rolled over and pounded her pillow. How could she ever undo the havoc she had caused by her own stupidity? How could she erase that look of disappointment on Graham's face, his suppressed fury at her outrageous behavior?

There was only one way. Apologize. First thing tomorrow she would go to him—grovel, if need be—and beg his forgiveness.

Worn out with worry, Avril slept deeply.

When she awoke, the room was bright with sunlight and she knew she had overslept. Hoping against hope that Graham had not already left the house on his plantation rounds, she dressed hurriedly and, leaving Becky still asleep, slipped out of the bedroom and down the stairs.

To her dismay she discovered she was too late to catch her guardian alone. As she entered the dining room, Auntie May, who was sitting at the table with him, greeted her with smiling affection.

"Well, here she is now! Good morning, birthday girl!" Then, turning to Graham, May asked, "Have you told her yet?"

Bewildered, Avril demanded, "Told me what?"

Auntie May seemed surprised. "You mean Graham hasn't given you your special birthday present yet?" She eyed the tall man at her left. "May I tell her the exciting news?"

"Why not?" Graham spoke indifferently, avoiding Avril's searching gaze. He drew an envelope from the inner pocket of his jacket and slid it across the polished surface of the table.

Still puzzled, Avril picked it up and withdrew the contents.

"Isn't it thrilling, Avril?" Auntie May exclaimed. "A year in Europe! Just imagine!"

Avril lowered her eyes. She was holding in her suddenly shaking hands a passenger ticket on a ship with a September sailing date only three weeks away.

"You see, darling, Hugh has to go to London—some complicated legal affair dealing with a client's estate. It's been held up in the courts for some time and the heirs are growing impatient for a settlement. So when I learned he might be gone for months, I decided to go along. We made some lovely friends when he took the boys over to enroll them in school, and of course Hugh has many friends in the legal profession there as well. So, quite naturally, we thought of *you!*"

Confused enough, Avril did not really see what she had to do with Judge Cameron's business. Before she could ask for an explanation, Auntie May went on. "A season in London, my dear! What a prospect. When I told Graham it was every young woman's dream, he consented for you to go with us. Oh, there will be all sorts of parties, places to go, and of course, sightseeing. We've already received an invitation to a country house from the parents of a classmate of Logan's there. So many people want to entertain us."

Avril turned stricken eyes on Graham. Surely he did not wish for her to be gone from Montclair—from *him*—for a full year?

But his eyes meeting hers were cool and impersonal, and he offered no rescue.

"And wait, my dear! The best part is that while Hugh attends to his business in London, we're going to the Continent! Actually it was Graham's suggestion. As long as we were already abroad, we should go on to France, Italy, and Switzerland!"

Shock and disbelief compounded Avril's already miserable state of mind. She wondered why they could not see it. But Auntie May did not seem to notice, and if Graham did, he ignored it.

This is my punishment, Avril told herself numbly. Auntie May's voice went on and on, but Avril was conscious only of an overwhelming paralysis of mind, heart, and body. She sat there like a stone while Hector placed her breakfast plate before her. Thus preoccupied, Avril was not aware that Becky had entered the room until Auntie May greeted her cordially.

"Good morning, dear. Come in and join us. We're just talking about the wonderful birthday present Avril's guardian has given her. A trip to Europe! A year to travel, to visit all the beautiful museums, art galleries, and historical sites. She will be accompanying my husband and me. Isn't that delightful?"

Becky clasped her hands together. "Oh, how lucky you are, Avril! How I envy you!" Then her happy expression changed. "But I'm afraid *someone* I know will not be at all thrilled at the prospect of Avril being gone for such a long time. My brother had hoped to see a lot of her now that she was back at Montclair. Jamison is finishing up his last year at William & Mary College," she explained to Auntie May.

"Oh, I see." Auntie May nodded and cast a questioning look at Avril. But Avril stared down at her untouched ham and eggs.

"Oh, yes, indeed!" Becky continued merrily, "Jamison has considered no one else since he first set eyes on Avril!"

At this Graham shoved back his chair, stood, and flung down his napkin in a gesture Avril recognized as irritation. But when he spoke his voice was as calm and courteous as usual.

"I'm sure you ladies will excuse me. I have an idea the subject of this conversation will soon turn to appropriate clothes for traveling and touring." A brief smile touched his mouth but did not reach his eyes, Avril noted. The mention of Jamison, she suspected, had touched off his annoyance over the unfortunate incident of the evening before.

Determined not to let him go without some chance to explain and apologize, Avril blurted out, "Graham, may I have a moment with you?"

He frowned. "I'm late as it is, Avril."

"I'm afraid I delayed you, Graham, by coming over so early and gossiping about the party and our trip!" Auntie May interjected.

"Not at all, May. You're always welcome."

"I suppose you want to thank Graham for his generosity don't you, dear?" May asked Avril. "Run along then. Becky and I shall have a nice chat."

Avril rose and followed Graham to the doorway. "Graham, about last night—I don't know what got into me. I'm very sorry I behaved in such a manner. It was unforgivable."

His face was impassive as he regarded her gravely. "There's no need for an apology, Avril."

"Oh, but there is! I know you were angry—"

"Not angry. Disappointed."

She reached out to touch his arm, but at that moment Hector appeared in the hallway. "'Scuse me, Mastuh Graham, but Miss Avril hab a caller."

Avril looked beyond and to her dismay saw Jamison standing inside the front door, his face aglow. He was holding a huge bouquet.

Oh, no! Avril thought. *Not now!*

Graham, following the direction of her gaze, turned and saw Jamison. He stiffened noticeably.

"Good morning, Avril," Jamison beamed. "Good morning, *sir!*"

"Good morning," Graham replied courteously, but he leveled an icy glare at Avril before continuing. "Since those obviously aren't for me, Jamison, I beg you to excuse me. I have business to attend to."

Bowing slightly, Graham strode toward his plantation office without a backward look.

chapter
22

AVRIL SAT at the desk in the apartment of the rented villa in Florence, her pen moving over the pages of the book in her lap.

> *The windows of my bedroom overlook the whitewashed wall of a monastery. Sometimes I can see brown-robed monks moving in single file through the arched cloister as the deep, clanging bell calls them to prayer.*
> *The colors here are so beautiful, the light indescribable—a kind of inner sunsoaked radiance of the very stones.*

Avril paused, lifting her head to gaze out the window, watching the shadows on the hills deepen from violet to purple, touched by the fading rays of what had been a glorious sunset.

> *Someday I shall have to come back to Florence when my heart is not so full of sadness.*

In the months since she had left Montclair to travel Europe with Auntie May there had not been a single day she had not felt the pangs of homesickness. Dutifully she had taken the tours, seen the sites, visited the museums, the castles, and even the catacombs in Rome. But in most of them, if only for a few minutes, she would think of Graham and wonder what he would make of this monument or that painting or this historical site. He was never far from her mind and heart, and now she began counting the weeks until they would be back in England and set sail again for America, for Virginia, for Montclair.

The last three weeks before they had started on their journey had been torturous for Avril. With Becky a houseguest and Jamison a frequent caller, there had been no chance to seek a time alone with Graham when she could try, at least, to recover the affectionate base of their relationship. Of course, she wanted more than that—a new status. Failing that, she was content to settle for the familiar camaraderie they had enjoyed for so many years—anything but the cool aloofness into which Graham had withdrawn.

With the frantic preparations for the tour, requiring several trips to Williamsburg, compounded by the appearance each day of Jamison, and Marshall, who was pursuing an eager courtship with Becky, Avril's time was filled almost to the day of leavetaking.

On the night before her departure from Montclair, Avril had dined alone with Graham. But she had been fearful of spoiling this rare occurrence by bringing up what had stood between them, unspoken, since the night of her debut. And yet to go without saying anything was like leaving an open wound unhealed.

So it was with studied caution that Avril kept the dinner conversation lighthearted in spite of her inner melancholy. Graham seemed to relax, dropping his guarded demeanor.

"You know, Avril, this is the opportunity of a lifetime. May has planned an itinerary that should increase your knowledge and appreciation of the art and culture of centuries of our civilization."

"Yes, I know, Graham. I only wish—"

"Wish what, Avril?"

"It would be even more pleasant if you could show me in person the things that meant most to you when you traveled in Europe."

"Ah, but I didn't see nearly as much as you will see. My time was limited and you will have a year."

His words struck like a knife into her heart. A year—a whole year before she would see him again.

After dinner they had walked for a while in the garden. The night was soft as blue velvet, the air fragrantly scented with the aroma of late-blooming roses. They strolled leisurely, though Avril knew the dreaded time for saying good-bye had come.

At length they walked back to the house. Graham leaned against the pillar of the veranda, the moonlight illuminating the noble structure of his profile as he studied the night sky.

Avril wanted to speak, to say something that would linger in his heart long after she had gone. But the words would not come. She stood there, memorizing his face, sensing that to express her love would only serve to drive him further from her. Should she then attempt another apology for the debacle on the night of her debut?

Graham himself had never brought up the incident again—not her arrogant behavior nor the scene in the garden with Jamison. She shuddered, even in the warmth of the soft Italian evening, remembering the cold fury in Graham's eyes when she had flaunted before him Jamison's open adoration.

At the core of it, she knew, was her jealousy of Clarice Fontayne. She had prayed for forgiveness for her smoldering resentment of that lady. She knew it was wrong—perhaps even groundless. Graham had only been fulfilling his role as a gracious host, perhaps escorting Clarice to the garden at her request. He had never given Avril reason to believe he harbored deep feelings for Clarice.

She picked up the travel diary Graham had given her on that evening, idly riffling through its pages. She had tried to write in it every day, if even just a sentence or two. She stopped here and there to reread what she had written:

Paris
Mont-Saint-Michel

The idea of such a cathedral stuns the imagination of one used to country churches. Standing on granite rock towering over a restless, churning sea, one looks two hundred and thirty-five feet down. Auntie May was quite overcome with vertigo. I felt as if we had somehow tumbled into the twelfth century.

Versailles

History comes alive here. When I think that it is not so long ago that Marie Antoinette lost her beautiful head, and the horrors of the guillotine are not so far removed from today, I felt faint. The Tuileries Gardens are lovely, or, I imagine, would be in full bloom. But with the approaching winter, Paris is much grayer and damper than I had expected. Everyone tells us we must come back in the spring. But all I can think of is Montclair in the spring, wearing a "bridal veil" of pink and white dogwood blossoms. . . .

Switzerland
Lake Leman

We are staying in a lakeside chalet in a charming village. From our hotel we can walk down to a spot where little benches are placed for one to enjoy the serene beauty of the vivid blue lake.

All Switzerland is sublimely clean and sparkling, its snowcapped mountains, its "toy towns" nestled in the valleys. All so peaceful and perfect, and yet I find myself thinking of the early Christian martyr, John Hus, whom we studied about at the Academy. Eager to bring about reforms in the church, he traveled to present his case to a council meeting in a town not far from here, in 1415. Having been promised safe conduct, he instead was cruelly betrayed and burned at the stake. What horrible things have been done in God's name throughout history.

Rome

The Eternal City. I know tourists are supposed to be awestruck by the buildings, the statues, the ruins here, but perhaps I was expecting too much, for I felt vaguely disappointed. Being herded along with crowds of people, often stepping on each other's heels as we were rushed from one site to the next, was most unsatisfactory. Then, too, there was so much to see that the mind cannot take it all in. However, I take notes wherever we go so that at tea back at Montclair, I can make adequate conversation: "Oh, yes, when I was in Rome, I saw. . . ."

Venice

Here I fell in love with Italy! It is beautiful and romantic. The graceful bridges over the canals, the long, slender gondolas sliding smoothly on the water, the boatmen standing at the stern, guiding them effortlessly along. I would love to ride in one, sit under the tapestried, fringed awnings, glide through the mysterious, winding waterways, listening to the musical Italian voices—

Auntie May is fiercely protective lest I swoon under the spell of all the dark-eyed, handsome gondoliers smiling boldly at the prim and proper English and American lady tourists!

Baveno

Auntie May is fatigued, so we are taking a week's rest in this neat, pleasant town on the edge of the Lago di Maggiore. She lounges on the sunlit piazzo while I stroll alone down to the lake. This is what I imagine Paradise must be like—quiet, still, infinitely beautiful. All the hustle, the confusion, the tiresomeness of endless travel simply melts away. Here the spirit is refreshed, nourished. A oneness with the Creator assures one that nothing more is needed, for He is sufficient. I stay until duty drags me back to take supper with the others in the small dining room. Even there, if one picks the right seat at the table, one can still bask in the tranquillity of the lake.

As she turned the pages slowly, stopping to read an entry here and there, Avril saw the one place where she had recounted an unusual incident. She had almost forgotten it in the months since, while traveling in other countries, but it was an incident she had evidently deemed significant enough to record.

She and Auntie May had been touring the Cathedral Notre Dame in Paris when, pausing to look more closely at one of the side altars, Avril had fallen a little behind the rest of the group. Quite suddenly she had felt the eerie sensation that someone was watching her. A shivery chill shuddered through her, and she turned slowly to look over her shoulder, aware of a movement in one of the shadowy arches.

It was such a fleeting glimpse, observed from the periphery of her vision, that she could not be sure what she had seen. Then, Auntie May, noticing her absence, called to her and Avril had hurried forward to rejoin her companions. Later, however, as they were gathering in front of the cathedral to take a carriage back to the hotel, Avril saw, on the fringe of the crowd, Claude Duchampes—the mysterious visitor of her school days, the distant cousin who had appeared, then vanished again after that one incident—until her graduation, when he had sent her a bouquet.

She stared at him, wondering what on earth he was doing in Paris. As their eyes met, it seemed to her that he started toward her. At that very moment their carriage arrived and Avril was jostled along in the press of boarding. When she looked out the window, she saw no sign of the man.

Had it really been he? Or perhaps some Frenchman with the same Gallic good looks?

Avril had never told Graham about Monsieur Duchampes' unannounced visit at Faith Academy, nor had she ever again worn the bracelet he had told her belonged to her mother. She did not know why exactly. Somehow the whole episode was cloaked in mystery and had a distinctly unsavory air that she felt was better kept hidden—like the moonstone bracelet.

Avril glanced at a few more entries, then closed the book. There were only a few blank pages left to fill.

She sighed, resting her head against her hand. This year had been a long one, but it was nearly over. At times she had thought it would never end. Recalling the kneeling "penitents" she had observed Easter week in Rome, she recognized the similarity. This had been her year of "penance" for her reckless behavior on the evening of the ball!

She had put the year to good use, determined to grow, to mature, to improve herself, to become the cultured, refined woman that Graham could love, accept as his life's companion. Above all, however, she had yearned to grow spiritually.

And she *had* tried, Avril told herself. She had been faithful in her devotions every morning, carrying her little New Testament and the Psalms with her everywhere. She had prayed earnestly and reminded herself often of the words she had taken as her talisman: "Delight thyself also in the Lord; and he shall give thee the desires of thine heart."

Yes, it had been a year of "penance," but it had also been a year of growth, evolving, and maturing. She had learned to be less selfish, giving in to Auntie May's plans and wishes when many times she would have preferred to assert her own. She had sought the Lord daily and asked to be conformed to His will for her life. And she had written regularly to Graham, putting down all the small, personal things she thought he would like to hear about her impressions of the people and places she encountered.

She began to imagine what it would be like to sit down with him in person so that they could discuss and laugh together about some of the things that had happened.

Avril smiled to herself as she left the window and went to dress for the dinner she and Auntie May would be attending at the home of some Italian friends. It wouldn't be long now until she would be back at Montclair, back with Graham. Just a matter of weeks!

But at the very moment she was happily anticipating going home, in England Hugh Cameron, on the eve of his departure to join them in Italy, suffered a serious heart attack.

chapter
23

"BUT IT IS SIMPLY out of the question, Avril! You cannot go back alone! I would be lacking in every respect as a substitute guardian to even consider such a thing. A young woman traveling without a chaperon? Oh, no, my dear, Graham would never hear of it!" Auntie May said firmly.

"But now that Uncle Hugh is out of danger and you are both so nicely situated here . . ." protested Avril, trying to control her own frustration. She had done her best to support, sustain, and comfort Auntie May during the weeks when Hugh Cameron had hovered between life and death, then all through the long days of his slow recovery.

It had been months since they had rushed to Hugh's bedside— months of idleness and boredom for Avril, since she could be of no real help. May was with the patient constantly, and he was attended by a nurse. There were no other young people and there was very little for Avril to do. She yearned to go home, longed to see Graham, to be at Montclair.

Some English friends had offered them the Dower House on their estate in Kent for the Camerons' use while Hugh recuperated. Everything had been supplied for their comfort. Now that she was no longer really needed, Avril was eager to leave.

"No, no, my dear! Graham entrusted me with your care and I would be shirking my responsibilities to contemplate such an idea.

You must be patient and we shall all go home together." Auntie May spoke as if the subject was closed.

Avril knew there was no point in further argument. Auntie May's stern resistance to her request was reinforced by Graham in his letters. To his urgings to render all the supportive help she could to his dear friends, the Camerons, she had no rebuttal. So, as cheerfully as possible, Avril resigned herself to the circumstances.

Their hosts had offered for her enjoyment any of the horses in their large stable. She accepted this gratefully, finding that the daily rides relieved some of her pent-up vexation at being stranded so far from home on this remote country estate.

One afternoon, upon returning from one such invigorating outing, Auntie May met her at the door with an expression of suppressed excitement.

"Avril, go right out to the garden! There's a wonderful surprise for you!"

An improbable hope sprang up in Avril. Could it be Graham come to fetch her home himself? *Oh, it must be,* she thought with a racing heart. *Why else would Auntie May look so delighted?*

Rounding the corner of the house, she saw a man's figure through the lattice of the gazebo at the end of the garden. Her head spun happily. It *was* Graham! He had missed her enough to come for her personally!

But at the sound of her boots on the flagstone path, the man turned and came to the archway of the gazebo and Avril felt all her excited happiness disappear.

It wasn't Graham after all. It was Jamison Buchanan.

Under the circumstances, her stunned expression must have appeared natural, because Jamison grinned broadly and came toward her, arms outstretched.

"Avril! I'm so glad to see you! You don't know how much I've missed you!" He put his arms around her waist and looked at her with love and longing. She was too shocked to protest when he drew her close. "You're even more beautiful than I remembered."

Before she realized it, she was in his arms, his lips pressed against her temple, and he was whispering words of endearment. The depth of her disappointment began to penetrate. Tears rushed into her eyes and she clung to Jamison, resting her head against his shoulder so that he could not see that she was crying.

Mistaking her emotion for gladness, he laughed tenderly. "Oh, my darling! I can't tell you how I've longed for this moment. This past year has seemed like an eternity." Then, holding her at arm's length, he said with shining eyes, "I've such plans! I'll soon be able to hang out my own shingle, have my own law practice. Father has offered me land to build on if I return to Pleasant Valley. At last I have something substantial to offer, Avril. That is—" Jamison paused. "I mean that is why I had to come and see you so we could talk about the future. I need reason to hope that—"

Automatically Avril put her fingers on his lips. "Jamison! Please! Let me recover from the shock," she murmured. "You are the very last person I expected to see *here*—of all places." She made a weak gesture.

"I know. It does seem strange for us to be together here hundreds and hundreds of miles from home." He was regarding her with a look of unconditional acceptance and love.

She turned away abruptly, knowing she did not deserve it. Neither his love nor his devotion. Certainly not his dreams of a shared future! But he was so sweet, so dear and special, and she did not want to hurt him, even though she knew that eventually she would break his heart.

Just then Auntie May appeared with a tea tray.

"I know I haven't given you two enough time alone, but Dora had the tea ready, so I thought we could have it out here where it's so pretty and pleasant. And to tell the truth, I'm dying to hear all the news and gossip from home."

Jamison quickly took the tray from her and set it on the low, round table inside the gazebo.

Turning to Avril, Auntie May went on, "Isn't this a lovely surprise, Avril? You and Jamison will have plenty of time to be together. He is staying the week. Now, isn't that a treat?"

Avril felt her throat constrict. A week, a whole week? How would she manage to avoid the one subject Jamison had come over three thousand miles to discuss?

"I think I'll go up and change before tea," she managed to say.

"Yes, dear, that's probably a good idea. I imagine you are warm from your ride and will feel better when you're refreshed. In the meantime, Jamison and I will have a nice chat."

Upstairs in her room overlooking the garden, Avril heard the murmur of their voices interspersed with occasional laughter. She would have to think of some way to get through the next few days of Jamison's unexpected visit.

Her mind whirled with possibilities. They could ride, go sightseeing, visit the ruined Abbey nearby, and he had already mentioned the fair to be held this weekend. If only Auntie May would not keep providing them with "time to be alone." Maybe she should confide her fear to Auntie May, enlist her help.

Yes! That was it! Auntie May was very clever at manipulating and arranging. She would be full of suggestions and advice.

As it turned out, telling Auntie May was a grave mistake. May had gazed at her in shocked dismay. "But why in the world would you want to discourage his suit?" she asked. "Jamison is a fine young man."

"That's just it. I don't want to hurt him, Auntie May," cried Avril, exasperated by May's lack of understanding. "Surely *you* know that it would be wrong to give Jamison the impression that a proposal would be welcome or, for that matter, possible!"

"Why ever not?"

"Have you forgotten that I am not free to marry anyone?"

Auntie May paled. Her eyes widened and she drew in her breath. "Have you forgotten, my dear, that your so-called 'marriage' was only a legal device to protect your property until you are twenty-one? There is no clause, no legality, that would prevent you from becoming engaged. Many engagements last two years or more. Why, my own to Hugh—"

"I am still married in the sight of the law," persisted Avril stubbornly. "As a lawyer, Jamison could certainly be aware of the situation."

"But *no one* knows!" protested Auntie May. "The— 'arrange-ment'—was kept secret so that you could make a suitable marriage when the time came. Graham discussed all this quite thoroughly with Hugh, and, of course, the 'paper marriage' will be quietly annulled when you reach the age of twenty-one."

"Perhaps I don't want an annulment," Avril said quietly.

"My dear child—" began Auntie May, looking distressed.

"And I am no longer a child."

Flustered, Auntie May tried again. "That marriage document is just that. A document! A scrap of paper. Nothing else, undertaken with no other objective but to protect you, not bind you."

"But it does, Auntie May," Avril said calmly. "And it binds Graham as well!"

At this May sat down as if her legs would no longer support her.

"Surely you don't think . . ." Her voice trailed off and she stared at Avril, speechless. When she spoke her tone was brisk. "Avril, I agree with you that you should not mislead Jamison. He is too good and honorable to deceive. But I must speak to you the way I feel in my heart is the best, even if I must dash your hopes and dreams." She cleared her throat. "I am well aware of your infatuation with Graham. Up until now, I felt you would eventually outgrow such a fantasy. It is, of course, absurd to think anything would come of it! It is out of the question, because I know Graham, and I know he would be embarrassed by such an idea! Now, you must put such thoughts out of your head once and for all. Set your sights on someone nearer your own age, someone who loves you dearly. That would cure your hopeless yearning for someone who can never be yours."

"I think that will be up to Graham," Avril said stubbornly.

Auntie May slowly shook her head. "Oh, my dear girl, you are heading for heartbreak."

"Better that than a loveless marriage!" replied Avril.

So the unsatisfactory conversation ended. But neither of them forgot what had been said.

At the end of the week when Jamison prepared to leave, he had secured no promise from Avril—only the hope that once back in Virginia he might persuade her to make him the happiest man in the world.

chapter
24

AT THE END of the summer Logan arrived to help his mother on the homeward journey with his still-ailing father. Their sailing date depended on the doctors' assurances that Hugh was strong enough to withstand the long sea voyage.

While they waited, Avril and Logan spent time together. It was a welcome change for Avril, who had been rather isolated in the country without the company of other young people. She had welcomed the chance to renew the warmth of this childhood friendship after such a long time.

Logan brought interesting news, which he shared with her a few days after his arrival. "My brother has been spending a great deal of time traveling back and forth between Virginia and North Carolina!"

"Oh?"

"Yes! Wearing the ruts off the road as a matter of fact."

Used to Logan's sometimes annoying manner of drawing out a story for all it was worth, Avril played along.

"How so?" she asked. "Any *particular* place in North Carolina?"

"One you are familiar with—a plantation in the eastern part of the state."

"Could I guess the name?"

"Perhaps."

"Does it have something to do with *timber?*"

"Quite."

"Woodlawn?"

"Right!"

They both laughed, then Logan continued. "It's your merry-eyed roommate, of course. Marshall hasn't written our parents yet because of father's illness. But he wants to speak to Becky's father. In fact, by now he may already have done so."

"I'm so pleased! Becky is perfect for Marshall!"

"And I've heard rumors about the same family as far as you're concerned as well!" Logan said, regarding Avril half seriously yet with the old teasing glint in his eyes.

"From whom? Auntie May?"

"Partly. But Marshall told me that Jamison's sole purpose in taking time out from his law studies was to come over here to see you and, I assume, to propose."

Avril shook her head. "I'm sorry if anyone got that impression."

"Then, it's not true?"

She hesitated. "Not exactly."

"You mean you refused?"

"Not exactly that, either," she sighed. "He may have come with that objective in mind but—"

"But?"

Avril turned to face Logan. "I'd really prefer not to discuss it, Logan. Let's just say there is no basis for any talk of engagements, except that of Becky and Marshall."

Logan gazed at her steadily, then gave her a mock bow. "Your wish is my command. Now, enough of seriousness. Tomorrow morning, let's go riding, just as in the old days!"

Avril paused before answering. "Tomorrow is Sunday, Logan. Since coming here, I've been attending the early service at the village church."

He looked startled.

"You're welcome to come with me, if you like."

Logan looked disconcerted. "I've never been much for church.

Chapel was compulsory when I was here in school, you know." He shrugged rather sheepishly. "I guess it just never took."

Avril did not reply to this comment and they began walking in silence until Logan said, "I know that school you attended was very strict, very religious. Is that where you got this church thing? I mean, we've always gone to services when we were in Williamsburg, at Christmas and Easter but . . ." He seemed puzzled.

"Maybe you never felt the need, Logan. But, yes, when I was at the Academy I did learn I needed God in my life. It's as simple or as complicated as that, I guess." They walked along in contemplation for a while. "There is something very special about this little church," she continued. "I've been in some of the great cathedrals on our travels, the most famous in the world, but somehow, it's here I feel closest to God."

"Well, that's very nice for you, Avril," Logan said with uncharacteristic stiffness. "It's good for ladies to be religious."

"Oh, Logan, you sound so pompous!" Avril laughed.

Logan looked offended. "I meant it's more to the taste of women—church and all that kneeling and praying—"

Avril shook her head, still smiling, but her eyes were grave. "No, Logan, you're wrong. It's for everyone. You just have to find it."

Logan squirmed uncomfortably, so Avril said no more. But she could not help wondering if all men—if Graham—felt as Logan did.

With her newly vitalized faith, Avril determined when she got back that she would open a discussion with Graham about spiritual things. If they were to have a future together as Avril was convinced they were, they would have to have a shared faith.

The sun had barely touched the tops of the trees when Avril set out early the next morning to walk the short distance to the stone church in the village. It was so comforting to be able to go to morning worship and evening vespers. Since leaving Faith Academy, she had not realized how much she had missed the comfort of regular church attendance.

In the dim interior of this ancient little church, she felt the peace of its stillness envelop her. Hearing the words of the Psalms read aloud by the rector in his refined English accent confirmed in her heart the verses that she had committed to memory. The order of worship was different from the one she had been introduced to at the Academy, but there was a unity in the Gospel that was universal and eternal.

Here "the desires of her heart" seemed possible. Here her faith was strengthened. In spite of what Auntie May said, or how "suitable" Jamison seemed to everyone else, Avril held firm to her belief that God would fulfill His purpose in her life. And that plan, she felt sure, included Graham.

At last the doctors gave the word that Hugh could travel, and the arrangements were made for their departure early in September. Everything went well and soon they were on board ship sailing for home, with fine weather, smooth seas, and agreeable fellow passengers.

With her husband improving rapidly and no longer the focus of her considerable energy and attention, Auntie May again turned them upon Avril. With more tenacity than tact she again raised the subject of Jamison Buchanan.

May joined her one sunny afternoon as Avril lounged in a deck chair. "It will be nice to be home again, won't it, dear?" she began.

"Oh, yes! It's been so long," sighed Avril thinking with mixed emotions of seeing Graham again.

"Has Logan mentioned Marshall's hopes to marry Rebecca?"

Avril nodded, smiling. "Yes, I'm happy for both of them."

"Their happiness could be yours also, you know," Auntie May ventured. "Jamison is so in love with you. It is obvious to anyone who sees the two of you together."

"Please, Auntie May, I've told you how I feel—"

"You've told me how *you* feel, Avril," replied Auntie May firmly. "But have you thought about how Graham feels? He loves you as he would a younger sister, his best friend's daughter. After all, Avril, he is nearly as old as your father, of another generation! You cannot believe anything will ever come of such a hopeless infatuation. It is impossible. Dear child, do be sensible and think of making a marriage with a kind, caring, young man who is devoted to you. Of course, as the third son in his family he will not likely receive a great inheritance but *you,* my dear, at age twenty-one will be an enormously wealthy young woman, and so you would both benefit."

Avril pulled the lap robe more securely about her against the brisk sea breeze. But nothing daunted Auntie May's litany.

"Since he knows nothing of it, I am not implying that Jamison's motives are anything but romantic love! And I cannot emphasize what a rare ingredient that is in most marriages! Which proves how wise Graham was to protect you, my dear," she said, raising a finger to make her point. "You, unlike some heiresses, have not been the target of fortune hunters. But that was what it was—an act of protection. An affectionate bond exists between you, I'll admit, but Graham has never intended a real marriage, of that you may be sure."

"Perhaps, when Graham sees me as I am now—a cultured, educated woman, well-prepared to become his wife and the mistress of Montclair—his intentions will change. When I tell him that I love him, that I do not want our legal marriage dissolved, I think he will agree."

Auntie May looked distressed. "Can't I make you understand how very unsuitable it is?" she begged.

Moved by her obvious dismay, Avril reached out and clasped the older lady's hand in both her own. "No, Auntie May. I'm sorry to upset you, but no."

"Then there is no way I can save you." Auntie May's eyes filled with tears and she turned away and quickly disappeared below deck.

Avril leaned on the railing and stared out at the dark blue ocean, its surface sparkling in the sun. The conversation with Auntie May had been disturbing, churning up all Avril's own fears and uncertainties. She did not know how long she had stood there lost in her thoughts before she felt a hand on her arm, and Logan's voice broke softly into her melancholy.

"Why so sad?"

She turned, lifting her face to his. "Auntie May wants me to marry Jamison Buchanan."

Something curious flickered in Logan's eyes as he looked at Avril, studying her. Then after a long silence, he asked, "Why don't you make everybody happy and marry *me?*"

"What? And lose my best friend?"

Part V

Homecoming
1816

Hold fast the confidence and the rejoicing of the hope firm unto the end.
Hebrews 3:6

chapter
25

As BECKY'S maid of honor Avril would be leaving for Woodlawn a week in advance of the wedding for the round of parties and other festivities preceding the ceremony.

The morning she was to leave, Graham was sitting at his desk in the library when she came down the stairs dressed for traveling. When he saw her, he drew in his breath.

Ever since Avril's return from Europe, Graham had found himself in an emotional dilemma. He had not been prepared for the impact of Avril's coming back into his life. His reaction to the stunning young woman, poised and possessed of an inner, quiet confidence, had shaken him.

She paused in front of the hall mirror to adjust the brim of her high-crowned hat, ribboned in two shades of green. The color set off her auburn curls and matched her traveling dress of apple green, corded Italian silk trimmed in dark green velvet.

Suddenly her eyes met his in the mirror and she smiled, knowing he had been watching her. Unembarrassed, she turned slowly around and walked toward the library.

At the doorway she stood for a moment. "Well? Do I pass inspection? Do you approve?"

Her eyes sparkled mischievously. Gold-and-amber earrings swung from the tips of her ears. Her shoes were bronze kid and she carried a bronze silk parasol.

He rose from behind his desk. "Forgive me for staring," he smiled. "You are a vision, but you don't need my approval. The compliments you are sure to receive from the Camerons will surpass anything I could say."

She looked pleased. "But it's *your* approval I want."

"You have it then."

He approached the doorway, his heart pounding as he drew near her. She looked at him and he felt he might drown in the depths of those sea green eyes. She was so close that her scent, like rain-washed roses, was intoxicating. Vainly he struggled against the desire that tantalized, the urge to take her in his arms. The moment stretched between them, then Avril rose on her tiptoes, ready to kiss him. Involuntarily he stepped back.

"Are you ready? Have you all your baggage?" she asked him brusquely.

"Yes, Hector took it down earlier."

"I had the carriage brought around. You'd best be off then." Graham felt his stomach knot with anxiety. These feelings he was experiencing were bewildering and must be banished immediately.

"You will be coming to Woodlawn in a day or two, won't you?" Avril asked.

"Of course." In a way he wished there were some way he could have declined the Buchanans' invitation. For several years, he had purposely avoided weddings. But this one was different, with the bride being Avril's closest friend, and the groom, the son of his longtime neighbors.

At the front door she stopped and gazed at him wistfully. "I hate saying good-bye to you," she sighed. "Why is it we always seem to be saying good-bye?"

There was a look in her eyes that undid him. How very lovely she was, how soft and vulnerable her sweetly curved mouth, Graham thought, then abruptly pulled his errant thoughts in line. Afraid he might betray his emotional turmoil, his voice harshened unintentionally.

"Oh, come now," he scoffed. "Why it's only for a short time, and you will soon be in the midst of a circle of admirers having a glorious reunion with your friends and any number of lively young people. Don't be so melodramatic."

Avril stepped back, her expression revealing her hurt, and Graham instantly regretted his offhand remark.

But she seemed to recover quickly and she lifted her face and brushed her cool, smooth cheek against his. "Yes, I know. But I shall still miss you—and Montclair!"

And then she was flying down the steps, a her rich russet curls bouncing, flash of green and gold, light as a feather or an autumn leaf.

Graham, feeling deeply troubled, stood on the veranda watching as the carriage rounded the bend at the turn of the driveway. What he was feeling was as familiar as it was disturbing. A man's feelings for a beautiful, desirable woman. Feelings he should not be having toward Avril.

He understood now the unrelenting loneliness he had felt all these months she had been away. The minute he had seen her it had all lifted. With her had come all the light and laughter, the gaiety and companionship he had missed. He felt as if he had recovered from a long, debilitating illness.

Graham stared down the now empty driveway lined with elms. He must be on guard from now on where Avril was concerned. There was much to think about, much to decide. At the end of August, when she turned twenty-one, she would come into her property. At that time his guardianship would end and with it the legal marriage he had entered into to keep her inheritance safe and secure.

Until August then, he must be very careful.

When Avril arrived at Woodlawn, even before she could alight from the carriage, the front door opened and Becky flew down the porch steps to greet her.

"It's so good to see you! I want to hear all about your trip to

Europe. You look so grand! That outfit must be from Paris. Oh, how exciting it all is!"

Becky hardly let Avril catch her breath or do more than give the briefest of greetings to Mrs. Buchanan before dragging her upstairs to the bedroom they were to share during Avril's visit.

"I am going to have you all to myself as long as I can, because the minute Jamie knows you have arrived, he will want to monopolize you!" Becky smiled knowingly. "Now, tell me, how was Paris?"

"Rainy."

"And Italy?"

"Sunny."

"Oh, come now, Avril." Becky giggled.

"All right, what do you want to know?"

Avril settled on the high four-poster bed opposite Becky, and they launched into a conversation liberally sprinkled with laughter and constant interruptions.

At length, Becky sighed. "Can you believe it? Here we are, just as if nothing had changed and we were back in our room at the Academy! Oh, Avril, let's always be friends, no matter what!"

"Of course! Why shouldn't we be?"

"I don't know. Maybe, now that I'm to be married, things will be different for us."

"Silly! No!"

"Oh, Avril, I wish you were getting married, too." Her eyes sparkled with inspiration. "Wouldn't it be wonderful if this were going to be a double wedding. Me and Marshall, you and Jamie!"

Avril said nothing but looked away from Becky's rapt gaze.

"Avril I know how much Jamie adores you. I know he went over to England on purpose to propose. Did he?"

Avril bit her lip and hesitated, then looked at her dear friend sadly. Should she break her long silence and tell her the truth? It seemed the only thing to do.

"Please tell me, Avril, why you won't give Jamie an answer. Don't you love him?"

"It's not that. I mean . . . I can't marry Jamie."

"Why can't you? I don't understand."

"It's a secret, Becky. I'm not supposed to tell anyone, but—," she paused. "I think you ought to know. I owe that to you. But you have to promise not to tell anyone else. Not now. Not ever."

Wide-eyed, Becky crossed her heart. "I promise!" she said.

"I can't marry Jamie, Becky, because—because I'm already married. *Secretly* married."

At these words Becky grabbed one of the posts to steady herself and gasped, "*Married!* When? Who? Someone you met in Europe?"

"No." Avril shook her head solemnly. "It's nothing like that, nothing romantic really."

"Not romantic? I think marriage is the most romantic thing in the world!"

"For you and Marshall, maybe. Not for me. You see, it was a kind of legal arrangement made when I first came to Montclair. Before I ever went to the Academy." And Avril explained about her "secret" wedding to Graham.

"Then it is just binding until you're twenty-one?"

Avril nodded.

Becky looked relieved. "Well, that's only a few months from now. Then you'll be free to marry whomever you choose!" She clapped her hands. "So there's still a chance for Jamie!"

Avril looked at her friend affectionately. She wished there were some way to soften the blow for Becky, but she knew she had gone this far and would have to tell her the whole truth.

"Becky, I wish I could make you happy by saying that perhaps, in time, I could learn to love Jamie the way he wants me to, the way you want me to—but it's Graham I love."

"But he's old enough to be your father, Avril!"

"It doesn't matter. Not to me. If he doesn't want our legal marriage to continue, if he insists on having it annulled, I don't know what I'll do. If I can't have Graham, I don't think I'll ever marry anyone else."

"Oh, you say that now, Avril. But—"

"I've loved Graham for years, Becky. I've just been waiting to grow up so I could tell him, so he could accept me as a woman, a wife." She wiped away a tear that had crept into her eyes. "That's just the way it is."

Becky's generous heart ached for her friend and she put her arms around Avril and wept with her. But even through her tears Becky felt a little guilty about her own happiness. Her own dreams of love were being fulfilled with Marshall, while Avril's for Graham were quite hopeless—as hopeless as Becky's dream that Avril would one day marry Jamison and be her sister.

Graham managed to slip into a back pew of the Pleasant Valley Community Church just before the bridal party entered. He had waited until the last possible moment, fighting his own reluctance to expose himself to what he knew would be a disturbing emotional experience.

The moment he saw Avril take the bouquet Becky handed her to hold during the exchange of vows and turn to face the congregation with the bridesmaids and groomsmen in a semicircle flanking the couple, Graham knew his apprehensions had not been ill-conceived.

Never had Graham seen Avril look so beautiful. Hyacinth blue, the color of her gown, complemented her lovely coloring. A halo-like headdress of twisted blue tulle intertwined with forget-me-nots crowned her glorious auburn hair.

As the minister began the ceremony suddenly everything else began to recede. Only Avril's face remained clear, her eyes finding and holding his so that he could not look away. It was as if they were the only two in the church and the words that were being spoken were for them alone.

The readings were from both the Old and the New Testament and these merged in Graham's ears as a special psalm of love and commitment—for his sole benefit to hear and heed.

"And it shall be from that day, saith the Lord, that you will call me 'My husband' . . . In that day I will make a covenant . . . I will betroth thee to me forever, Yes, I will betroth thee to me . . . in lovingkindness . . . in faithfulness."

As he heard the marriage vows, Graham realized now that he had been so young at his first marriage, so dazzled by his unexpected luck in winning the equally youthful bride that the solemn beauty of the ceremony had skimmed over him. His marriage had been too tragically brief for those promises ever to be tested. He knew now that to undertake such vows again, he would know full well their sacred intent and purpose.

His knuckles were white as he gripped the railing of the pew in front of him, still unable to pull his eyes from the grip with which Avril's gaze held him.

He felt himself grow warmer; his collar and cravat felt too tight; his knees trembled. He hoped no one else noticed his discomfort. He was as one paralyzed. Was it his imagination? Or could Avril's unwavering gaze mean what her eyes seemed to be saying? Was it possible that Avril was reminding him of the similar bond they had contracted in that secret legal ceremony nearly eight years ago?

Graham felt perspiration bead his brow, his palms grew clammy, his heart pounded painfully. The church was stifling, making it difficult to breathe. He wished desperately for escape.

He must get hold of himself, Graham resolved. Blinking hard, and by an effort of will, he turned his head straight ahead just as the minister entoned, "What God hath joined together let not man put asunder. . . ."

Graham had little recollection of how he got from the church to the reception at the Buchanans' country home, Woodlawn. There, hospitality of the most gracious, expansive kind was manifested. The Buchanans must have had dozens and dozens of relatives as well as a limitless number of friends streaming through the seemingly endless receiving line, then spilling out from the large house onto the lawn and garden.

Under the trees a long table decorated with masses of flowers and loaded with all sorts of food held a punch bowl at either end.

Graham found himself treated with immediate acceptance by everyone, as though he were either a member of the family or an old friend. There were no strangers at the Buchanan home.

When at last Mrs. Buchanan gave the word that the guests had all been received and the bridal party could break up the receiving line and join in the festivities, Avril searched the crowd for Graham.

Just as she spotted him and started to thread her way through the maze of wellwishers to him, she heard Mrs. Buchanan inquiring of Auntie May, "Mr. Montrose is such a charming, handsome man. Why is it he's not married?"

Avril felt herself stiffen and halted instinctively, waiting to hear Auntie May's reply.

"He is a widower, my dear. Such a tragic story. His bride died within a few months of their wedding. And as you know, he has had the guardianship of Avril these past years. He has made her welfare his priority."

"But surely there must be many ladies who would be glad to help him exchange his bachelorhood for wedded bliss?" Mrs. Buchanan continued.

Auntie May laughed. "Oh, my yes! Many! There is one in Williamsburg who, I believe, is simply biding her time."

"And is Mr. Montrose a willing victim?"

"Well, he takes his responsibility as guardian seriously and as an honorable gentleman would not ask anyone to wait and wait but—"

"But Avril is the same age as Becky, isn't she? And Becky just turned twenty-one."

"In a few months, at the end of the summer—"

"So, either when his ward is twenty-one or should she herself choose to marry, I suppose then *he* would be free."

"You could assume so—" Auntie May was skillfully avoiding giving Mrs. Buchanan a direct answer, Avril thought, but the woman's next words caught her off-guard.

"Well, if my Jamison has anything to say about it, it will be the former, not the latter!" she laughed. "He is completely determined to marry Avril. Has been since he first set eyes on her."

Avril moved away. She did not want to hear any more. She felt her cheeks flame at being the subject of such a discussion. They both assumed so much. About Graham, about Clarice Fontayne, about herself. In the end, she would prove them wrong! They would all be surprised at the end of the summer when her marriage to Graham, instead of being annulled, would be blessed by a church ceremony—a ceremony as sacredly beautiful as the one taking place today. Hadn't she seen Graham's expression when Becky and Marshall made their vows? She could not have been mistaken. She had read a message in his eyes that told her without words that he was feeling what she was feeling. Of that she was certain.

She looked for Graham again but saw that he was now involved in a conversation with a wedding guest. She started toward them, but it was announced that the bridal couple were about to cut their wedding cake.

"And we shall now have the toasts!" Becky's father said loudly as people gathered around.

Mr. Buchanan made the first. His jowly, jovial face was red with pleasure and excitement, his speech eloquent and loquacious, heightened by a liberal helping of the special wedding punch. At the end, he waved his hand in a welcoming gesture to the guests assembled around him.

"And I invite you all back in the not-too-distant future for another wedding in the family, that of my son and the lovely girl he has not yet had the courage to ask to be his wife!"

To Avril's horror, he was looking directly from her to Jamison, who, although flushed with embarrassment, was smiling broadly.

There was a hearty round of laughter, though some, unaware of his meaning, did not appear to be taking Mr. Buchanan's announcement seriously. But Avril, darting a quick glance at Graham, saw the grim set of his features.

The crowd was too dense for Avril to make her way to him without rudely elbowing her way through, so she had to stay put until Becky and Marshall had sliced the first piece of wedding cake and the guests hovering near had moved away.

Again, however, Avril was delayed. Someone was calling her name. Turning to acknowledge the greeting, she was caught up in an exuberant hug by one of her former schoolmates who had been invited to the wedding. The ensuing exchange took another several minutes and when she started over to Graham, she saw that he was engaged in a serious conversation with Jamison.

For some reason Avril felt a shiver pass over her, even in the warmth of the June day.

By the time she finally made her passage through the tight little clusters of people socializing, Graham himself was striding purposefully toward her.

When he reached her, the look on his face made her lighthearted greeting fall flat. "I have made my excuses to the Buchanans, Avril, because I must go now. My plans are to leave for Montclair in the morning. May wants you to accompany her, as Logan is going on to visit friends in Charleston, and of course, Marshall will be on his honeymoon."

"But, Graham, I thought—" she began.

"Plans change, Avril," he said shortly. "I did not know Logan did not intend to go back with his mother." He paused for a moment. "I'm sure the Buchanans will enjoy having you as their guest a little longer, especially since young Buchanan has a special interest in your staying. He has just asked my permission to marry you."

Avril shuddered, bringing the violent reaction under control only by iron willpower. Through stiff lips she asked, "And did you give it?"

"I saw no reason to withhold it," Graham admitted. "In fewer than three months you will be twenty-one—free to make your own decisions."

"Is that all you told him?"

"I think that was sufficient."

Just then a stir of excitement rippled through the party, followed by a laughing remark made by a feminine voice. "Oh, look! The bride's going to throw her bouquet!"

Avril felt herself pushed and jostled forward until she found herself in the front of the line of guests gathering in front of the porch steps where Becky and Marshall were standing. Looking over her shoulder and finding Avril, Becky lifted her bouquet and flung it unerringly in her direction. Before she knew what was happening, Avril mechanically put up her hands and caught the fragrant, lace-encircled missile.

"You'll be the next!" came the laughing predictions all about her.

From behind, she felt strong arms go around her waist, felt a kiss on her cheek, heard Jamison's whispered words, "Say, yes, Avril! Do say yes!"

In a frantic attempt to offset the seriousness of Jamie's request, Avril whirled out of his impulsive embrace and raised the bouquet high above her head to show the smiling onlookers. As she did so, she saw Graham standing on the fringe of the crowd. The expression on his face wrenched her heart.

In a single second's passing, their eyes met. Then he turned abruptly and the crowd swallowed him from her sight.

chapter
26

ON THE PRETEXT of wanting to give Aunt Laura a full account of the wedding at Woodlawn, Avril insisted on going immediately to Williamsburg instead of remaining with the Buchanans. Auntie May seemed amenable to her suggestion and would drop her off there, though Jamison did his best to persuade her to stay.

But Avril needed time to collect herself, to do some serious thinking about her future. With her twenty-first birthday only a few weeks away, she must make some alternate plans if her hopes and dreams for a life with Graham were not to be fulfilled.

In Williamsburg, Avril gave a charming recital of the events of the preceding few days, but she had not counted on Aunt Laura's canny perception. Her eyesight might be failing, but the old lady's heart was still tender, her insight clear.

One day when she and Avril were in the garden gathering herbs, she suggested that they pause for refreshments. "My, but the sun is getting hot. Why don't we sit in the summerhouse for a while to cool off?"

Seated in the charming gazebo, she gave Avril a searching look. "Now, my dear, what's really bothering you?"

Avril sighed. "Growing up, I guess. Trying to decide what to do next."

"Ah, but that's a lifetime task," declared Aunt Laura, smiling gently.

"Even if you feel something is right for *you*, how can you know it is right for another person? Or, if it's right for another person, it may not be right for you! Oh, dear, it is all so difficult!"

"Yes, life is difficult. And perhaps it was meant to be. Or else, to quote the poet, 'What's a Heaven for?'" Laura shook her silver head. "We must live by faith and lean not on our own understanding."

Growing bolder, Avril blurted out her dilemma. "I love someone, Aunt Laura, but I don't know if he loves me. Someone else loves me, but I don't love him, at least not in the way he wants me to— and I don't know what to do!"

"You're still young, Avril. You've plenty of time to choose a life's companion."

Avril shook her head. "No, I don't, Aunt Laura. I have only a few weeks. At the end of the summer, everything will be different, everything will change."

"Then all you can do is trust in the Lord, Avril. Ask Him to show you the way."

Avril kissed Aunt Laura's wrinkled cheek in gratitude and within a few days, made preparations to return to Montclair.

On the long carriage ride home, there was time for contemplation. While confiding in Aunt Laura had eased some of her tension, Avril found that it had also made things more complicated. Now, she must accept the responsibility of her own conscience.

Aunt Laura's oft-repeated admonition to "seek God's will in His Word, to listen to the still, small voice, to pray for guidance" seemed reasonable. But when Avril tried to follow that advice, her emotions took over and she found herself more confused than ever. She began to wish that something would happen that would take the decision out of her hands.

Avril was still debating with herself as the carriage rounded the bend of the drive and Montclair came into full view. There, in front of the house, was another carriage, its driver lounging in the shade of one of the giant elms. As they drew nearer, she saw that this was no carriage she had ever seen before, but a hired hack.

Puzzled, she stepped down, mounted the steps to the veranda, and went inside, quite unprepared for the scene taking place in the front hall.

Locked in furious argument were two men. One was Graham; the other, to Avril's shocked surprise, was Claude Duchampes.

Duchampes' voice was thick with anger. "A fine scandal when it becomes public knowledge that you coerced an innocent child to sign over her property. The oh-so-honorable member of the Montrose clan conniving to get his greedy hands on such valuable land! You would stoop to any device—even a surreptitious wedding ceremony—to transfer her rights to your own dubious control. And who were the witnesses? Your best friends and some now deceased lawyers whose credentials cannot now be scrutinized."

"You dare accuse me of fraud?" Graham's tone was icy with contempt, but Avril recognized the fury seething beneath it and shuddered.

"Fraud and more!" Duchampes flung back. "I don't think the documents you claim to have will stand up in any court! A child, under duress, made to sign away her birthright! If you had not acted so furtively, I could have been named her guardian, and the property would have remained in the family. I, too, could have devised a mock marriage to get full ownership. But you deceived this child into a belief that all you wanted to do was safeguard her. I say, when this is brought out into the open, when the light of day exposes your true motives—"

"Enough, sir! Out of my house! If it must be, we shall meet in a court of law and the thing will be settled!"

"Indeed it will be!"

As the two men turned, they saw Avril pressed against the doorframe, her eyes wide with alarm.

Duchampes seemed startled at first, then his countenance lightened, and his manner became smooth and affable.

"Well now, here she is herself, the lovely lady in question. Perhaps we should ask her opinion of your latest business transactions *in her behalf*." His last words were heavy with sarcasm. "Did you know, for instance, that your guardian was selling your priceless heritage in Natchez, letting the house and land go to strangers—land that has been in the Duchampes family for generations?"

Avril looked at Duchampes, then at Graham.

"You signed the papers, Avril. I explained at the time the lease-option agreement about the house—the land," Graham reminded her.

"Of course, Graham." She drew a long breath and fixed her gaze on Duchampes. "I do not know where or how you got the impression that I was coerced or manipulated or in any way forced to agree to, or to sign, anything. Whatever has been done in regard to the Duchampes' land and property has been done with my full knowledge and consent. And, as far as I am concerned, our 'mock marriage,' as you choose to call it, was entered into with my complete understanding. It still stands as legal and binding, and my guardian and *husband* is entitled to conduct my affairs in any way he deems right. He has my entire confidence."

As she spoke, Avril felt a surge of strength giving her an articulate expression she did not know she possessed.

Duchampes seemed to shrink before her eyes. His pale face, drained of color, became a sickly gray, then flooded with bright crimson.

"You've not heard the last of this!" He shook his fist at Graham, his mouth twisted in an angry snarl. Then, shaking with fury, he brushed past Avril and was out the door, the sound of the carriage wheels spinning as he made a hasty exit.

Avril went limp, feeling her knees buckle beneath her.

"My dear Avril, I'm so very sorry you had to witness all that!" Regarding her, his solemn expression changed to one of frank admiration. "I'm very proud of you. I never supposed I had such a champion!"

"Oh, Graham, don't you know how much I love you?" she burst

215

out, not realizing what she was saying until the words had left her lips.

"And I love you, Avril. You are a brave, courageous girl—I suppose I should say *woman* since you will soon be twenty-one." But by his intonation, she knew he did not mean the kind of love she had for him, only a fond affection for his loyal ward. Then he frowned. "At least this unfortunate episode has precipitated the necessity of drawing up some new papers for you to sign. I shall see Judge Cameron soon. In the meantime, my dear, try to put this whole ugly incident out of your mind."

With that, Graham walked into the library, leaving Avril feeling weak and frustrated, leaning heavily against the door. She looked after him helplessly. Hadn't he heard what she had said? *I love you, Graham. What more must I do to prove it?*

chapter
27

ON THE MORNING of her twenty-first birthday, Avril awakened to the sound of a bird trilling merrily on a tree branch right outside her bedroom window. Below, she could hear the low tones of the gardener directing his young helper.

Outside her bedroom door were the sounds of scurrying feet and muffled voices as servants bustled along the hallway. The household was humming with preparations for the party that night.

As she came slowly into full consciousness, Avril remembered the date and all that it signified—the real end of her girlhood, the beginning of independence. It was the day she came into her inheritance, a day alive with promise. Today she could win everything she had hoped for, or perhaps lose her dream.

A light tap at her door interrupted her half-formed thoughts. "Miss Avril, is you 'wake?"

"Yes, come on in, Dilly," Avril instructed her old nurse, sitting up as Dilly opened the door cautiously and came in, carrying a tray.

The lined mahogany face was all smiles as she set the tray on the table by the bed. Propped against the silver coffeepot was an envelope addressed to her in Graham's bold hand: "Let me be the first to wish you a Happy Birthday," and beside it, a single scarlet rose, still sparkling with dew.

Avril picked it up, held it to her lips, its delicate scent wafting to her nostrils. She breathed in its sweetness.

"Now, sit up, chile, so's you can eat. Busy day ahead," Dilly warned, plumping an extra pillow to wedge behind Avril.

There were berries and cream, fluffy hot biscuits, and honey. "Done pressed yo' party dress," Dilly told her. "Miz Cameron already sent over some peaches from dey orchard. Cookie been up since dawn bakin'." Dilly shook her head, chuckling, as she closed the louvered shutters against the morning sun.

Sipping her coffee Avril watched her old nurse. Dilly moved stiffly now, plagued with arthritis.

With a new jarring awareness of the passage of time, Avril realized that the same years that had seemed so slow to her, impatient to grow up, had brought Dilly swiftly to old age. Suddenly she had a new appreciation for the years of devotion lavished on her. She must do something for Dilly, Avril decided, not sure of just what.

There was another knock on the bedroom door. At her summons, one of the maids entered, bringing a bouquet and note just delivered from Becky and Marshall, who were back from their honeymoon. They were staying temporarily at Cameron Hall and would be coming over for tonight's celebration.

All day long messengers came, bearing flowers, notes, gifts, and tokens of affection for Avril. As she bathed and dressed, she could not help thinking how richly blessed her life had been since coming to Montclair as a lonely orphan.

She remembered her first birthday party here, and realized that all the same people would be celebrating with her tonight—Auntie May, Uncle Hugh, Logan, and Marshall, with the delicious addition of Becky. And as indicated in Becky's birthday note, Jamison would be with them, also.

Jamison! Coming, Avril felt certain, to demand an answer from her.

Ever since the wedding at Woodlawn Avril had felt more and more pressure. Jamison, gentle as he was, was becoming understandably impatient.

Not intending to use Jamison as a shield for her real love for

Graham, she had nonetheless avoided giving him a direct answer to his continued pleas for her hand in marriage. But she needed time to plan, time to bring up the subject of their secret marriage, tell Graham she did not want it annulled, and open the way for him to confess his love for her.

Avril had been caught up in the web of misunderstanding that had swirled around her at Becky and Marshall's wedding, with everyone assuming that she and Jamison would soon be making an announcement of their own. She had smiled through all the little jokes, playful banter, and innuendos people make under such circumstances. She had pretended a gaiety she did not feel, all the time seeing that spark of anger in Graham, that sudden flash of truth in his eyes.

What she had seen in Graham's expression during the marriage ceremony and later blazing in his eyes even as he had calmly told her of Jamison's request to propose, convinced her of his true feelings. In those few moments Avril had seen Graham's soul stripped bare. He *did* love her. Why, then, had he not been able to tell her? Why had not God freed them both to declare their love?

Contritely Avril remembered something Aunt Laura, in her gentle wisdom, had once said: "God never tells us 'why.' He only asks us to trust Him."

Trusting came hard for Avril. She had to work at her faith. But more and more she understood enough about herself to know that what she had told Becky was true: "If I cannot have Graham, I won't have anyone else."

Still, Avril was not ready to face the possibility of life without him. And if it did come to that, then she would have to leave Montclair.

But if she left, what would happen to Graham? What would become of Montclair without children to grow up here, to fill the rooms with laughter, to ride ponies in the meadows, to someday inherit this beautiful place? Would Graham live here alone? Or— and this thought chilled her—after she left, would Graham marry Clarice Fontayne?

Reluctantly Avril recalled what she had heard May and Logan discuss on the long trip from Woodlawn to Virginia after Becky's wedding. At the last minute, Logan had changed his mind and accompanied his mother and Avril in the Camerons' carriage. Worn out, Avril had fallen asleep during one part of the journey and had half-awakened while Logan and his mother discussed a subject not intended for her ears.

"But why *Clarice?*" Logan asked. "It would seem a man of Graham's intelligence could see through that lovely façade."

"Oh, I admit Clarice is somewhat frivolous—"

"Frivolous?" scoffed Logan. "She has a sharp, malicious tongue and a small mind."

"Logan, that's terribly harsh, isn't it? It may seem she rarely gives a thought to anything beyond the moment, what gown to wear to the next fête or what to have for tea, but don't underestimate her cleverness."

"I don't underestimate her, Mama, not at all. She would turn Montclair into a circus," Logan said glumly. "Or let it go to seed. She enjoys the Continental-style life. They'd probably travel two-thirds of the year."

"Graham has a plantation to run," Auntie May chided. "And remember, Graham has been alone for a long time. Her companion-ship might be just what he needs."

"What Graham needs is right in front of his eyes if only he could see it," was Logan's brisk rejoinder.

Dear Logan, Avril thought affectionately. Had he seen all these years what everyone else had somehow failed to see?

She and Logan had become closer than ever during the weeks they had spent together in England while his father was recuperating. When at last they had been given permission to take Uncle Hugh home, Logan had teased Avril on her elation at the prospect of returning to America.

"I had no idea you were such a patriot!" he remarked with exaggerated surprise.

"I've been away for a long time!" she retorted. "Months longer than you, Logan," she reminded him archly.

"Ah, yes." He nodded solemnly. "But something tells me it is less America, Virginia, and Montclair you have been longing to see than it is Graham."

Avril gave him a quick, sharp look. Did Logan suspect? She started to protest, defend herself.

"When are you going to realize life is not a fairy tale with storybook endings?" Logan asked gently.

Again Avril started to say something but Logan had already turned away. His question rankled. Still, Avril stubbornly clung to her hope. Why wasn't a "storybook ending" possible? Why couldn't they—she and Graham—"live happily ever after"?

Not wanting to waste a minute of this very special day, Avril left her recollections and made quick work of bathing and dressing, then slipped down the back stairs and out into the garden. She took the shallow wicker basket hanging on a hook by the door and walked along the paths, selecting flowers. Morning dew still sparkled on the petals and leaves as she cut them carefully.

Avril wondered if Aunt Laura had taught Graham the same language of the flowers she had taught Avril. If so, would he recognize the message in the bouquet she arranged and placed on his desk to be found when he returned from plantation rounds—this mixture of marguerites, blue cornflowers, heartsease, and in the center, one perfect yellow rose? Together they spelled hope, faithfulness, love. Avril did not realize until that moment that they also symbolized the three spiritual virtues spoken of by the apostle Paul in the thirteenth chapter of his first letter to the Corinthians.

"And the greatest of these is love," she quoted to herself as she set the vase on his desk.

She had so much love to give him that her heart was bursting with the desire to tell him so, to have him receive it.

All that day Avril's excitement mounted. The importance of what she intended to do sent shivers of nervous anticipation trembling through her as she dressed for the evening.

She had chosen to wear the other gown Graham had commissioned for her in Paris. Fashioned with classic simplicity of line, it featured a peach-colored slip beneath a filmy lace overskirt. Its short, puffed sleeves and low, rounded neckline were trimmed with satin ruching in the same color, so complementary to Avril's rich auburn hair and creamy complexion. As a finishing touch she fastened in the aquamarine-and-pearl earrings and pinned the fleur-de-lis pin to her bodice.

As she descended the stairway at the sound of the first carriage on the crushed shell drive, she saw Graham going out to greet them, and she paused on the landing. Someday, if all went as she planned, they would be going together to welcome guests as Master and Mistress of this great house. Unconsciously she glanced again at the framed portraits of the brides of Montclair along the wall, envisioning her own among them.

As she hesitated there caught up in her own fantasy, the grandfather clock in the hallway below struck the hour of seven. The strokes echoed strangely and Avril, without knowing why, shivered. For some reason she felt an eerie sensation, as if the clock were sounding a warning knell.

Passing off her momentary discomfort as nervous excitement, Avril flew down the rest of the stairs, hurrying toward the music, the laughter, the happy voices.

Avril moved through the evening with a heightened sense of destiny. Soon her future would be assured. Graham would know of her love and finally all would be settled. The thought acted upon her like a stimulant. She laughed and chatted happily with everyone. She opened her gifts with delight, and kissed each giver. Jamison beamed, and in her own happiness, Avril did not realize he assumed her mood reflected the fulfillment of his hope.

No one watching Avril would have guessed that she was impatiently waiting for the evening to be over.

Every time she glanced at Graham she could feel her heart quicken its beat. To her, he seemed more attractive than ever. The silvery strands that now tinged the dark, wavy hair did not age him at all. He was still the most handsome man she had ever seen. Each year the strong, well-bred face, the fine, clear eyes grew even more appealing.

That evening Graham seemed to be observing her in a new way, seemingly confirming her conviction that he loved her.

At last the evening came to an end. The thought that soon she and Graham would be alone made even her parting thanks and good-nights to each guest warmer than usual.

"May I come tomorrow so we can speak in private?" Jamison whispered as he clasped her hand before he left with the Camerons.

"Oh, yes!" agreed Avril happily, feeling sure that by the next day it would be possible to break her news to Jamison in a way that would not break his heart. How could he not rejoice in her happiness if he really cared for her?

Logan's farewell did give her pause, though. As he leaned down to kiss her cheek, he said in a low tone, "Remember, Avril, if we do not like a storybook's ending, we can write one of our own. There is always an alternative, even if it is bittersweet."

She stared at him in puzzlement. "Is that some kind of riddle?"

"Just as life itself is a riddle," he replied enigmatically.

Avril tried to brush aside Logan's remark and shrugged.

But then he said something she could not ignore. As he pressed her hand, he murmured, "I'm always here, if you need me, Avril, remember that. Second choice does not have to mean second best."

Then he was gone and Auntie May stepped up to embrace her.

"There has never been such a delightful party!" she declared as she kissed Avril an affectionate good-night. "And you, my dear, have never looked lovelier." She gave her a little pat on her flushed cheek.

At last she stood on the veranda with Graham, watching the last carriage disappear down the drive.

"Well, was it a happy birthday for you, Avril?" Graham asked.

"Yes, almost perfect!" she replied. She walked over to the balustrade and leaned against it.

"*Almost?*" Graham asked. "Was there something . . . someone . . . missing?"

"No, not that." She turned away, unable to see his face. "It's not over yet. There's something we must discuss, Graham."

"Yes, I know," Graham replied. His tone became crisp. "Young Buchanan cornered me early in the evening. He is anxious to have things settled between you."

Startled by having the course of the conversation surprisingly wrested from her, Avril straightened, tensed.

Graham continued. "I told him that there were some legal matters—I was not specific—that had to be attended to regarding your future before I could consent to a formal announcement of your engagement."

The words fell with deadly precision on Avril's unwilling ears. At the moment she could find no words to refute the implication of his statement. This was far from the way she had planned their private conversation.

"I also told him that your happiness was my primary concern and he emphatically stated that it was also his. He has finished his law studies. His father is helping him set up practice in Pleasant Valley as well as giving him land on which to build a house—"

Finally Avril found her voice. "Wait! Stop, Graham! This is all happening too fast. You have given Jamison permission—" She broke off, took a long breath, and started again. "You are saying that you want me to accept his proposal of marriage?"

"If you love him . . ." Graham left unfinished the unanswered question.

Waves of emotion flowed over Avril. Should she speak now? Even as she tried to gain possession of herself, she felt dizzy and held onto the balustrade to steady herself.

"As I said, your happiness is my main concern."

At these words Avril wondered what Graham would say or do if she told him where and with whom her true happiness lay. But his voice was grave and level as he went on.

"Once the legal matter that binds you from making any other

commitment is resolved, I will want to go over with you the things you will need to know about your inheritance, your property in Natchez—and then after your betrothal, Jamison will have to be instructed, advised on how best to handle the transfer from me, as your guardian, to him, as your husband-to-be. His law training will make it easier to understand—" Graham cleared his throat, then repeated, "Again, your happiness is my primary concern."

Avril replied coolly, "I am very touched by your concern for my happiness."

"Your happiness has always been my concern—your welfare—has always been my concern."

"Oh, there is no doubt of that," she interrupted, sarcasm sharpening her words. "It made me very happy to spend so many years away at boarding school and nearly two years in Europe . . ." She felt rather than saw Graham stiffen. She stopped, her throat tightening, glad that the darkness hid from Graham her unshed tears. Suddenly she knew she had to escape before she broke down completely. She moved toward the front door.

"Avril, my dear,—" Graham's voice sounded husky. "Is there something else you wished to talk to me about?"

She halted, then turned and made a gesture of dismissal. "It doesn't matter—I think I am too tired tonight to be clear-headed about any of this. Perhaps, tomorrow—" Again the threat of tears closed off her words. "Good night, Graham." She started inside, then called over her shoulder, "And thank you for my happy birthday."

Her feet were like leaden weights as she mounted the stairs, clinging to the banister as she climbed, the sobs she was trying to suppress choking her. At the top she started running down the hall to reach the haven of her bedroom. There she flung herself on her knees beside her bed in despair.

All Auntie May's warnings about eventual heartbreak had come true. She felt such a sense of hopelessness that even the healing tears would not come. She realized her helplessness in a profoundly painful awakening of reality. She might be twenty-one—an adult in every sense of the word—yet her life, her future was still being dictated as if she were a child.

Avril knew it would probably not have made any difference if she had tried to tell Graham what was in her heart tonight. It would only have humiliated her and embarrassed him, putting even more distance between them. Whatever he felt, he had decided not to tell her. Not ever. And since their relationship was no longer that of guardian and ward—they had nothing. Nothing at all.

Avril did not remember afterward how long she had remained on her knees, half-despairing, half-praying. Finally she had risen, gone over to the window, and sat there.

Moonlight flooded the room, giving her a sense of unreality. She did not feel sleepy nor especially tired. In fact, she felt more alert than she had felt earlier. There was not a sound anywhere, neither in the house nor in the garden. It was as if everything were suspended, waiting . . . for what, she did not know.

Avril gazed out the window and in her mind's eye, like pages of a book turning too fast, she tried to imagine what it would be like living away from Montclair. How could she bear not to see the fields golden with daffodils in the early spring or the orchards dressed in pink "fairy lace" for one brief week in May when the trees were in bloom, or the gold, crimson, and bronze of the elms and maples along the fences in the fall?

All sorts of memories marched through her mind, bits and pieces of conversations, incidents, events small and large, all the assorted things that had made up her life since she had come to live at Montclair when she was ten. Graham was a part of every memory— the biggest part of her life for the past eleven years. What would it be like without him?

For now, Avril knew, if she could not be his wife, she would have to find a life, some kind of happiness without him. She would have to leave Montclair, of course.

Gradually the sky became light, the pale dawn replacing the dark night. With it came the flickering revival of hope. She had to follow the dictates of her heart.

Then she realized she had not even tried to tell Graham how she felt. Had not wished to risk his rejection. But love was a priceless gift, to be offered before it could be accepted.

This was a new day. All she could do was to be truthful with Graham. Be truthful with Jamison. If she had been mistaken, misread God's plan for her life, then she would have to accept that and wait for Him to show her the next step she should take. She would trust and obey.

Finally Avril went to bed and slept so long and peacefully that when she finally went downstairs, she found that Graham had already left for the day.

"Did he say when he would be back?" she asked Hector as he served her breakfast.

"No, ma'm, he sho' didn't. He said he had to see Judge Cameron on some business matters. Doan know how long he's likely to be."

The "business matters" he wanted to discuss with Uncle Hugh must concern their secret marriage, Avril felt positive.

Well, no matter. Nothing could be annulled without her consent and signature, she was sure. In the meantime, before anything was definitely decided, Graham must be confronted with the truth.

Avril felt the stir of impatience. It might be hours before Graham returned. How would she pass the time until then?

That, however, did not prove a problem. That afternoon Avril had two callers. Logan came first.

He had sauntered in, unannounced, with the familiar freedom of years of friendship. Without prelude he launched right into what he'd come to say. "Father and Graham have been closeted for hours," he told Avril. "And I have the decided feeling it has something to do with you."

Avril waited for him to go on.

"Mama is fluttering about like a nesting bird, but when I asked her what was going on, she just shook her head and said, 'You'll know soon enough!' So I thought I'd ride over and see if I could pry something out of you."

"I think perhaps it is about my inheritance," she explained. "Now that I'm twenty-one—"

"Yes, I know all that!" he said impatiently. "You're a wealthy young lady. I've known it for years. That's why I've come now, before you do anything rash, before you are officially an heiress."

Logan paced the room restlessly. "I want you to know that I've loved you for years. And I don't give a tinker's dam for your fortune. We shall both have to marry someone and I don't want you running off to North Carolina in case—" He stopped abruptly, looked at Avril sternly,—"in case you don't get your storybook ending."

She looked at him aghast.

"What I'm saying is that we two would get on well together. We're friends and that's important. I don't think you really love Jamison. And if you married me, you could stay in Virginia and—" He grinned—"perhaps 'live happily ever after'"?

Avril opened her mouth to speak, but Logan waved a hand. "There's no need to give me an answer now. I just wanted you to know."

Almost as quickly as he had come, he left.

Bless Logan, Avril thought as she watched him ride off in the direction of their childhood trail through the woods. This was just the sort of reckless, impulsive gesture she might have expected from him. Since Jamison was staying at Cameron Hall, Logan probably knew what their guest might be planning when he came to call this afternoon. That's what had prompted Logan's unexpected proposal—to head off any rash acceptance on her part. She smiled, fond tears misting her eyes.

Knowing her heart's desire lay elsewhere had not deterred him. His attempt to offer her this alternative was a noble one, but useless. She could never give a leftover love to someone as kind as Logan.

Logan's surprise visit and all that had passed between them lingered in Avril's mind when Hector announced Jamison's arrival.

The minute Jamison stepped across the threshold, Avril felt her heart sink. All his hope was in his eyes, his smile, his entire happy demeanor. He handed her a beautiful bouquet of roses fresh from Auntie May's garden.

"How lovely. Thank you, Jamie," Avril said, accepting the gift. Then capturing her free hand, he brought it to his lips and kissed it fervently.

So there was to be no preliminary conversation, no easing into a more serious discussion, she thought with dismay. She could not prolong this hopeless situation. She must do it at once, and as gently as possible.

"Oh, Avril, there is so much I want to say, I hardly know where to begin." Jamison was speaking hurriedly, his heart in his eyes. "I believe you know my feelings. They could hardly be a secret. What you must know is that I have already spoken to your guardian, and he—"

Avril drew her hand away. "I know, Jamie. He has told me, but my dear friend, I must refuse."

Now there was a gasp from Jamison. "But he gave me to understand—"

"Then he misunderstood."

"I thought I had made my intentions very clear," protested Jamison, looking puzzled.

"Oh, yes, they were clear. I meant Graham misunderstood *my* feelings. Jamie, I care for you—but more like a brother—"

She saw the hope fade from his eyes and her own heart wrenched painfully.

"A *brother!*" He sounded crushed.

"Yes, Jamie." Avril rushed on. "Becky is my dearest friend. All your family is especially precious to me. And you—well, I feel great affection for you, Jamie, but not love—at least not the kind of love that leads to marriage."

"But, Avril, listen to me. I've heard that love does not always come right away but, in time, grows. And I love you so, Avril, enough for both of us. I can make you happy. I know it!"

"Oh, dear Jamie, I wish it could be different. Truly I do. I know you think now that your love is enough for both of us, that I might learn to love you in the same way. But it could never happen. Perhaps I'm too much the romantic, but I believe that two people, joining their hearts and lives for always, must feel they can't live apart before they try to live together."

"But, Avril, I've thought of nothing else for years and years—from the moment I met you, in fact. I've worked to become someone you could be proud of, could love. Now I can offer you all you deserve—"

"Don't, Jamie, please! I don't deserve anything! Certainly not the kind of love you're offering. What woman could live up to what you think of me? You've put me on a pedestal, Jamie, and I deserve that least of all!"

His face revealed the depth of his disappointment. "Can't you even try?" he asked bleakly.

"Try what? Try how? Oh, Jamie, how can one *try* to love someone differently than one does?"

"Is there someone else, then? Or would it be possible for me to continue to hope—that your feelings for me might change?"

Avril hesitated. What good would it do to tell Jamie about Graham? Her future was too uncertain. Later, she would give Becky permission to tell Jamison about the "secret." Now she must make her plans to leave if her own hopes were dashed.

"Jamison, it isn't *you*," she said. "It's *me*. You are a fine man, a loving, sensitive person. Any young lady would be proud to be your wife. I am proud that you cared enough to ask me. Someday you will find someone else who will appreciate and love you the way you should be loved."

When at last he left, Avril felt emotionally drained. She went outside onto the veranda and, leaning against one of the pillars, watched the azure sky darken into dusk.

She drew a long, uneven sigh. Her heart ached for Jamison. She knew only too well what it was like to love someone in vain. She prayed Jamison would, in time, get over her. Perhaps, before the evening was over, she would be praying the same prayer for herself, she thought ironically.

Just then she heard the sound of an approaching rider on horseback. She moved to the edge of the porch and saw Graham cantering up the driveway on Chief. At the sight of him, Avril felt the sweet, familiar pounding of her heart.

One of the stable boys came running to take the reins of the horse as he dismounted. Avril moved out of the shadow of the column and came to the top of the steps. Graham seemed surprised to find her standing there.

"Avril! I didn't see you!"

"Good evening, Graham," she said quietly.

Graham removed his wide-brimmed hat and smoothed back his hair in a characteristic gesture. "I passed young Buchanan on the road on his way back to Cameron Hall." He squinted up at her. "I assume he got his answer."

Avril pressed her hands together against her breast, where she could feel the throbbing within. She moistened her lips nervously.

"Yes, he got his answer."

A moment passed, then Graham leaned over a rosebush near the steps as if intent on examining it and with elaborate casualness said, "And—I assume—rode off happily?"

Avril did not answer. Instead, she moved to the side of the porch where he was inspecting the roses. Her pulses raced, her chest hurt as she took a deep breath. The rest of her life depended upon the next few minutes.

"Graham," she began, "I've wanted to talk with you about my plans."

He nodded, still looking down.

"I want to go to Natchez. I'd like to visit Mama's and Papa's graves, see the house again. I thought I'd take Dilly home. She's getting older and would like to see her sisters."

Graham lifted his head to regard her with a frown. "You mean— go alone or after you and Jamison are married?" His voice was rough-edged.

"I'm not going to marry Jamison, Graham. I sent him away. That's what I wanted to tell you. I've been waiting to tell you—"

"How long have you been waiting?"

His question struck her as almost laughable.

"How long have I been waiting, Graham?" she repeated.

With that, she moved slowly down the steps until she stood only one step above him. Placing her hands on his shoulders, she slid them down to his coat lapels and tugged gently. "You ask how long have I been waiting for you? I think I've been waiting for you most of my life." Then, holding his head between her hands, she gazed into the face she had loved for so long and kissed him, slowly and sweetly.

When the kiss ended, Graham, unable to speak for the tumult of emotions clamoring through him, put his arms around her and held her close to his thundering heart. All the love and longing he had felt intensifying over the last year and a half, but had held in check, now flooded over him.

Her eyes traveled over his face, then searching deeply into his eyes, Avril said, "I need you to love me, Graham—not as a child, nor someone for whom you feel responsible, but as a woman. Tell me if I'm wrong, if what I see in your eyes isn't real. Even if you deny it, I don't think I can believe you! My heart tells me something else. If you don't love me, cannot love me, tell me now and I'll go away. But I must hear you say it."

"Oh, my dear, my very dear," he whispered huskily.

He felt the silken cascade of her hair fall about his shoulders as she leaned down again to kiss him. And it was no child's kiss, but softly yielding and exciting.

Afterwards Graham sighed. "I *do* love you. I have always loved you, but I've never dared say it."

Avril's heart soared in glorious triumph. Honor and restraint had kept Graham from declaring himself, but now she knew what her heart had told her was true.

His arms tightened around her and he began to kiss her, her temple, her cheeks, her eyes now closed in ecstasy, then finally her lips. His kiss was passionate but infinitely tender.

"Beloved . . ." he murmured.

Part VI

The Waiting
Fall 1816

Delight thyself in the Lord, and he shall give thee the desires of thine heart.

Psalm 37:4

chapter
28

WHEN AVRIL awakened the next morning, she lay still for a few minutes, wondering if the events of the evening before had really happened or if she had dreamed them, after all.

Had Graham really said those words she had waited to hear? Or was his declaration of love some fantasy her own longing had created? Avril drew in a deep breath. Slowly the scene on the moonlit veranda became reality and her heart lifted with joy.

She threw back the covers and bounded out of bed. Anxious to get downstairs and see Graham before he set out on his rounds, Avril made quick work of bathing, then brushed her hair, tying it back with a ribbon. When she found herself lingering indecisively before the contents of her armoire, she impatiently pulled out a simple blue cotton chambray. Still buttoning the bodice, she ran out into the hall and flew down the stairs and into the dining room where she found Graham already at breakfast.

A sudden shyness swept over her when he looked up and saw her standing on the threshold. One look assured her it had been no dream. It was true! Graham's eyes spoke everything she had ever hoped to see in them.

She slid into her usual place beside him, then leaned forward to kiss his cheek. "Good morning, darling Graham!" She smiled. "Isn't it a glorious morning? The most beautiful of my entire life!"

Graham smiled at her indulgently, reached over, and patted her hand. "Beautiful indeed. But we have some serious matters to discuss."

"*Serious!* But, Graham, how can you possibly expect me to be serious when I am so deliciously happy?" she asked, spooning sugar onto the sliced peaches in the cut-glass bowl on her plate. "And how can you look so solemn? Or do you already regret saying what you said last night?" A tiny furrow marred the smooth forehead for an instant.

"Hardly *that,* dearest girl. I never meant anything more. But there are some things we must settle about the future." He tapped a pile of papers beside his plate. "Some legal matters—"

Avril interrupted him with a groan. "Oh, no, Graham! Do we *have* to? Surely, not *today!*"

"We must, Avril. Our getting married depends upon it—"

"*Getting* married? I thought we were already married, Graham." Avril looked puzzled.

"On paper, Avril. But there is much more to be settled before we can actually live together as man and wife. Let me explain." With that, Graham launched into a complicated exposition of the legal arrangement they had entered into to protect her property and inheritance when Avril was a child. The binding effect of Graham's guardianship had ended on her twenty-first birthday, automatically annulling their "secret marriage" contract. They must now proceed not only with a legal annulment but with the premarital requirements necessary for marriage in the Anglican church.

Avril felt as if a cloud had eclipsed the sunlight of the lovely morning. "So, Graham, how long will all this take?"

"I will begin procedures at once, of course, but these things always take longer than one hopes." He cast her a wary glance, then brightened. "But you will need time to make plans for the wedding . . . and May Cameron will want to be involved—"

"Graham!" exclaimed Avril, flinging down her napkin. "What kind of a wedding? If Auntie May has her way, you know what that will mean! She'll want all sorts of fancy arrangements and . . . goodness knows what else! Can't we just go quietly into Williamsburg and have Reverend Price marry us when all this legal tangle is straightened out?"

Graham shook his head firmly. "No, Avril, we cannot. Besides, you must leave Montclair as soon as our intentions are known."

Avril gasped. "Leave Montclair?" Her words sounded hollow and dull as if she were speaking them into a cavernous vault. Leave, after everything they had experienced together—after the long years of separation—after a lifetime of waiting? "Leave, Graham?" she repeated. "Why should I leave *now?*"

Graham's tanned face reddened slightly. "Come, Avril-all-grown-up! Were your tutors at Faith Academy so remiss that they failed to instill in you the proprieties? Our situation has changed completely. There's a formal engagement period to be observed. It would not be proper for an engaged couple to remain under the same roof, unchaperoned."

"But where would I go? I don't want to stay with Auntie May at the Camerons, Graham, dearly as I love her—"

"I suggest you go to Great-Aunt Laura's. She'd love to have you and you'd be a great help to her. In that way we would be living far enough apart to satisfy protocol. Not even the whisper of gossip should touch us, Avril. Our announcement will provide quite enough talk as it is. No, I want everything done strictly according to social decorum."

Avril could not resist a pout. "Oh, fie on society!" she said. "I think all those rules and regulations are stupid! But I suppose I *must* agree to it . . . that is, if the waiting is only a matter of weeks—"

"I'm afraid, my dear, that it will be more a matter of months."

Avril pushed back her chair and stood to her feet. "*Months?* Graham, I can't believe you would be willing to wait months for us to be married!" She crossed her arms and faced him furiously.

To her amazement Graham threw back his head and laughed. "You remind me of the stubborn little redhead who didn't want to be sent away to school."

"And now you're sending me away again!" she retorted. "If you loved me, you'd be eager to—"

"I *am* eager to marry you, Avril. I have just learned that there are some things in life worth waiting for, being patient about—"

"I *have* been patient! For years and years! I've waited all this time for you to love me, and now you want me to wait even longer?" Avril flounced over to the French windows overlooking the garden and stood rigidly, her back to Graham.

He walked up behind her, putting his arms around her waist and leaning his cheek against hers. "Youth is so impetuous, so impatient," he said softly.

Avril pulled away from him and whirled about, hands on hips, her eyes flashing green fire. "Don't do it, Graham!"

"Don't do what?" he asked, surprised.

"Don't patronize me."

"I didn't intend to insult you, Avril."

"I don't like having everything arranged for me. I don't like being told what I must do. I'm twenty-one, Graham! I want to be treated like an adult. Have some say in the decisions about my own wedding . . . since it appears there must be a wedding."

"And so you shall, my darling," Graham assured her. Pausing, he continued more deliberately. "I suppose we could be utterly selfish, go into Williamsburg, as you mentioned, be married quietly, exclude everyone who loves and cares about us and would like to share our happiness. Is that what you really want?"

Avril gave a long sigh of resignation. "I didn't mean to be unkind," she said at length. "I suppose we shall have to have some kind of wedding . . . invite guests . . . yes, I *would* like Becky to be here . . . and, of course, Great-Aunt Laura and—" She stopped and eyed Graham warily. "You *do* have a way of having the last word, don't you?" she challenged.

"That's my dear, sensible girl." He held out his arms and she went into them.

"You know I'm not just trying to be difficult, don't you, Graham?" She sighed. "It's just once Auntie May takes over, she's sure to want all sorts of folderol and—"

"Darling, nothing would make me happier than to have you all to myself and dispense with all the folderol, as you call it. On the other hand, I think you deserve a beautiful wedding to remember the rest of our lives."

"I guess I'm just disappointed. I really thought you would want to be married as soon as possible too. If you loved me as much as you say you do, as much as *I* love *you* —"

Graham's finger touched her lips, stopping her words.

"Now, you *are* being childish, Avril." He looked out the window over her head and said, "I love you more than I can say . . . I didn't think I had to convince you of that. But I don't want us to do anything rash that would set any more tongues wagging than the fact of our getting married at all surely will. We are *not* going to marry in undue haste." He paused before saying gravely, "Perhaps, Avril, you need time to reflect on whether this is what you want to do with the rest of your life. There *is* the matter of our ages, which may often cause us to respond differently to every situation, as we have just now—" There was another long pause. "If that seems a problem . . . maybe it is well we face it now."

Avril fought a rising flood of exasperation. "Oh, all right, Graham—you're *right*. And what's more, you probably always will be! I will agree to the wedding as long as it isn't more than six weeks from now!" Then tilting her head back, she looked up at him with a hint of mischief in her smile. "You're right, that is, except about *one* thing. I don't need time to think about our marriage, Graham. I've never been so sure of anything in my life. I love you and want to be your wife. Nothing—not time nor anything else—will ever change that!"

To Avril's dismay, *even* the very date of the wedding became the subject of great discussion and debate. Ample travel time must be allowed for those relatives and friends living a distance away. Graham was especially eager to invite his Uncle Rowan Cameron, his father's youngest brother and Graham's godfather, to stand up with him as best man. The travel time needed for the Rowan

Camerons to come from Wilmington, North Carolina, must be calculated.

As predicted, Auntie May appointed herself consultant in charge of the myriad details she assured Avril must be arranged. The list of "things to do" grew longer each time she rode over from Cameron Hall. Soon the private ceremony Avril had envisioned became an elaborate, colorful event requiring endless discussions, planning, and appointments. Though May expressed shock at the brevity of the time to accomplish it all, she reluctantly agreed to try.

The day Avril was to leave for Aunt Laura's home in Williamsburg, Graham called her into the library, a place with many rich memories for her. From the expression on his face, she guessed he was feeling as melancholy as she at the prospect of their parting. At her entrance he retreated behind the desk, as if for protection.

His smile was as tender and loving as ever, but taking her cue from his formality, Avril seated herself and waited for him to tell her what he wanted to say.

"As you know, I haven't asked what kind of an engagement ring you want," he began hesitantly. "We haven't had much time to ourselves since May became involved, have we?" He gave her a wry grin. "Perhaps you have a preference. But, in any case, I want to show you something—"

Graham then cupped his hands and extended them across the desk. In his palm was a ring of unusual beauty—gold, with a deep amethyst stone set in two tiny sculptured hands beneath a small gold crown.

"This is the traditional Montrose family betrothal ring," he explained, "fashioned from an ancient design dating from the fifteenth century in Scotland. My grandmother, Noramary, was the first to wear it as a bride, but since she was still living when my father and mother married, my mother did not wear it, nor did my first wife, Luella." He ducked his head in an uncharacteristic gesture of embarrassment. "I just thought knowing that would make your decision easier."

"*Of course* I want to wear it. It's lovely!" The ring symbolized so

240

much—the past, the future—that it seemed to seal all their promises to each other. Furthermore, Avril was certain of one thing. She had no desire to leave Montclair that morning without some tangible reminder that all that had transpired between them was not just a beautiful dream.

Graham brightened and, rising, came from behind the desk. Taking Avril's hands, he drew her to her feet, took her left hand, and slipped the ring on her third finger.

Something beautiful and meaningful trembled between them. Cradling her face between his hands, he leaned down and kissed her—a kiss so sweet and tender that she shivered.

At last he reluctantly released her. "You must go now, darling," he said. "The carriage has been brought around, and Josh is waiting to drive you into Williamsburg. I'll come in later in the week and we'll attend the Sunday service together. Then we can talk with Reverend Price and make arrangements to have the banns of our coming marriage announced."

Avril did not trust herself to speak. She merely put on her bonnet and allowed Graham to lead her out to the waiting carriage.

He leaned inside and said, "Until Friday, darling!" then stepped back, closing the carriage door and signaling Josh to drive on.

Avril waved at Graham from the rear window for as long as she could see him. When the carriage rounded the bend in the drive, she lost sight of his tall figure standing on the porch. The tears that had threatened all morning began to roll, unchecked, down her cheeks. How she hated leaving him.

Then, as she glimpsed the ring on her finger, her sadness gave way to a deep sense of peace. This would be the last farewell. The next time she returned to Montclair, it would be as Graham's bride.

chapter
29

THE SIX WEEKS that had loomed tiresome and tedious *before* the wedding soon took on a feverish quality. Duties, errands, appointments, and pressing decisions filled virtually every waking hour so that Avril had little time to call her own.

As she had learned during her summer visit with Great-Aunt Laura, the sprightly old lady was a delightful companion, and often seemed hardly more than a girl herself. She was merry and cheerful, without being intrusive as she helped Avril with her plans.

Feeling younger and more inexperienced than ever in the face of her impending marriage to Graham, Avril welcomed Aunt Laura's discreet suggestions and genuine friendship, in contrast with Auntie May, who was so overpowering at times, issuing orders like a commanding general before battle.

On a rare day when there were no errands to run, no fittings for her trousseau, Avril and Aunt Laura sat in the small parlor, satin-stitching her future monogram, *ADM*, on some new linens.

Avril's thoughts wandered to the other Montrose brides who had probably been similarly employed at this prenuptial task. Looking up from her embroidery hoop, she asked, "Did you know Graham's stepmother?"

"Arden Sherwood? Oh yes, dear, quite well."

"Tell me what she was like."

"Very beautiful, elegant, intelligent." Aunt Laura's needle flashed in and out of the fine fabric, completing a French knot embellishing the final initial. She lay the piece down and rethreaded her needle with shell pink floss before continuing. "Arden was born and grew up in a house designed by Thomas Jefferson, but her ancestors were even earlier settlers to Virginia than the Montrose family. The couple who founded the family dynasty here were Colton Sherwood, who had been a palace guard, and Lady Rachel Perry, who had been a lady-in-waiting to the Queen of England. Her father objected to the marriage, so they ran away to America."

"How romantic!" exclaimed Avril.

"Ah, yes. Very romantic indeed." Aunt Laura clucked her tongue as if to say that not all such escapades were so successful.

"They lived happily ever after, didn't they?" demanded Avril, unconsciously using the fairy-tale ending to childhood stories.

"I suppose so," Laura replied cautiously. "They had a splendid family, who prospered, and had fine families of their own. Arden was one of three daughters, all beauties. A year or so before she married Cameron Montrose, her fiancé was killed. Perhaps it was the tragedy that brought the two of them together—" She lifted her head and peered at Avril over her spectacles—"for, as you know, Cameron's *first* wife, Graham's mother, also died unexpectedly at a very young age."

"Yes, I know. Lorabeth. Graham barely remembers her, he says. Please tell me more." She set aside the pillowcase she had just completed and leaned forward, all attention.

"Ah, Lorabeth—" Aunt Laura's voice grew mellow. "Lorabeth was . . . special. Very sweet, very precious. A sad loss to us all. She was dearly beloved by everyone who knew her. Her death nearly broke my mother's heart. Lorabeth was—although not in actual fact—a granddaughter, she was devoted to Mama, and Mama to her."

"What happened, Aunt Laura? I'm not sure I remember the details."

"Lorabeth went to England when her mother, my sister Winnie, was supposedly seriously ill and required nursing. Actually, Winnie was not Lorabeth's real mother but . . . well, that's another story best left untold." Aunt Laura's lips tightened. "At any rate, Winnie recovered, but poor Lorabeth died!" The old lady sighed. "But what kind of conversation is this on the eve of a wedding? Let's talk of happier things, shall we?"

There were many such pleasant times together as the lazy September days passed, each one bringing Avril closer to her heart's desire. But in this lovely interlude, she experienced a stormy encounter that left disaster in its wake.

The incident took place at Chez Luise, the dressmaking establishment where her bridal gown was being made.

Madame Luise had once been the chosen dressmaker for the socially elite of Williamsburg. A Frenchwoman of great style and skill, she was more than a mere seamstress, Avril had been told. Studying the latest French patterns from the Paris salons, Madame often recut them, giving them her own inimitable touch. She prided herself on her ability not only to adapt the styles, but by a change in material or design, to make them more suitable to the Virginia climate without losing the French flair.

She was so adept in accentuating the individuality of her clientele so that no two ladies who patronized her boutique need ever fear the humiliation of arriving at a ball or fete to find another guest wearing an identical gown! In a short time Madame Luise became the undisputed arbiter of taste and fashion in the town. Though the lady was now quite elderly, she had had the foresight to train a member of her family, her niece Charmaine, who was now managing her business. And Auntie May had lost no time in enlisting her services to design the gown for Avril's special day.

In the salon, fitting rooms were strategically placed, with little parlors provided with private doors leading out to the street so clients could come and go with anonymity if they chose. Although ostensibly for the convenience of the customers, Avril had heard the rumor that these "petite salles" had also become the trysting place for faithless wives and lovers. She shook off such a shocking thought.

Armed with some sketches of her own, Avril discussed the design of her wedding gown with Mademoiselle Charmaine. Now the gown had been cut, basted, and pinned, and was ready for the first fitting.

On a glorious autumn afternoon, splashed with the first riotous colors of fall, Avril walked from the Barnwell house to Chez Luise for her fitting. On such a day as this, she would have much rather been cantering through the autumn woods near Montclair. She would be happy when all this fuss was over, and she and Graham were married to everyone's satisfaction and living there, free to spend their time in the old happy ways.

A maid in frilled cap and ruffled apron opened the door to Avril's knock, and an attendant, attired in rustling black taffeta, showed her into one of the tiny parlors adjacent to a fitting room.

"Mademoiselle Charmaine is with a client at the moment, but she will be with you presently, Miss Dumont. May I have tea brought in for you?"

"No, thank you."

Seating herself on a velvet upholstered settee, Avril picked up one of the fashion books lying on the round, gilt inlaid table beside it. She leafed idly through the pages. The models pictured were wearing such exaggerated costumes, festooned with feathers, furbelows, and frills, that Avril almost giggled aloud. Her silent amusement was interrupted by the sound of a strident voice coming from behind the closed door of the fitting room.

"No, no, this will not do! It won't do at all!"

This outburst was followed by a conciliatory murmur as the luckless fitter tried to pacify an obviously outraged client.

"I want to see Mademoiselle Charmaine immediately, you stupid girl! I thought I had made my wishes clear about this gown at my last fitting! Now it is all wrong! I would never be seen in this—this monstrosity! Well, don't just stand there staring! Go and get Charmaine! Now!"

Avril glanced up from the book, cocking her head. There was something oddly familiar about that voice. Surely not. Surely *that* lady, with all her fine manners and silken tones would never stoop to shouting. Or would she? Could it possibly be? Clarice Fontayne screeching like the proverbial fishwife?

Avril held very still, straining to hear what would happen next. The door opened and closed; then came the sound of scurrying feet down the hall, followed by a frantic consultation in French. Then all doubt as to who the irate customer was disappeared as, from the fitting room, Avril heard the clear, softly accented voice of Mademoiselle Charmaine inquire soothingly. "Now, Madame Fontayne, what seems to be the problem?"

Avril let out her breath. So! She was right. It *was* Clarice. Wouldn't Auntie May and Graham be surprised to have overheard such a tirade? Avril took a naughty satisfaction in having inadvertently discovered an unpleasant underside of the woman's gracious façade, exposing a crack in her careful veneer.

But within minutes the truth of the adage, "Eavesdroppers never hear well of themselves," was brought painfully home to Avril.

"Certainly, madame," she heard Mademoiselle Charmaine say. "We will make all these adjustments immediately, and have the dress ready for another fitting as soon as possible. When must you have the finished garment?"

"In three weeks! It is to be worn to the wedding of a friend . . . unless he comes to his senses before it takes place. I suppose you have heard that Graham Montrose is marrying his ward? I couldn't believe it when I heard it myself! What fools men are! So easily taken in by flattery, adoration, appeals to their masculine vanity, their protective instinct—"

Avril jumped up, her hands clenched in fury. How dared Clarice say such things? She felt her face flame, but there was more to come.

"His bride? A silly chit of a child, and he a man of such intelligence, sophistication, and charm. I cannot see how he was tricked into it. Of course, some mean-spirited people are saying— not that I am one to listen to gossip, you understand—that it is for her fortune he is marrying her. But I really don't see how that could be true," the shrill voice continued, "since the Montrose family has been among the wealthiest in Virginia—" Her next words were muffled—probably under yards of fabric in the process of being removed or put on, Avril assumed—and she leaned nearer the wall to listen.

"—needs an heir to carry on the family name." Clarice's voice rose again. "Whatever the case, I am absolutely sure he is not marrying the girl for love! Why, she's hardly out of the schoolroom. Oh, he'll soon tire of her silly prattle, her childish ways. It appears she'd be better suited to preside over the stables of Montclair than the grand ballroom!"

Avril put shaky hands over her ears. She had already heard enough to bring angry tears to her eyes. How dreadful of the woman to repeat such lies, make such terrible accusations!

Furious, Avril resisted the temptation to fling open the fitting room door and confront Clarice on the spot. But retreat seemed the wiser strategy. From past encounters, Avril knew she was no match for the worldly sophisticate.

She stepped out into the hallway, bent on making it to the door leading to the street. But in her haste and confusion, Avril turned the wrong way and at that very moment the fitting room door flew opem, and there was Clarice, standing only a few feet away.

For a heart-stopping instant, it seemed to Avril that the woman's face blanched, the violet eyes widening in shock. Then almost immediately the smooth features rearranged themselves into a bland expression.

"Why, Avril, what a charming surprise, my dear," she purred. Not waiting for a reply or comment, she swept by in a swirl of mauve taffeta and lace and the musky scent of perfume.

Avril did not remember the walk back to the Barnwell house. Still seething with indignation, the next thing she knew she was pushing through the front gate and running up the steps and into the hall.

Inside, all was still. Aunt Laura was napping upstairs, and no one else was about. Avril stood for a moment, breathing hard, frustrated, and bewildered by her confrontation.

Just then her eyes fell on a large envelope lying on the silver platter on the hall table. She recognized Graham's fine penmanship immediately. There was no mistaking his flourishing script. The letter was addressed to her. She picked it up, turned it over, and saw the red wax seal with the Montrose crest.

All of Clarice Fontayne's spiteful accusations echoed in Avril's mind. What if Clarice were right? Would Graham grow bored with a younger wife? Regret his declaration of love? Their plans to marry? Not willing to face Avril in person, had he written to tell her what she feared most?

She broke the seal and opened the envelope, withdrew the letter, and began to read.

Beloved,

Today this house resounds with emptiness, and I know once again in acute awareness how you have filled my home, my heart, my life with your sweetness and light. I miss everything about you—your voice, your smile, your step on the stair, the sound of your laughter.

I'm counting the days, begging the hands of the clock to move more swiftly, each hour bringing the moment of fulfillment nearer.

I am at a loss when I try to express my love. All I can say is that my life was without meaning before you came into it, nor can I imagine what it would be without you.

I thank God for you, my darling.

Ever, your devoted Graham

Impulsively Avril pressed the letter to her lips, kissing it. If only Graham could know how much his words meant to her at this moment!

Suddenly all the unnerving doubts, the feelings of uncertainty disappeared. There was no mistaking the passionate longing between the lines of this note. Graham loved her. Nothing anyone could say or do could change that. And nothing else mattered except what only they two knew in their hearts.

The Wedding
October 1816

My beloved spake, and said unto me:
"Rise up, my love, my fair one,
And come away.
For lo, the winter is past,
The rain is over and gone.
The flowers appear on the earth;
The time of the singing of birds is come,
And the voice of the turtle
Is heard in our land."

—Song of Solomon 2:10–12

chapter
30

"OH, IT'S JUST last-minute megrims!" Becky declared when Avril confessed her recurring doubts about Graham's love for her only two days before the wedding. "I had them, too—at least a few, even though I knew Marshall and I loved each other to distraction!"

The friends were perched high on the tester bed in the guest room at Cameron Hall where Auntie May had insisted on holding the garden wedding, to be tailored in keeping with the Scottish traditions of the Montrose family. "Just the sort of wedding I would have planned for my own daughter if I had been fortunate enough to have one," she had twittered when Avril arrived from Williamsburg with Great-Aunt Laura.

"But I haven't seen Graham in ten days!" Avril moaned, jumping from the bed and padding over in stocking feet to the armoire to see for herself that her wedding gown, swathed in tissue, was still safely inside. "With the harvest to oversee, he's been much too busy to make the long ride in to town. Maybe—"

Despite his eloquent expressions of love, his letters, Avril could not quite escape the gnawing fear that Graham would realize his mistake in marrying one so much younger. Suppose Clarice were right, after all? Surely the older woman knew a great deal more about him, about managing a plantation like Montclair, about . . . everything! Suddenly Avril was a child again, feeling familiar pangs of heartache and abandonment. She cast a stricken look at Becky, who was still sitting on the bed amid a confusion of billowing petticoats and pillows.

"What . . . you . . . need," Becky said slowly, with the old glint of mischief in her eye. Picking up one of the lace-lavished rectangles, she took careful aim—"is . . . a . . . good . . . old-fashioned . . . pillow fight!"

The soft missile landed squarely in Avril's midsection. What followed rivaled any misdemeanor from Faith Academy days. One after another, a volley of pillows was fired and returned until both Avril and her childhood chum were convulsed in spasms of laughter.

"Oh, Becky!" gasped Avril when she finally caught her breath. "That was just what I needed! What would I do without you? I thank God for your friendship all these years. And now it will be even more perfect. With you married to Marshall, and me to Graham, we'll be neighbors for the rest of our lives!"

Dilly tried to slip quietly into Avril's bedroom at the Camerons' that morning, but Avril's sleep had been shallow the night before her wedding, and she opened her eyes and smiled tenderly at her old nurse. Sunlight flooded through the windows as Dilly pulled back the draperies.

"Happy de bride de sun shine on!" quoted Dilly, shaking her kerchiefed head as she gazed over at Avril sitting up in bed. "Cain't believe my baby's gettin' married!" she declared.

"I know, Dilly! Isn't it wonderful?" Avril responded happily. "And what a perfect day!"

She got up, went to the window overlooking the Cameron gardens, and pushed open the casement. She stood, breathing in the air tangy with a touch of fall crispness.

From below came a strange cacophony of sounds. Leaning farther out, she saw that the source of the discordant strains was four professional bagpipers Auntie May had found to play at the wedding. Everyone had thought it impossible, but May had managed it somehow. Avril remained a moment longer, saying a little prayer of thanks for the gift of this lovely October day with its clear, china-blue sky—so perfect for a garden wedding.

She turned from the scene to begin her preparations. Becky would be in soon, no doubt, to help her dress, and Avril needed these few minutes while Dilly was fetching her bath water to reflect on the life-changing event that was to take place this day.

She moved calmly now to the armoire and took out her wedding gown for a final inspection. At least here she had had her way, she thought with a smile of satisfaction. The gown was simply styled, cut in the high-waisted French Empire fashion, its oyster-white silk folds falling into a short train. Her only jewelry would be the matching fleur-de-lis pin and earrings Graham had given her, and a dainty, seed-pearl necklace that had belonged to her mother. She lifted the veil from its nest in a large hatbox. It was of gossamer tulle to be attached to a coronet of her own thick russet hair, braided and garlanded with tiny yellow rosebuds. So simple, so right. She hoped Graham would be pleased.

Avril draped the gown across her bed, returned the tulle illusion to its place, then picked up the small, now well-worn Bible she had unpacked and placed on her bedside table. Thumbing through the velvety pages, she paused at a passage in the book of Ephesians: "Wives, submit yourselves unto your own husbands, as unto the Lord. For the husband is the head of the wife, even as Christ is the head of the church: and he is the saviour of the body. . . . So ought men to love their wives as their own bodies. He that loveth his wife loveth himself. . . . For this cause shall a man leave his father and mother, and shall be joined unto his wife, and they two shall be one flesh. . . . Nevertheless let every one of you in particular so love his wife even as himself; and the wife see that she reverence her husband."

Avril's heart gave a leap. Did Graham love her as he loved his own body? Suddenly a warm sense of belonging swept over her. God was giving her—not only the home of her heart—but a true husband. Did she "reverence" Graham, as the Good Book admonished? Oh, yes! Had she not looked up to him, admired him, depended upon him, held him in the highest esteem for as long as she could remember? Of course. And she could easily do it for the rest of her life.

Becky's knock and joyful greeting brought Avril's quiet time to an abrupt end. "Lazybones! You're still in your nightie! You want to be late to your own wedding?" asked Auntie May bustling in behind Becky. Docilely, Avril submitted docilely to the ministrations of her friend and aunts as they flitted about her like bright butterflies among the late-blooming roses in the garden. They helped her into her camisole and petticoats, brushed and arranged her hair, and at last settled the gown over her head, and buttoned it up the back, proclaiming her the loveliest of all the Montrose brides.

"I just can't wait for Graham to lay eyes on you," breathed Becky, radiant in a mousseline dress of lemon yellow. "He'll never let you out of his sight!" Auntie May beamed with pride and pleasure to see her "creation," while Great-Aunt Laura's eyes misted over as she handed her niece a bouquet of flowers and herbs from her own garden, symbols of joy, love, faithfulness, and hope, and tied with plaid ribbons.

But it was Graham who took Avril's breath away as she started up the garden path on Judge Cameron's arm to the piping of the Highlanders.

Resplendent in traditional Scottish dress, he stood waiting for her at the steps of the gazebo where arrangements of fall flowers— lavender asters, yellow marguerites, and feathery white chrysanthemums—flanked the makeshift altar. Above the white ruffled jabot, his tanned face was the same dear face she had loved for so long. The features, bold and chiseled, had never seemed more striking— the aquiline nose, the strong jut of jawline, the proud brow.

He wore his pleated kilt and tartan with all the stalwart manliness of his Montrose forebears. The fringed tartan, in gray, purple, and black, was draped over one shoulder and secured by a large, silver brooch embossed with the family heraldic crest.

All this Avril saw in a single glance, but as she approached, she was drawn by the love in Graham's eyes. The wedding party—

Logan and Marshall in the Cameron tartan, Uncle Rowan, dear Becky, beloved friends and family—all faded away. It was Graham and Graham alone she saw and knew and loved and rejoiced in.

Then, as the pipers ceased their playing, she was at her groom's side, her hand in his.

"Graham, my lad, I consider it a high honor indeed to present Avril to you. I feel as if I were giving my own daughter to become your bride," Judge Cameron was saying.

The balding minister, rosy-cheeked above his starched surplice, beamed benevolently from the top step.

"Dearly beloved," he began. "We are gathered in the sight of God and this company—"

Through the mist of her veil, she looked up at him—this man she had known most of her life, her beloved guardian and protector, who would, from this day forward, be even more.

"Avril, wilt thou—"

She heard her name and slowly spun out of her dreamy reverie. Reverend Price was repeating her name, his wispy eyebrows lifted in some surprise. "Avril Dumont, wilt thou have Graham Montrose to be thy lawful, wedded husband?"

"Oh, yes, of course!" She heard a ripple of amusement from the assembled guests behind her and felt her cheeks grow warm as she glanced sidelong at Graham.

His fingers tightened reassuringly on her hand as he gave his own promise.

The liturgical ritual completed, Reverend Price took both their hands in his. Looking directly into Graham's eyes, he spoke firmly. "In the name of our heavenly Father, receive Avril as a gift, for the Word of God declares that every good and perfect gift is from above, and comes down from the Father in whom there is no variation, nor shadow cast by His turning. It was Jesus' first miracle at Cana that embued marriage with a sacred quality.

"I pray that from this moment on, the two of you may be knit together in love, braced and encouraged by faith—to live side by side, blessed by His mercy, strengthened by His grace, guided by His Spirit."

He turned to Avril. "I pray, Avril, that Graham will always love you as his wife, being in a new sense part of him, and that you will respect, reverence, regard, honor, prefer, venerate, esteem, and defer to him, praise, love, and admire him above all earthly others." Avril smiled to herself, remembering her morning devotions. "I pray that you may always stand together in unity of spirit and purpose, obeying God in His commandments and in the truth of His Spirit."

"The ring, please," Reverend Price asked, and Graham took out the gold band, and as the minister directed, Graham repeated, "With this ring I thee wed, and do pledge my troth, and all my worldly possessions—"

Avril felt the ring slide over her finger, her happiness complete.

"In the ceremony of candles," the minister explained, "we have a tangible expression of the vows you have just taken, the covenant you have made." Leading them to a three-branched candelabrum on the altar, he continued. "These two candles represent your separate lives as you have lived them to this time." Handing Graham a lighted taper, he motioned for him to light one of the end candles, then nodded for Avril to do the same. "Now that you have pledged your lives to one another, you will each take your lighted candle and ignite the middle candle, symbolizing the merging of your separate lives. From now on," he admonished, "your thoughts shall be, not for self, but for the other; your plans, mutual; your joys and sorrows shared and halved alike.

"You are, in God's sight and in the eyes of the world, truly man and wife. And what God has joined together, let no man put asunder. God bless you. Go in peace."

At the conclusion of the ceremony Graham drew Avril's arm through his, looked down at her lovingly, and covered her hand with his own. Then together they turned to face the congregation of gathered family and friends.

So many well-wishers clustered around them that a formal receiving line was never formed. A steady stream of people pressed forward to kiss Avril affectionately, pump Graham's hand, and offer congratulations with predictions of great future happiness.

Dazed and excited, Avril was suddenly taken aback when she saw Clarice Fontayne approaching. Immediately she felt a knot of apprehension at the sight of the woman she had always considered her rival and whom she had feared might become Graham's bride and the mistress of Montclair.

Honesty forced Avril to admit that Clarice had never looked lovelier. With a twinge of jealousy she recognized that not even the advantage of youth could compete with such exquisite grace and beauty.

What magic kept the woman from betraying any signs of aging in the past ten years? Avril wondered, observing her. Of course, she was clever enough to wear a wide-brimmed hat of lacy straw which shadowed her face. It was not only flattering but softened any faint lines that might possibly have marred the smooth porcelain complexion. Her slender neck was still firm, and besides, the highstanding ruffled collar and pearl choker would have hidden any telltale wrinkles.

Mademoiselle Charmaine had surely outdone herself in the gown she had designed for Clarice. Of watered silk, it was made in the newest Parisian fashion in a shade of rosy peach that was extremely becoming to Clarice's vivid brunette beauty.

Unconsciously Avril held her breath as Clarice stopped first in front of Graham. Putting her head to one side and smiling up at him coquettishly, she said, "Well, do I get to kiss the bridegroom, or does that privilege apply only to gentlemen congratulating the bride?"

"Not at all, dear lady." Graham laughed and leaned down to kiss the upturned face.

Clarice lifted one lace-mitted hand and patted his cheek. "Ah, Graham, I hope you won't disappear completely now into domestic bliss on your lovely but so remote estate and deprive Williamsburg of your charming company."

"Of course not, Clarice. As a matter of fact, when we return from our wedding trip, we intend to give a large party at Montclair, to which you are invited. I certainly do not intend to be a recluse nor to keep Avril from enjoying an active social life."

"Ah, yes, she is so very young." Clarice sighed. "She will want companions her own age."

Listening, Avril bristled. She darted an indignant glance at Graham. Couldn't he see what Clarice was insinuating? Under that silken-smooth manner, such barbed innuendos! But Graham was simply laughing, continuing the bantering exchange.

Finally Clarice moved over to Avril. A cool smile briefly touched her lips as she held out her fingertips to the bride.

"So, Avril, here you are. You have achieved your heart's desire. But do you know how to keep it? It takes more than poetic words, legal contracts, or names scribbled on a scrap of paper, to make a marriage . . . successful. I wish you luck, my dear. You will surely need it."

Before Avril could respond to Clarice's murmured invective, the lady drifted away, and the crowd closed behind her elegant, departing figure. If Logan had not appeared to claim her for a dance at that precise moment, she might just have vented her anger.

"Do you remember the first time we danced together, Avril?" Logan asked as he swept her into the steps of the lively music.

"Of course! How could I forget? You taught me!"

"And lived to regret it!" he countered teasingly.

"How so? What do you mean?"

"Well, ever after that, at all the parties we attended, your dance card was so full that I never again had a chance to be your partner."

"Oh, Logan, not true!" Avril laughed, looking up at her old friend. Then, detecting something curious in his expression, she added, "You always exaggerate so!"

"Not always. And perhaps I find myself regretting something else today."

"What could that be?"

"That I didn't make you take me seriously when I proposed to you," he said, and the laughter left those intensely blue eyes.

"But, Logan, you surely guessed . . . in fact, you *knew*, didn't you, that it was Graham I loved?"

"Yes, but I suppose I thought it an impossible love and lived in the hope that you, too, would come to realize that and settle for second best. Me."

"Oh, Logan, I would never have considered you second best—," she protested, "I'm not sure I would ever have married at all if Graham had not loved me, too." Then she said, "And some lucky girl will soon make you see that what you felt for me was . . . perhaps, a little more than friendship, but a little less than love . . . at least the kind of love one needs to spend a lifetime together."

Just then the music came to an end, and Graham appeared at Avril's side. "May I have the next dance with my wife?" he asked, bowing to Logan, and feasting his eyes on her.

Logan relinquished her with an answering bow, and Avril moved into Graham's arms as the music began again.

When Avril and Graham at last led the crowd of well-wishers into the dining room to cut the cake, she saw that Auntie May had carried the Scottish theme throughout the rooms, decorating the buffet table with the combination of Cameron and Graham tartan ribbons.

The cake, a delicious confection of fruit and nuts with a burnt sugar frosting and decorated with rosemary, lavender, and thyme from Aunt Laura's garden, was a product of her household. Baked from a recipe that had been handed down through the first Montrose bride by her sister-in-law, Janet, it was another tangible evidence of Great-Aunt Laura's thoughtfulness. Even the herbs garnishing the cake, symbolizing health, happiness, and good fortune for the new couple, had been selected with care. How like her! Avril, catching the old lady's eye across the expanse of the room, smiled her gratitude.

It was late in the afternoon when, by a silent exchanged glance, a mutual unspoken decision, Avril knew that it was time to leave for the short trip to Montclair. She whispered to Auntie May, who signaled the small band to strike a flourish of chords announcing that the bride was about to toss her bouquet.

As all the unmarried guests clustered on the veranda, at the foot of the steps, Avril spun around and threw her flowers over one shoulder. Then, in a pelting of rice and rose petals, the couple ran down the steps and into their waiting carriage.

At her first sight of Montclair as they rounded the bend of the drive, Avril slipped her hand into her husband's.

"We're almost home," she said softly as their eyes met.

They had left on their wedding trip to England and the Continent in the late spring, waiting for fair weather for the ship's crossing, and had been away all summer. Now Avril saw that the giant elms lining the drive bore the first tinges of autumn gold; here and there she saw a flash of scarlet where the maples were. They were back in time for Indian summer, that last reprieve before winter, when the sunny days lingered into long afternoons, when the scent of ripening fruit from the orchards mingled with the spicy fragrance of chrysanthemums and purple asters in the still-blooming gardens.

Soon the house came into full view, and Avril sat forward, eager for the carriage to stop, realizing how much she had missed this place.

As part of their honeymoon trip, they had traveled down the Mississippi on a luxurious riverboat. It had been a journey rich with threads of the past interwoven with her new-found happiness.

Visiting the house where she was born, Avril had stepped back into her childhood. She had laid a bouquet of flowers upon the stones bearing her parents' names, the young couple she scarcely remembered. Everything had seemed strange, even foreign to her. The one constant had been the quiet, loving man who accompanied her. In some ways it had been a disturbing experience, but finally she had said farewell to all that had composed the first ten years of her life.

Now that she was returning to Montclair, Avril was aware that the vague restlessness of which she had always been conscious began to subside. The closer they came to Montclair, the greater her sense of tranquillity and peace.

When the carriage came to a full stop, Graham gave her hand a reassuring squeeze. Avril looked at him with shining eyes and confident smile. She belonged to him now and he to her, and it gave her a comforting security she had never known before.

Avril gazed up at the stately mansion before her, poignantly reminded of that lost, lonely, little girl who had stood with the gentle young man years ago just like this. He had held out his hand to her then as he was doing now, offering her his love, care, and protection, and she had placed her small one in his, sensing that with him she would be safe.

That child's heart has never changed, Avril thought.

Graham took her hand. His long fingers closed around it, their palms touching, and she felt that warm sensation of belonging that was infinitely sweet and familiar.

"Come, my darling, let's go home."

Part VII

Epilogue—Entry from Avril's Journal
Summer 1821

He maketh the barren woman . . . a joyful mother of children.
—Psalm 113:9

TODAY WE HAVE received news of great sadness. Graham's Uncle Rowan, his wife Gladney, and their baby daughter have all been lost at sea. Returning from a visit to her parents in Bermuda, their ship encountered a terrible storm and ran aground, taking the lives of all aboard.

Only their little son, Clayborn, who was staying at the home of a schoolmate, survives. A dreadful tragedy.

Graham left immediately to go to North Carolina and fetch the child back here to live with us. . . . We have been wondering why God has not seen fit to answer our prayer for children these five years. Perhaps, today, he has—

Avril watched from the landing as the tall man and the little boy approached the house. Her thoughts raced back to another day when she had first seen Montclair, clinging to Graham's hand, as this child was doing.

Deeply touched by his tragedy, so like her own, that had orphaned him at the same tender age, Avril's heart contracted painfully as the child gazed up at her where she stood in the curve of the stair.

Their eyes met—his, round and dark and filled with anxiety; hers, clear and serene and full of reassurance. Something wordless passed between them at that moment—something they never spoke of afterward nor ever needed to express. Heart to heart, loving spirit to longing need.

Aware of Avril's presence, Graham called to her. "We're here, dear. Come down and meet Clayborn."

Avril lifted her skirts and skimmed lightly down the steps. Holding out both hands to the boy, she said, "Welcome to Montclair, Clayborn. This is your home now."

Over the dark head Avril looked at Graham, smiling ... remembering.

Family Tree

In Scotland

Brothers GAVIN and ROWAN MONTROSE, descendants of the chieftan of the Clan Graham, came to Virginia to build on an original King's Grant of two thousand acres along the James River. They began to clear, plant, and build upon it.

In 1722, GAVIN's son, KENNETH MONTROSE, brought his bride, CLAIR FRASER, from Scotland, and they settled in Williamsburg while their plantation house—"Montclair"—was being planned and built. They had three children: sons KENNETH and DUNCAN, and daughter JANET.

In England

The Barnwell Family

GEORGE BARNWELL first married WINIFRED AINSELY, and they had two sons: GEORGE and WILLIAM. BARNWELL later married a widow, ALICE CARY, who had a daughter, ELEANORA.

ELEANORA married NORBERT MARSH (widower with son, SIMON), and they had a daughter, NORAMARY.

In Virginia

Since the oldest son inherits, GEORGE BARNWELL's younger son, WILLIAM, came to Virginia, settled in Williamsburg, and started a shipping and importing business.

WILLIAM married ELIZABETH DEAN, and they had four daughters: WINNIE, LAURA, KATE, and SALLY. WILLIAM and ELIZABETH adopted NORAMARY when she was sent to Virginia at twelve years of age.

KENNETH MONTROSE married CLAIR FRASER. They had three children: KENNETH, JANET, and DUNCAN.

DUNCAN married NORAMARY MARSH, and they had three children: CAMERON, ROWAN, and ALAN.

CAMERON MONTROSE married LORABETH WHITAKER, and they had one son, GRAHAM. Later CAMERON married ARDEN SHERWOOD, and they remained childless.

The Saga Continues!

Be sure to read all of the "Brides of Montclair" books, available from your local bookstore:

Valiant Bride

To prevent social embarrassment after their daughter's elopement, a wealthy Virginia couple forces their ward, Noramary Marsh, to marry Duncan Montrose. Already in love with another, Noramary anguishes over submitting to an arranged marriage.

Ransomed Bride

After fleeing an arranged marriage in England, Lorabeth Whitaker met Cameron Montrose, a Virginia planter. His impending marriage to someone else is already taken for granted. A story of love, conscience, and conflict.

Fortune's Bride

The story of Avril Dumont, a wealthy young heiress and orphan, who gradually comes to terms with her lonely adolescence. Romance and heartbreak ensue from her seemingly unreturned but undiscourageable love for her widowed guardian, Graham Montrose.

Folly's Bride

Spoiled and willful Sara Leighton, born with high expectations, encounters personal conflicts with those closest to her. Set in the decades before the War Between the States, the story follows Sara as she comes under the influence of Clayborn Montrose, scion of the Montrose family and Master of Montclair.

More books in this series due soon! Look for Yankee Bride/Rebel Bride: Montclair Divided, Gallant Bride, *and* Destiny's Bride.